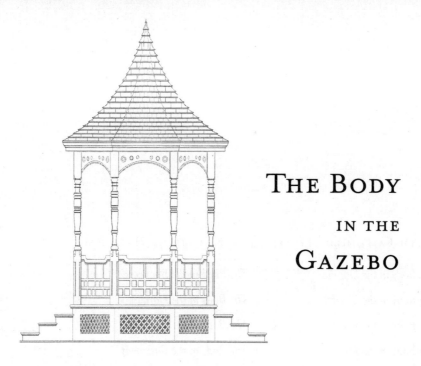

THE BODY

IN THE

GAZEBO

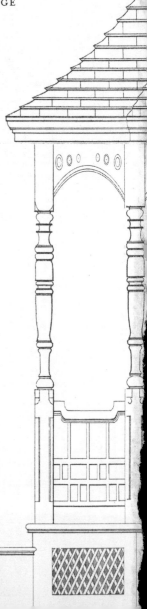

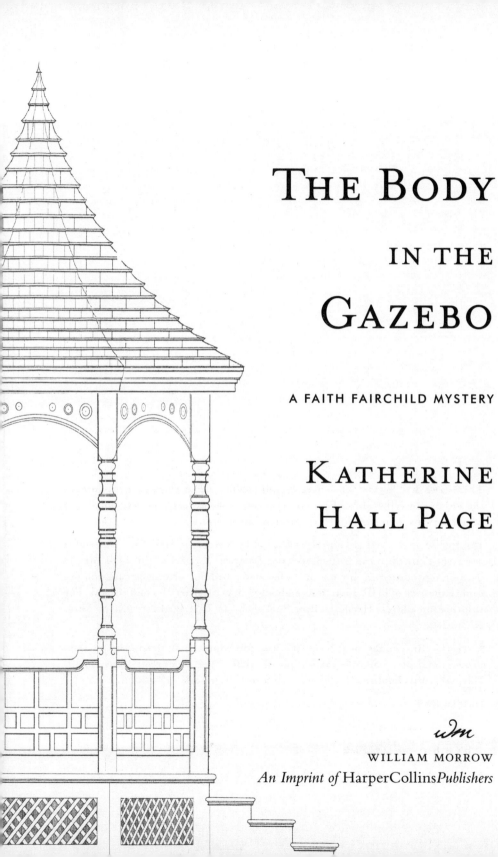

THE BODY
IN THE
GAZEBO

A FAITH FAIRCHILD MYSTERY

KATHERINE
HALL PAGE

wm

WILLIAM MORROW
An Imprint of HarperCollins*Publishers*

THE BODY IN THE GAZEBO. Copyright © 2011 by Katherine Hall Page. All rights reserved. Printed in the United States of America. No part of this book may be used or reproduced in any manner whatsoever without written permission except in the case of brief quotations embodied in critical articles and reviews. For information address HarperCollins Publishers, 10 East 53rd Street, New York, NY 10022.

HarperCollins books may be purchased for educational, business, or sales promotional use. For information please write: Special Markets Department, HarperCollins Publishers, 10 East 53rd Street, New York, NY 10022.

FIRST EDITION

Library of Congress Cataloging-in-Publication Data has been applied for.

ISBN 978-0-06-147426-2

11 12 13 14 15   OV/RRD   10 9 8 7 6 5 4 3 2 1

For my dear husband, Alan
Happy 35th Anniversary

Truth is stranger than Fiction, but it is because Fiction is obliged to stick to the possibilities; Truth isn't.

—MARK TWAIN, *Pudd'nhead Wilson*

Acknowledgments

My thanks to Dr. Robert DeMartino, Jean Fogelberg, Nicholas Hein, Amalie Kass, Kathy and Peter Winham, Valerie Wolzien, and the Poison Lady, Luci Zahray, for help from their various areas of expertise. Also many thanks to my agent, Faith Hamlin, and to my editor, Wendy Lee.

The idea for this book originated during a glorious week on Martha's Vineyard with my friends of over forty years, Kate Danforth, Mimi Garrett, Virginia Pick, and Margaret Stuart. Always, my thanks to them.

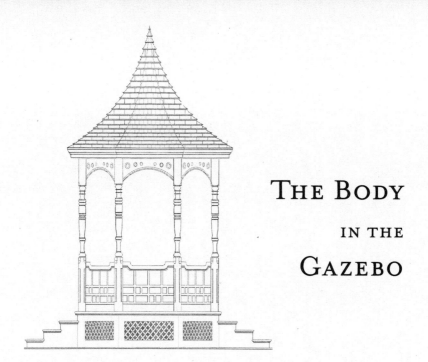

The Body
in the
Gazebo

CHAPTER 1

The first letter arrived on a Tuesday. Ursula Rowe had no need to read the brittle, yellowed newspaper clippings that were enclosed. She knew what they said. But the few words on the single sheet of white stationery in the envelope were new. New and succinct:

Are you sure you were right?

She went upstairs to her bedroom—hers alone for too many years—and sat down on the antique four-poster bed they'd bought when, newly married, they'd moved into this house. The bed had pineapples carved on the finials—symbols of hospitality. She reached up and traced the intricately carved wood with her fingers. Pineapples. A great luxury for those early colonists—her long-ago ancestors. How had such exotic fruit made its way to New England? She'd never considered this before. Wouldn't they have rotted in the hold of a ship on the voyage from South America? Perhaps the pineapples came from the Southern colonies. That must have been it.

Her mind was wandering. No, her mind was trying to take her

away from what was clutched in her other hand. The letter. She closed her eyes. Arnold had joked that the pineapples were fertility symbols. Certainly the bed had borne fruit—two children—and been the site of years of pleasure. He had been gone for such a long time, but she could still recall his touch, his whispered endearments, the passion. She'd never wanted anyone else.

Ursula read the words again—a single sentence written in a shaky hand. You couldn't duplicate it; it came only with age. So, the writer was old. She looked at her own hand. The raised blue veins were so close to the surface of her powdery, thin skin that it seemed they would burst through. Her fingers, once long and straight, were knobbed and for some years she'd removed all her rings except her wedding band, worn thin. An old woman's hands. The change had come so gradually—the brown spots first appearing as summer freckles to her mind—that even now she could scarcely believe her age. She loosened her grip and put everything back in the envelope, tucking the flap in securely.

Where could she hide it? It wouldn't do to have her daughter come across it. Not that Pix was nosy, but she sometimes put Ursula's wash away, so the Sheraton chest of drawers was out. And the blanket chest at the foot of the bed that had been her grandmother's was out, too. Pix regularly aired the contents. There wasn't much furniture in the room. Some years after Arnold died, Ursula had removed his marble-topped nightstand—the repository of books, eyeglasses, reading lamp, alarm clock, and eventually pill bottles—replacing it with a chaise and small candlestick table, angled into the room. It felt wrong to get into bed during the day, but she'd wanted a place to stretch out to read and, increasingly, to nap. Somehow the chaise made her feel a bit more like a grande dame than an old one. There was a nightstand on her side of the bed, but her granddaughter, Samantha, often left little notes in the drawer and might notice the envelope. Ursula always saved the notes—bits of poetry Samantha liked or just a few words, "Have sweet dreams, Granny." Generally Ursula did. Her days had been good ones and she felt blessed. Arnold, the two children, although Arnold junior lived in Santa Fe and she only saw him and his wife during the summer in Maine and on her annual visit out there. Three grandchildren, all healthy and finding their ways without too much difficulty so far. But you never know what life will hand you. She stood up, chiding herself. The six words—"Are you sure you were right?"—had entered her system like a poison, seeping into the very marrow of her bones and replacing her normal optimism with dark thoughts.

The mail had come at noon when the bright sun was still high in the clear blue sky. She walked to the arched window that overlooked the backyard. It was why they had chosen this room for their own, although it was not as large as the master bedroom across the hall. Each morning this uncurtained window beckoned them to a new day. And it had a window seat. The window seat! She slid the envelope under the cushion. Done. She gazed out the window, feeling herself slowly relax. The yard sloped down to the Concord River, which occasionally overflowed, flooding the swing set that was still in place. Arnie and Pix had gleefully waded out to it as children, getting gloriously wet sliding down the slide into the shallow water. The family had always kept canoes there, too, under the majestic oak planted by design or perhaps a squirrel. It didn't matter. The tree was perfect for climbing, and a succession of tree houses. The grandchildren had added kayaks to the fleet and given her a fancy new one for her eightieth birthday, or had it been her eighty-fifth? Today the river flowed gently, its slightly rippled surface like the glass in the windows of Aleford's oldest houses. A good day to be on the water. However, she'd promised Pix never to go out for a paddle alone. Perhaps she'd do some gardening. Yes, that was the thing. Start to clear some of the dead leaves left by winter's ravages from the perennial border around the gazebo that Arnold had insisted they build near the riverbank. She'd been reluctant about it—no, not reluctant. That was the wrong word. Too mild. "Opposed." That was more like it.

Ursula had never wanted to see another gazebo again, not after that earlier summer. Not after the image that had still appeared unbidden and unwanted in nightmares—and her waking thoughts. Arnold had told her this one would replace that other gazebo. It would be a symbol of their new life and their future together, blotting out the horror forever. She could call it a pergola or a garden house instead if she liked. She'd given in. And he'd been right, of course. It had brought the family much pleasure— especially, screened in, as a refuge from the mosquitoes and other insects that living by the river brought. The grandchildren loved it, too.

Yet, Ursula had never loved it.

She left the room and went downstairs, heading for the back of the house and her gardening trug in the mudroom. She stopped outside the kitchen door. Suddenly she didn't feel like gardening or going outside at all. Suddenly she felt sick to death.

"My mother is never ill! I can't possibly leave now." Pix Miller was sitting in the kitchen of the house she'd grown up in; her friend and neighbor Faith Fairchild was across the table. They were both clutching mugs of coffee, the suburban panacea.

"I'll be here and you know Dr. Homans says the worst is over. That there's nothing to worry about. Never really was. A bad bout of the flu." Faith found herself imitating the doctor's very words and clipped Yankee tone.

"Dora will keep coming nights for as long as we want." Pix was thinking out loud. Dora McNeill was an institution in Aleford, Massachusetts, the small town west of Boston where Pix, Faith, and their families lived. Dora, a private-duty nurse, had cared for Aleford's populace for as long as anyone could remember. Her arrival at a bedside brought instant comfort, both for the patient and kin. "Dora's coming" was tantamount to a sickroom lottery win.

"I'll keep bringing food. I know she makes breakfast and what she thinks Ursula can tolerate for other meals, but Dora needs heartier fare." Faith was a caterer and her thoughts normally turned to sustenance before all else.

"Maybe I should skip Hilton Head and just go to Charleston. I could go down for the shower—it's in the afternoon—and come back the next day."

"Let's start with the fact that Ursula would be very upset if you didn't go for the whole time, which means both places. You wouldn't be able to tell her—she'd send you packing instantly—so the only way you could see her would be when she was asleep, or by sneaking a peek through the door. So, there's no point to staying on her account.

"Besides, she'll want a blow-by-blow description of everything. Sometimes I think she's more excited about the wedding than you are."

"I'm very excited about the wedding," Pix said defensively. "Our firstborn—and Rebecca is wonderful. I couldn't ask for a better daughter-in-law. Sam thinks so, too."

"Her parents will be wonderful, as well." Faith knew Pix was worried about meeting her prospective in-laws, even with her husband and offspring by her side. "They couldn't have produced such a lovely daughter if they weren't the same."

She then rushed on before Pix could come up with all the exceptions to this parent/child rule they both knew.

"You can't skip either week. Hilton Head is the whole bonding thing. They've even planned it so you're going during Dan's spring break from Clark. Samantha can work on her thesis anywhere, but Mark and Becca have been making all sorts of arrangements so they can take the time off."

Mark Miller worked on the Hill as a congressional aide; Becca, or rather Dr. Rebecca Cohen, was an environmental scientist with the EPA. A blind date had very quickly moved into a lifelong commitment with both sets of eyes wide open. Pix had thought the oldest of her three children would follow the pattern of so many of her friends' offspring and postpone marriage treacherously close to ticking clocks. Tying the knot at twenty-seven might mean grandchildren much sooner than she had imagined. It was one of those thoughts that was helping her to cope with the wedding.

"I'm sure we will enjoy spending time with Becca's parents and the rest of her family." If the sentence sounded as if she were reciting it by rote, it was because it was one Pix had repeated to herself many times.

"You're not still thinking about that picture, are you?" Faith said sternly. "Yes, her mother is younger than you are and, yes, she dresses well, but I'm sure she'd kill for your gorgeous long legs, and don't forget all the new clothes we bought. You'll look terrific, too."

Cynthia Cohen, "Cissy," was a petite brunette, and at first glance it was hard to tell the mother from her three daughters. The photo had been taken during Mark's first visit to the Cohens' in Charleston and he was in the center of the group beaming. Becca's father was presumably behind the camera. Mark had e-mailed it to his mother, who had promptly printed it out to show Faith what she was up against.

"Her makeup is perfect."

It had taken Faith a number of years to move her friend away from a dab of lipstick for formal occasions to mascara, eye shadow, blush, and gloss. Pix still favored nothing more than a swipe of Burt's Bees gloss on her lips for everyday.

"So is her hair."

"She'd probably just had it done—the picture was taken during the holidays—and besides, you have lovely hair," Faith said loyally.

Pix *did* have good hair—chestnut colored and thick. She kept it short, and the only problem was its tendency to stand on end after she'd run her hand through it while engaged in contemplation, a habit hard to break.

"I still don't think I needed all those clothes. And you'll have to go over what goes with what again. At least I don't have to worry about where to get something to wear at the wedding. They want to use the same place for my mother-of-the-groom dress as the rest of the bridal party's attire, so that's settled. I have to make the final choice, though, and you know I hate to shop. Plus I'll be shopping with strangers."

"Samantha will be with you, remember."

"Thank God, I'd almost forgotten," Pix said, grasping at the lifeline her daughter's presence would afford. Samantha, her middle child, had always been the calmest, plus she was wise in the ways of the world of fashion, often to Pix's bemusement. The last time she'd had lunch with Samantha, Pix had offered to sew up the rips in her daughter's very short dress only to be told that they were on purpose. She was wearing it over a kind of leotard. Pix could not believe someone would pay money to buy what would be a dust cloth in her household.

Faith looked at her friend, drank some coffee, and wished she could grab Harry Potter's cloak of invisibility to accompany skittish Pix. Meeting new in-laws was nerve-racking, but it would be beautiful at Hilton Head this time of year and better to meet now than at the wedding, where there wouldn't be a chance to get to know one another with all the inevitable commotion. Faith should know—she'd catered enough of them. After the week at Hilton Head, everyone who had to get back to work was leaving, but Pix and Samantha were continuing on to Charleston for fittings, wedding plans, and a bridal shower. It was late March and the wedding itself would be in early June—before the real heat set in. Pix had to check out the place Faith had helped her find for the rehearsal dinner—as well as make the final arrangements for all the out-of-town guests from Mark's side of the family. Considering this was a woman whose idea of a good time was birding at dawn in Aleford's Willards Woods and dressing up meant exchanging L.L.Bean khakis for a Vermont Country Store wraparound skirt, her nervousness over the nuptials and face time with belles from the South was understandable.

"You'll love Charleston, and I know the street their house is on—Hasell Street. It has to be one of the old houses, since Mark told you the family has been in Charleston for generations." Faith was grasping for any straw she could find. Charleston's fabled cuisine—the thought of chef Jeremiah Bacon's shrimp and grits with andouille gravy at Carolina's was making Faith salivate slightly— would cut no ice with Pix. Much as she adored her friend, there remained a huge gap in their respective food tastes. Pix's kitchen cabinets and freezer were filled with boxes that had "Helper" printed on them, while Faith's were jammed with everything but. Pix worked for Faith at her catering company, Have Faith, but kept the books. She'd accepted the job some years ago with the understanding that it would involve no food preparation of any kind except in dire emergencies such as pitching in to pack up cutlery, china, and napkins for an event.

Faith soldiered on. "You'll find out about the house when you get there. And don't forget the gardens. You know you love gardens. . . ."

Faith suddenly felt as if she were trying to convince a toddler to eat spinach.

"Anyway, everything will be fine," she concluded lamely.

"Except for my mother. She might not be fine."

She'd said it out loud, Pix thought. The dread that had been with her ever since she'd gotten the phone call from Dr. Homans that Ursula had suddenly spiked a high fever and was severely dehydrated. He was admitting her to Emerson Hospital for treatment, fearing pneumonia. It wasn't pneumonia, thank goodness. He'd discharged her as soon as possible—so she wouldn't pick anything else up—but she had been quite ill and still hadn't recovered. Pix knew her mother would die someday. It was all part of the plan and she didn't fear her own death. She just didn't want her mother to die.

Reading her friend's thoughts, Faith reached over and covered Pix's hand with her own, marveling as always at her soft skin treated with nothing more than Bag Balm. Faith felt a momentary pang of guilt at all the expensive creams of Araby that filled her medicine chest, but efficacious or no, Bag Balm was the cosmetic equivalent of a New England boiled dinner—lines she would not cross.

"I'm going to see if Mother's still sleeping," Pix said.

"If she isn't, I'll say a quick hello. I have to pick Amy up and take her to ballet." Amy Fairchild, a third grader, and her older brother, Ben, in his first year of middle school, both required a great deal of chauffeuring, and Faith had not taken kindly to this suburban mother's chore—although the fact that Ben would be driving himself in a little over two years filled her with dread.

"I'm sure she'll want to see you. She's been asking for you," Pix said.

"Tom told me the same thing when he came home last night."

Faith's husband, the Reverend Thomas Fairchild, was the minister at Aleford's First Parish Church. Ursula was a lifelong member, as were the Millers. Faith was a more recent arrival, born and raised in Manhattan. The daughter and granddaughter of men of the cloth, she and her younger sister, Hope, had sworn to avoid that particular fabric and the fishbowl existence that went along with it. Over the years they had observed congregations—composed of ordinarily reticent individuals—who felt perfectly free to comment on the way the minister's wife was treating her husband and raising her children. At First Parish there were a number of women Faith termed "Tom's Groupies" who were sure they would do a far better job than Faith at keeping him in clean collars and doing other wifely chores. They regularly dropped off dubious burnt offerings—casseroles featuring canned soups and tuna fish. Faith ceded the collar cleaning—amazing how hard it was to keep track—but stood her ground on the culinary front.

The fact that she succumbed to the Reverend in the first place was due to good old love at first sight. He was in New York to perform the nuptials for his college roommate and Faith was catering the reception. Shedding his ministerial garb, Tom had been in mufti by the time the poached salmon and beef tenderloin appeared on the buffet tables along with Faith bearing pâté en croûte. Whether it was the platter she was carrying or her big blue eyes that attracted him was soon moot. Later that evening in Central Park, during a ride in one of the touristy but undeniably romantic horse-drawn carriages, when she discovered his calling—he'd assumed she knew—it was too late. The heart knows no reason.

She left the Big Apple for the more bucolic orchards of New England and, like Lot's wife, looked back—often. Faith, however, did not become a pillar of salt, even the delicious French *fleur de sel* from the Camargue kind. What she did become was a frequent traveler back to the city for visits to the three Bs: Barneys, Bloomingdale's, and the late great Balducci's, as well as the lox counter at Zabar's.

"Maybe she wants me to cook her something special," Faith said, although, she thought, Ursula could have given the message to Tom, or Pix. More likely it was a request that Faith urge Pix not to change her trip plans. Pix was as easy to read as a billboard and Ursula had, no doubt, picked up on her daughter's reluctance to leave.

As they moved out of the kitchen to go upstairs, the doorbell rang.

"I wonder who that can be?" Pix said. "I'm not expecting anyone."

She opened the door and Millicent Revere McKinley stepped into the foyer. She was carrying a brown paper bag similar in size and shape to those sported by individuals in New York's Bowery before it became a fashionable address. Faith knew that Millicent's did not contain Thunderbird or a fifth of Old Grand-Dad. And it wasn't because Millicent had joined the Cold Water Army around the time Carry Nation was smashing mirrors in saloons. No, Faith knew because Millicent's earlier offerings still filled the shelves in Ursula's refrigerator. The bag contained calf's foot jelly, the Congregationalist equivalent of Jewish penicillin, chicken soup.

Pix took it from her.

"How kind of you. I know Mother appreciates your thoughtfulness," she said. "Let me go up and see if she's awake."

"She doesn't need a roomful of company. That's not why I'm here, but you go check on her and I'll talk to Faith."

Pix handed Faith the bag. Millicent led the way back into the kitchen. She knew Ursula's house as well as her own, a white clapboard Cape perched strategically on one side of Aleford's Green with a view from the bay window straight down Main Street. Not much got past Millicent, who had been admitting to being seventy for many years now. Her hairstyle was as unvarying as her age. She'd adopted Mamie Eisenhower's bangs during Ike's first term and stuck to them. Millicent's stiff perm was slate gray when Faith met her and it now appeared as if she'd been caught in a heavy snowfall—yet a storm that left every hair in place.

Although not a member of First Parish, Millicent behaved like one, freely offering Faith advice she didn't want. Their relationship was further complicated by several incidents. The first occurred when Faith, early on in Aleford, had discovered a still-warm corpse in the Old Belfry atop Belfry Hill. With newborn Benjamin strapped to her chest in a Snugli, Faith did what she supposed any sensible person would do. She rang the bell. It produced immediate results, although not the capture of the murderer. That took Faith a while and came later. The most long lasting of these results came from Millicent, who was appalled that Faith had dared to ring the venerable icon—cast by Paul Revere himself, Millicent's many times removed cousin. It had sounded the alarm on that famous day and year. Subsequent peals were restricted to April 19, Patriot's Day, that curious Massachusetts and Maine holiday; the death of a President; and the death of a descendent of one of those stalwarts who faced the Redcoats on the green. None of these categories, Millicent was quick to point out, applied in Faith's case. Rapidly running down the hill screaming loudly would have sufficed.

The other incidents involved Millicent's saving Faith's life not once but twice. Since then, Faith had labored in vain to repay this debt, hoping to drag Millicent from the path of an oncoming train—the commuter rail passed through Aleford—or else surprise a desperate burglar intent on purloining Millicent's collection of Revere McKinley mourning wreaths, intricately woven from bygone tresses.

For the moment, all she could do was follow her savior into the kitchen if not meekly, then obediently, and put the Mason jar of jelly in the fridge.

"I'd like to give you the recipe, Faith, but it's a treasured family secret."

Faith could never understand why families that treasured their recipes wouldn't want to share them with the world, but in this case, she would not expect otherwise. Millicent hoarded information like the Collyer brothers hoarded newspapers—and everything else. Prying anything out of the woman was well nigh impossible. Faith had tried with varying success. As for calf's foot jelly, she had her own recipe. It called for a lot of boiling and straining, but when you added lemon juice, cinnamon, clove, and some sherry to the gelatin and put it in a nice mold, the result was quite pleasant. She'd recently come across the actor Zero Mostel's recipe, which was similar. An epicure, he never met a gelatin or—judging by his girth—a pudding, he didn't like.

Millicent got herself a cup and saucer from the china closet in the butler's pantry. Miss McKinley—not Ms., thank you very much—didn't do mugs, and poured herself a cup of coffee before sitting down. Faith had had enough caffeine for the day, but joined her at the table. She didn't have to pick Amy up for another half hour. In any case, it was a command performance.

"I hope Pix isn't upsetting her mother about this trip. The last thing Ursula needs is her daughter moaning about having to go away. Why these people want to spend all that time together with people they'll rarely see after the wedding is another story. In my day you got married and spent one holiday with one set of in-laws and another with the others. None of this bonding business."

Faith was interested in Millicent's remarks. The woman had never been married—"never cared to"—but brought her eagle eye to the institution. There was something to what she said, Faith thought. Tom's parents and her parents liked one another, but contact was limited to things like a grandchild's christening. They did live far apart, but Faith sensed it would be the same if the Fairchilds were a few blocks away down Madison in Manhattan or the Sibleys on the other side of Norwell, the South Shore town where Tom had grown up and his parents still lived. Their children had bonded to the point where they got married and that was enough for their elders.

"It's hard for Pix to go away now when her mother isn't completely recovered, but she's definitely going," Faith said.

"Problem is she won't admit Ursula is getting to the point where she may not be able to stay here. This flu business should be a wake-up call."

Faith had thought the same thing herself. Pix had a severe case of denial when it came to her mother. Pix's father had died suddenly in his early sixties, and for most of her adult life,

Pix had had only Ursula. The idea that she wouldn't be in this house forever, frozen at some age between seventy and eighty, was anathema to Pix. Faith had never brought up the subject of Ursula's future. And Pix herself hadn't. It was obviously too painful. She was the exception to Faith's friends who were Pix's age—in their fifties. The subject of aging parents had replaced aging kids, although Faith had learned some years ago from these same friends that you're never going to be finished raising your children.

"She won't be able to do those stairs much longer." Millicent was complacently going down a list she had certainly reviewed before. "However, the staircase is straight, so they could get one of those chair-elevator things."

Faith pictured Ursula regally rising up past the newel post. Not a bad idea. Millicent was barreling on.

"The place is big enough for someone to live in, but she'd hate that. Could turn the library into a bedroom, but you'd have to put in a full bath."

"You seem to have thought this over pretty thoroughly," Faith couldn't help commenting.

"One does," Millicent replied, looking at Faith sternly. "*Semper paratus.*"

Millicent's bedroom was on the ground floor of her house. Faith doubted it was foresight. More likely just plain "sight," as in looking out the window past the muslin sheers.

"She has a lot of friends at Brookhaven. She could go there," Faith suggested, thinking two could play the preparedness game. Brookhaven was a life-care community in nearby Lexington.

"You know she'd never leave Aleford," Millicent said smugly.

Match to her.

This was true, Faith thought, and a problem for many of Aleford's older residents. A group had tried to interest Kendal, the retirement and assisted-living communities associated with the

Quakers, in coming to Aleford. So far, nothing had happened, and if it did, it would be too late for Ursula. Faith almost gasped as she thought this. Not that Ursula would be gone soon. No! But a decision would have to have been made. She had to admit Millicent was right—an admission she generally tried to avoid. This last illness had shown that Ursula really couldn't continue as she had. Faith had been shocked to see the change in the woman after she'd come home from the hospital. It was dramatic, especially when Faith looked back at last summer. Ursula had climbed Blue Hill in Maine with them, setting a pace that left several gasping for a second wind.

Blue Hill was close to Sanpere Island in Penobscot Bay, where the Fairchilds had vacationed, at the Millers' urging, the summer after Ben was born—Pix was a third-generation rusticator. Eventually, enchanted with the island, the Fairchilds built a cottage of their own, an event that a younger Faith would never have predicted. "Vacation" meant the south of France, the Hamptons, Tuscany, and the Caribbean—balmy waters, not the rocky Maine coast's subzero briny deep.

And Ursula had seemed all right for most of the winter. As usual, she'd participated in the Christmas Audubon Bird Count, snowshoeing deep into the woods to do so. But when Faith saw her when she was discharged from the hospital, Ursula looked years older, her face an unhealthy pallor, her thick white hair limp and lifeless. What was the worst was the change in her eyes—those beautiful deep topaz orbs had acquired a milky film.

"When Pix gets back from gadding about, you're going to have to talk to her about all this."

"Why me?" Faith protested. Millicent was the one with all the ideas—and probably brochures.

"It's not my business," Millicent said firmly.

Faith didn't know whether to laugh or cry. Instead she got up.

"I have to pick Amy up at school."

Millicent nodded. "Yes, it's her day for ballet. You'd better get going."

The woman knew everything.

Pix came into the kitchen. She looked ill herself.

"She was awake, but she's drifted off again. She seems to be sleeping so much of the day now. But she said to thank you for the jelly, Millicent, and Faith, she wants you to come spend some time with her. 'A real visit,' she said. That's a good sign, don't you think?"

"Yes," Faith said. "And Dora can let me know when. She has my cell or she can leave a message at home."

"I'll tell her," Pix said. "But do you really think I ought . . ."

Faith nodded slightly toward Millicent.

"Don't tell me you still haven't decided whether to get those sandals we looked at for the trip."

Momentarily nonplussed, Pix picked up on the signal.

"They were expensive and I'd never wear them in Maine. I don't think I ought to get them."

Millicent looked suspicious. She said, "Shoes," sounding eerily like Margaret Hamilton as the Wicked Witch of the West saying "Slippers," before Faith cut her off with a "Good-bye" as she left to get her daughter.

The parsonage was quiet. Both children were asleep. Faith realized the nights when Ben went to bed before they did were numbered. Even now he'd still be awake except for soccer practice. Nothing like a coach who believed in laps and lengthy practice drills. Bless her.

"Hungry, darling?" she asked Tom, who was stretched out on the sofa next to her. They'd lit a fire in the fireplace, as they had for several nights, each time declaring it would be the last one until fall. Rather, Tom had made the pronouncements. There had been a blizzard on Easter Sunday her first spring in Aleford and Faith hadn't trusted New England weather ever since. The battle of the thermostat was ongoing and at times ugly—at least to Faith.

"Hmmm," Tom said. "I could go for a little something. What did you have in mind?" He got up and reached for his wife.

"Save that for later?" she said, settling into his arms. "For now how about some of that broccoli cheddar soup and a sandwich—pastrami on dark rye?"

After a scary bout of pancreatitis in November, Tom had been advised to eat small meals throughout the day and avoid alcohol. Faith had always teased him about being a cheap drunk—half a glass of pinot grigio and he was singing "O Sole Mio," so he didn't miss the sauce. It explained why she'd been sipping some Rémy Martin without him, though.

"Great."

"Stay put and I'll bring it in here."

"No, I'll come and keep you company."

Earlier they had been discussing Faith's conversation with Millicent and hadn't come to any conclusion other than gently trying to talk to Pix about future choices for her mother, with husband Sam there, too, once they returned from South Carolina. As Faith heated the soup and spread Tom's favorite horseradish mustard on the bread, she found herself returning to the subject.

"Ursula is determined to go to the wedding in June," she said.

"I know, and that means she'll do it." Ursula was one of the parishioners waiting to welcome the new minister at the parsonage upon Tom's arrival in Aleford a year before his marriage. She held the distinction of being the first female warden at First Parish and had served on the vestry several times.

"The drive is so long that the best thing would be for her to go down in stages, staying overnight or longer," Tom went on. "Or she could fly, but that's pretty taxing these days. She'd insist on standing in the security line—no wheelchair."

"Because of this," Faith said, "I wish they were getting married on Sanpere. But aside from the problem of where to house all the guests, Becca quite naturally wants to get married in her own temple."

Tom nodded. His mouth was full. He swallowed.

"And it's not just any temple," he said. "Her family have been members for generations. Kahal Kadosh Beth Elohim is the oldest synagogue building in the country after Touro in Newport, and the congregation is the fourth oldest. It's a place I've always wanted to visit and I'm honored that they want me to be a part of the ceremony."

Faith had been in Charleston several times before Tom appeared on the scene and since for the business. This was his first trip, and although the wedding was still many weeks away, Faith had already planned what they would see in the area when not involved with wedding events. It was a rare getaway for them. Ben and Amy were going down to Norwell, where they would be blissfully happy exploring their grandparents' attic and garage—the cars had never been parked in it. Why waste the space? In true New England fashion, the Fairchilds saved *everything,* carefully labeling containers, no doubt one with the proverbial contents "String Too Short to Be Saved." Weather permitting, there would be canoeing and fishing with Grandpa on the North River and perhaps a visit to nearby Plimoth Plantation with Grandma, who was a longtime volunteer.

Meanwhile Faith had booked their stay at one of Charleston's historic bed-and-breakfasts—from the picture, a delightfully furnished large room, kitchenette, and bath with a private garden below. She'd advised Pix on the venue for the rehearsal dinner—the Peninsula Grill in Charleston's fabled Planters Inn. It was romantic in that way only Southern places can be. While there might not be magnolias in bloom, somehow you smell them and, in your mind's eye, see women in low-cut gowns with powdered shoulders fending off beaux in the soft candlelight. Besides, the Grill made the best coconut layer cake in the universe—a towering confection that managed to be both decadently rich and still light.

Tom got up, rinsed his dishes, and put them in the dishwasher.

"Okay," he said to his wife, taking her in his arms. "I've had enough to eat, but I'm still hungry."

"Hmmm," she said. "Funny thing. Me, too."

Faith did not get a chance to go see Ursula until Friday. Dora went home for a few hours after lunch before returning for the night and Faith had arranged to come then. Ursula didn't need constant daytime care anymore—there was a Medi-Alert system next to her bed—but as it turned out she was seldom left completely alone. Pix was so uneasy about going away that she had enlisted her mother's friends to keep an eye on her, something they'd been doing as soon as Ursula had been up to receiving visitors. Faith had promised she'd be dropping in frequently. It was no chore. Over the years, both Faith and Tom had come to love Ursula dearly. She seemed—and acted—like a member of their family.

Dora had said her charge was awake, so as Faith ran up the stairs—ever so slightly worn in the center of each tread by years of use—she called out, "Ursula, it's Faith. Would you like a little company for a while?"

The answer came as Faith entered the sun-filled bedroom. "How lovely. And just the person I've been wanting."

Ursula was sitting up in bed. She looked better than the last time Faith had seen her, but still much too thin—the skin stretched over the high cheekbones her daughter and granddaughter had inherited looked translucent. She was wearing a quilted bed jacket; no doubt from Makanna's, that venerable, and now lamented, Boston ladies' lingerie emporium, Faith thought. It had served several generations, especially for their trousseaux. The peau de soie lacy slips and nightgowns may have left more to the imagination than Victoria's Secret garb, but perhaps they were even sexier. What was the line? "Putting all your goods in the shopwindow"? Keeping some of them behind the counter wasn't a bad idea.

"I'm at your disposal. Tom is picking up the kids and my dinner is all made. I just have to pop it in the oven." She pulled the slipper chair that was next to Ursula's bed up closer and took her hand. Ursula gave it a slight squeeze and let it drop.

"When I was young, we almost always had cooks. And when we didn't, Mother opened cans. She wasn't at home in the kitchen and I suppose that's the source of my lack of enthusiasm."

One passed down to *your* daughter, Faith finished mentally.

"But I didn't ask you to come to talk about recipes," Ursula said.

"I didn't think you had," Faith said, smiling. Ursula was looking so serious. She had to cheer the woman up. "Even though I *have* tasted your rum cake [see recipe, p. 251] and it's fabulous." The rum cake gave off such a heady aroma that you felt you had imbibed even before a moist, buttery morsel crossed your lips.

Ursula didn't respond for a moment and Faith wondered if she was up to visitors, after all. Ursula's next words confirmed the thought.

"I'm a bit tired today."

Faith started to get to her feet.

"No!" Ursula said vehemently. "I need to talk to you!" She reached toward Faith and seemed agitated. "Don't leave."

Faith settled back into the chair. "Of course I won't. I just thought you might want to rest."

"I do. It's horrible. That's all I ever do, but I'd like you to come back in the morning. Pix will be gone by then—be sure to wait until the cab takes them to the airport—and besides, mornings are my best times."

"That's no problem. I can come tomorrow."

Ursula sank back against the pillows and closed her eyes briefly.

Opening them again, she said, "I have to tell you something. A story."

Faith nodded.

"It's about something that happened a long time ago."

"To you?"

Ursula ignored the question. "We'll need a lot of time. It's a long story and I must start at the beginning. When we get to the end, I will need your help."

"Anything," Faith said, softly stroking Ursula's hand.

"And Faith, you can't tell my family what I say."

"Not Pix?" Faith was surprised.

"Especially not Pix."

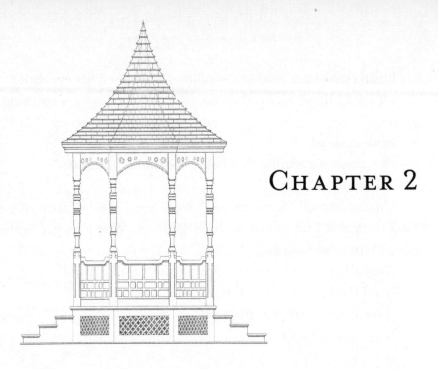

CHAPTER 2

"No, Pix, you will not need these." Faith plucked a pair of extremely worn sneakers from her friend's hands.

"They're in case I get a chance to go bird-watching in a marshy area. My other sneakers are too good."

Having packed the other sneakers herself, Faith would have employed another description. She'd gingerly wrapped them in tissue to keep them away from Pix's mostly new apparel and accessories.

"There are stores in South Carolina. If you go wading in any marshes"—Faith shuddered slightly at the thought—"you can make the ones already packed your 'marshy' sneaks and buy new ones to wear other places."

Pix looked at the two suitcases, filled to the brim, and ran her hand through her hair, a gesture she had been repeating frequently since Faith arrived to help her finish getting ready for the trip South. Her thick, short locks now resembled a pot scrubber.

"I really don't think I need to bring this much stuff. I'm sure I can get away with one suitcase. Sam is."

"Sam is staying less than a week and men can get away with

less—nobody notices that they're wearing the same pants, and a navy sports jacket is all he needs for dinner so long as he brings a few different ties. Plus, he'll be on the golf course with Becca's father most of the time."

"It's very expensive to check bags these days." Pix's mouth curved down.

Faith repressed a sigh. "Samantha has checked all three of you in online, so you saved some money—and, in any case, it's non-refundable."

That did it and Pix glanced about the room looking for something else to tuck in now that the money had been spent: her good bedside reading lamp? Some of the forest of framed family photos that covered every flat surface? An afghan?

Meanwhile, Faith was zipping the cases shut. Even though Pix was frugal—and generous—it wasn't the baggage fee that was upsetting her. It was leaving Ursula, hence Faith's inward sigh. She knew how Pix was feeling, how torn her friend was, and wished the timing for the trip had been earlier or later.

"As soon as the cab leaves, I'll head over to your mother's. I promised her I would wait to see you all off."

As Faith said that, she wondered why Ursula had been so emphatic that Faith witness Pix's departure. Did she think Pix would cancel at the last minute?

"And you've promised me that you'll call instantly if you think I should come home," Pix said. "Though she was looking better last night when I went to say good-bye."

"It's not going to happen; you're not going to have to come back, but you know I'd call you. And yes, when I saw her yesterday I thought she looked good and so did Tom. He stopped in at noon. He said he particularly noticed she wasn't as pale as when he'd last visited. She was quite cheerful—telling him that she planned to wear the same dress for Mark's wedding that she'd worn for yours."

Pix laughed. "We were married in December, so I'm not sure how appropriate garnet satin is for June. She can still fit into it is the point she's not so subtly making. My mother *does* have a streak of vanity."

"And with ample reason. She's beautiful still, but from the pictures, I can see she was a knockout when she was younger," Faith said. "Now, Ms. Mother-of-the Groom, you'd better get going. Look in that pocketbook of yours once more and be sure you don't have anything that airport security could mistake for a weapon—your Hiker Swiss Army knife, for example."

Sam had given it to Pix on their last anniversary and it had everything save the keg that a Saint Bernard carried. While Faith's notion of anniversary gifts ran more to things with carats, it had been exactly what Pix wanted and she toted it everywhere.

"It's in my suitcase."

Samantha came running into the room.

"The cab is here and Dad's already outside. Go to the bathroom and I'll tell them you're on the way!"

"I thought I was the mother," Pix said, heading for the toilet nevertheless.

Faith and Samantha exchanged glances and a hug.

"You'll have a wonderful time. And everything here will be fine," Faith said.

"I know. Becca's great. I've always wanted a sister and, even though she has two of her own, she's made me feel like one more already."

Pix emerged and grabbed her suitcases. She'd obviously glanced in the mirror and her hair was back to normal, but she'd forgotten lipstick. Faith decided now was not the time for makeup advice.

"Where are your bags?" Pix asked her daughter.

"In the cab, and let me take one of these. We have plenty of time, Mom, don't worry."

"Again, it's too early for role reversal. You've got a few more years to go." Pix had recently read an article about this female child/parent phenomenon and told Faith to be ready when Amy hit her twenties. The good news was that with such dutiful daughters, they would both have someone to do things like cut their toenails when they hit their twilight years.

"And I'm not worried, just being practical. There could be traffic on the Mass Pike." With that she squared her shoulders and set off down the hallway.

Soon Faith was standing in the driveway watching per Ursula's instruction. The cab turned out of sight onto Main Street and she ducked through the opening in the boxwood hedge shared by the Millers and the Fairchilds. Over the years, the space had been widened by numerous crossings between the two yards. She went straight to the garage. Tom was doing parent duty at the kids' soccer games, so Faith got in her car and drove the short distance to Ursula Rowe's.

A story. A long story, Ursula had said. She could hardly wait.

Ursula was out of bed and in her chaise, tucked under a duvet. Before she left, Dora had brought a glass of some sort of smoothie that she set on a small table, admonishing Ursula to finish "every last drop."

"It's my special protein shake," she'd told Faith. "She loves them."

Ursula had made a face, but as soon as the nurse was gone, she took a sip.

"If this is what it takes to get me up and around, I'd be a fool not to do it—however loathsome it tastes. I think Dora's secret ingredient is chalk."

Ursula took another swallow.

"I'm sure it will work Dora's magic," Faith said. "Let me get your water, so you can sip some after you finish. It might help."

Faith got the carafe and glass from the nightstand next to Ursula's bed. The preamble was continuing. Ursula was apparently waiting to start her story until after she'd finished the drink.

"Samantha wants me to get one of those cell phones. As if I needed one! There's a perfectly good phone in the hallway. She says she'd like to be able to talk to me when I'm in bed."

It was a good idea, Faith thought—and not just to talk to Samantha. Ursula had reluctantly given up her dial phones upstairs and down for touch-tones, but neither landline was a portable.

"I think the Millers have a family plan where they can add you as another number. It wouldn't be expensive," Faith commented, correctly guessing that Ursula was not only concerned with the newness of the technology, but the cost. While Faith knew Ursula was "comfortable," which in Aleford parlance meant many pennies both earned and saved, she also knew Ursula did not like to spend those pennies except on things like presents for her grandchildren and a number of charitable institutions. Some of Ursula's clothing, especially outerwear, had belonged to her mother: "Perfectly good tweed. It will last until I'm gone and then some." Frugal—and generous—just like her daughter.

Soon Ursula had drunk "every last drop" and taken several sips of water. She started in immediately.

"I was born in Boston, as you probably know. Not at home, but at the old Boston Lying-in Hospital. My Lyman grandmother was apparently shocked. She was a bit of a snob, perhaps more than a bit, and thought it rather common not to have the doctor come to you in the sanctity of one's own boudoir. Thank goodness my parents had more sense. Apparently I gave my mother a rather difficult time and there were no more babies after me.

"My father was in business and we lived on Mt. Vernon Street on the South Slope of Beacon Hill—the only side, again Grandmother Lyman's opinion. Sundays we walked up and over the Hill, past the State House with its big golden dome, to church at King's Chapel. Boston has changed enormously since I was a girl, but not that walk, I fancy. The rest of the town is barely recognizable to me today. In my early years, there was no skyline. Just one skyscraper—the Customs House Tower. You can barely make it out now, so many buildings have risen up around it, and we certainly never imagined that anything as tall as the new John Hancock building could exist except in the imagination. Father's office was down the street from the Customs House. Peregrine falcons nested in the tower—and still do. I imagine they find it more aesthetic than some of the other buildings nearby. Father always grumbled about the clock on the tower—it never kept accurate time. This was the sort of thing that mattered to him, and his associates, I dare say. The area was, and is, Boston's financial district, convenient to the wharves, although the old buildings are expensive hotels and condominiums today, not a bit like the places where we'd go watch the ships dock. Father would sometimes take me with him when he went in on a Saturday and we'd go down to the harbor after he'd finished whatever it was he had to do.

"He used to joke that if the wind was right, we could smell molasses. I'm sure you've heard about the terrible Molasses Flood in 1919. The tank where it was stored exploded and killed more than twenty people. Over two million gallons spilled out in a wave that was over thirty-five feet high. Father always mentioned the statistics. Ten years later—the story I'll get to eventually starts in the summer of 1929—people would still claim some of the downtown alleys got sticky when it was hot, and perhaps it was the power of suggestion, but I *did* think I could smell it on those long-ago walks.

"Father was always so well turned out. Not dapper, never that. I could tell the change of season by his hats—homburgs turned into straw boaters with broad black bands in the late spring and summer. Top hats for evenings out. His shoes came from London. I believe a man actually came to the house to show him the styles and measure his feet. He had a gold watch that his father had given him for not drinking or smoking until he was eighteen, not that he did much of either afterward. One of my first memories is of listening to the watch tick at the end of its long, gold fob.

"Mother didn't work, of course. Women of her class didn't then. But she was very busy running the household. Unlike many of her peers, she had been an ardent suffragist, although I'm not sure my father was altogether happy about it. It's odd to think that I was born before women could vote. Although Mother could never have been described as a radical, she raised me to believe that men and women were equal and entitled to the same rights. She did a great deal of charity work and was an active member of the Fragment Society, the oldest continuous sewing circle in Boston. It was started during the War of 1812. Pix and I are members, too— although what we do is quite different from Mother's day. Mother might not have been able to do more than boil water for tea, but she did beautiful handwork, and I'm sure the indigent new mothers who received what she made for their layettes were thrilled.

"She had been a well-known beauty in her time and had a delicious sense of humor. She always smelled of lilies of the valley. It was the only scent she used. The only cosmetic. My father wouldn't have stood for rouge or even rice powder. I don't think she much cared. She was very interested in what she wore, though. Father had given her a pearl collar similar to Queen Mary's for a wedding gift and the pearls became Mother's signature jewelry, too."

Ursula paused before taking up the thread again.

"You're sitting here so patiently and I know you're wondering where I'm going with this, but I promise you, it's going somewhere. My story has a number of pieces, which will come together at the end. Just now with this piece, I'm trying to give you a sense of what it was like in Boston—for my parents and for me. They grew up in another century and the changes the twentieth brought were rapid and must have been bewildering to them at times. Especially the changes during the 1920s. I've often thought this was the beginning of the notion of a generation gap. Young people in the Jazz Age were so very different from the kinds of young people their parents had been in what was still the Victorian Age. Maybe it's a little like Samantha and her cell phone— all this new technology. We had 'talkies' and Lucky Lindy flying across the Atlantic. Pix thinks Samantha's frocks belong in the rag pile and the flappers' mothers must have thought the same way. Despite everything that was going on around me, though, as a little girl, my day-to-day life wasn't so far removed from that of my mother's growing up.

"We skated on the Frog Pond on the Boston Common in the winter, and the arrival of the swan boats in the Public Garden was the first sign of spring for us, along with snow drops in Louisburg Square. My brother and his friends sculled on the Charles River straight through until late autumn when the water started to freeze."

Ursula looked straight at Faith.

"Pix has never mentioned an uncle, has she?"

Faith shook her head. Ursula drank some water and leaned back again on the large down European square pillows Dora had arranged for her patient's comfort.

"My brother Theodore. He was always called 'Theo.' "

"Come on, Sis. All you have to do is slip downstairs once the mater and pater are asleep and unlock the side door. I'll lock it up again. Don't worry. I'm not about to risk the family plate."

Ursula Lyman cocked her head to one side and pretended to think. She knew—and Theo knew—that she'd do anything her adored big brother asked.

"Once the break is over and I'm back on campus, I won't have this kind of bother."

"*Just the regular kind of bother—your studies.*" *Ursula tried to look stern. Theo's first-semester grades at Harvard hadn't even been gentlemen's Cs. Their father had threatened to cut off his son's allowance if they didn't improve markedly. He'd stopped short of demanding that Theo move home. Leaving Westmorly Court, one of Harvard's "Gold Coast" houses on Mount Auburn Street, which Theo had opted for over the more plebian, and shabbier, freshman housing in the Yard, would make Theo's failings too public.*

"*I've been burning the midnight oil, don't you worry your pretty little head. A fellow has to have some fun, you know. So, what do you say—will you do it?*"

Ursula nodded. Theo lifted his sister up and swung her around. She had been as much a surprise to him nine years ago as he imagined she must have been to their parents.

"*But do be careful—and good, Theo, won't you?*"

"*I'm always good and careful,*" *he said, laughing.*

*Theo set his sister down and looked in the tall pier glass mirror at the end of the broad front hallway where they'd been standing. Their reflection could have been a painting by Sargent—*Master Theodore Speedwell Lyman and sister, Ursula Rose. *Theo's hair was carefully parted in the middle and slicked down; he was wearing evening clothes. To please his parents, he was dining at their Cabot cousin's home on Beacon Street before making an appearance at one of the many debutante balls to which he and his very eligible friends were continually invited. But that dinner and the ball would merely mark the start of his evening. Later he and some of his chums were treating a few of the beauties from the Old Howard to a post-show supper at Locke-Ober—upstairs in a private dining room, the only part of the restaurant where women were allowed. He'd ordered Lobster Savannah, the house specialty, and they'd have to bring in their own magnums of champagne thanks to Prohibition—damn it all. Of course the ladies would be wearing considerably more than they would have been earlier. He hoped those dreary guardians of* the public morality from the Watch and Ward Society wouldn't have stopped by to interrupt the show, which would push supper up later. The irony was that some of last season's debs, who were officially launched and therefore granted more leeway now, would be wearing outfits at the ball that were almost as revealing as the strippers'. He chuckled to himself and pulled a Butterfinger candy bar—her favorite—from his pocket for his sister.

Ursula was studying herself in the mirror. She was clad in the blue serge skirt, black lisle stockings, and long middy blouse she'd worn to school. Winsor had moved to the Longwood area of Boston some ten years ago and Mrs. Lyman regularly complained about the distance. "When I was a student, it was so convenient. Right here on the Hill. We could walk."

Ursula rather liked the commute. She wasn't allowed to explore Boston on her own yet, but she yearned for the day when she could go to the opposite side of the Hill to the West End and perhaps even down to Scollay Square. She was pretty sure that was where her brother would be for at least part of the evening. She'd seen the giant two-hundred-pound steaming teakettle that hung above the Oriental Tea Company not far from the Square down Tremont Street several blocks away from King's Chapel, but it was the limit permissible in that tantalizing direction. She wasn't interested in what her brother sought in Scollay Square. What she wanted to explore were the bookshops on nearby Corn Hill. But her world was carefully circumscribed by the Common and the Public Garden with occasional trips to the Boston Public Library in Copley Square, the Museum of Fine Arts in the Fenway, or Symphony Hall.

Each morning Mr. Lyman's chauffeur returned from dropping his employer off at his offices to drive his employer's daughter to school. While Ursula thought taking the subway would be great fun, she found plenty to entertain herself looking out the window of the big Packard.

"I wish Mother would let me bob my hair," she complained,

turning away from the mirror and eagerly accepting her brother's proffered treat.

Theo yanked one of her braids. "Don't be in a hurry to grow up, squirt. It's not all that it's cracked up to be."

Although the evening promised to be great fun—Charlie Winthrop was picking him up after dinner in the Stutz Torpedo he'd just bought, plus Charlie always had the best hooch—Theo had a moment's longing for the days when he was a schoolboy at Milton, coming home on weekends with nothing much to worry about except beating Groton's football team. He hadn't made Harvard's team, but it would have been rare for a frosh. He missed playing, which was maybe why he was making up for it by all this other playing. Ursula was holding out the white silk scarf he'd dropped when he'd put on his overcoat. Her serious little face was crinkled in a smile. He promised himself he'd buckle down and give up the late nights at Sanborn's Billiards and Tobacco Parlor, hit the books, and make everyone proud—especially the girl standing in front of him.

"You're a brick," he told her, and with a wave, walked out into the dusk.

Faith drove slowly through the streets of Aleford to the outskirts of town where her catering kitchen was located. Her thoughts were so firmly fixed on the early twentieth century that she was startled when a Toyota Prius glided by. The car would have seemed like something from a science fiction novel in 1929. Nineteen twenty-nine. That's when Ursula had said her story started, although so far she'd been describing the years prior, her childhood, and Faith had been captivated by the picture of this bygone era drawn by someone who had lived it. Both Tom's and Faith's parents were younger than Ursula. And of those closer to her in age who would have remembered that significant year, only Faith's paternal grandmother was still alive—Olive Sibley. She lived in New Jersey with her daughter, Faith's aunt Chat, short for Charity. Sibley women had been named Faith, Hope, and Charity since Noah. Faith's parents had stopped with Hope. Whether this was due to an aversion to the third name on the part of Jane, Faith's mother, or the decision that two children were enough, Faith did not know. However, she did know that no one on the branches of the family tree had ever gone beyond Charity. What would it have been? Chastity, no doubt.

Listening to Ursula today, Faith regretted not having spent more time asking her grandmother about her childhood—or asking her mother and father about theirs. She resolved to take a recorder with her on her next trip to the city. And yes, Jersey—to Aunt Chat's. Charity Sibley had made a name for herself—and a great deal of money—in advertising. The firm she founded was a household name, as were the products in her account portfolio. Her colleagues and friends were astounded when she sold the business, retired early, and purchased a small estate in Mendham, on the wrong side of the Hudson. She had been contentedly raising miniature horses and prize dahlias ever since. The fabulous parties she'd hosted at her San Remo apartment in one of the towers overlooking Central Park continued in the new locale. New Yorkers, for whom the Garden State was a less likely destination than Mars, were soon happily crossing the George Washington Bridge.

The big question, Faith thought as she pulled up to work, was why Pix—who had revealed details of her life ranging from the name of her kindergarten class pet (Eleanor, a guinea pig) to where and when she and Sam first did "it"—had never mentioned having an uncle. *Theo*. It was a lovely, old-fashioned nickname. There were several possible answers to this question: He was the despised black sheep of the family, although Ursula's description of him so far had been very affectionate; he died well before Pix was born;

or finally, Pix didn't know of his existence. Was this last what Ursula didn't want Faith to reveal? That Ursula had a brother? In the course of her story were other siblings going to emerge? Up until now, Faith had assumed Ursula was an only child. She'd indicated that there weren't any more babies after her birth, but what about older siblings besides Theo?

She'd reached the catering kitchen. Faith unlocked the door, hung up her coat, and took out some sweet butter from the refrigerator and flour from the walk-in pantry. Ursula clearly could not talk for long without tiring and Faith had left her dozing. It meant she now had time to prepare some much-needed puff pastry, *feuilletage,* for the freezer. *Feuilletage,* from the French for "leaf," was tricky and involved folding, rolling, and folding the buttery dough over itself again multiple times in order to get those ethereal, leaf-thin layers that would literally melt in your mouth. It was a task she had always loved—something about the repetitive motion was soothing. Not that anything particular was bothering her at the moment. She quickly knocked wood, tapping the counter with her wide rolling pin. Sure, Amy was dealing with a small group of mean girls in her grade, but she said she had only told her mother to show how well she and her friends were handling them. "We just laugh like crazy at everything they say and Sarah says stuff like, 'Aren't they hysterical,' and they get mad and go to the other side of the playground." It *was* a good strategy, but Faith, remembering some of the recent tragic outcomes of bullying, had called both the school principal and Amy's teacher, asking each to keep an eye on the situation.

After a very rough start in middle school, Ben had discovered that he loved English—although it might have something to do with the very young and very pretty student teacher who had recently arrived. He was currently turning out short stories about vegetarian vampires for his writing assignments. They were actually pretty funny, although that might not be Ben's intent. And Tom, thank goodness, was his hale and hearty self again. So, knock wood, no worries. Well, there was the economy and the fact that Faith's business was off by over half. In addition, clients for the events they were catering were substituting things on sticks and cheese plates for passed mini beef Wellington and lobster spring rolls; opting for wine and beer without the exotic cocktails that had formerly been all the rage.

Some of the puff pastry in front of her was for an event Have Faith was catering for a yacht club on the North Shore. The Tiller Club had an annual game dinner in the fall and an old-fashioned clambake in the summer, both of which Faith had catered for years. The chairman had called Faith late last summer and told her there would be only one dinner this year and it would be a "Spring Fling" in late March. Faith thought he was being rather optimistic with the name—not the "Fling" part; the "Tillies," as the men called themselves, were nautical party animals, but March didn't suggest spring to her. However, just this week the plow guy had removed those long sticks he used to avoid running off the Fairchild's driveway during a heavy snowfall. This was a more accurate harbinger of the season than the poor crocuses that struggled to bloom, so the Tillies had been right.

Their first course would be a *champignon Napoléon*—delicious, but plain old button mushrooms sautéed in butter with a bit of cream and sherry added at the end, not the medley of wild (expensive) mushrooms she normally used. And the chairman had opted for chicken roulade, not prime rib, as Faith had first suggested, knowing from the game dinners the amount of red meat they gleefully scarfed down.

Two things wouldn't change on the menu. The dessert—boys at heart, they always wanted chocolate layer cake—and plenty of dinner rolls served throughout the meal, since tossing them, and rolled-up napkins, at one another made up much of the evening's entertainment. The club supplied the booze and, recession or no, Faith was sure it would flow as amply as it had in other years. One had to maintain standards, after all. The dinner was next Friday and she made a mental note to remind Scott and Tricia Phelan, who worked as bartender and server at most of her events. Scott's day job was at an auto body shop in nearby Byford, and Trish was working as an occasional apprentice for Faith, hoping to gain enough skill to find a job in a restaurant kitchen, bringing in some much-needed additional income. Their two kids were both in school full-time now and Faith wished she could put Trish on salary. Maybe in a few months.

Faith knew business would pick up. History repeated itself. There had been a big slump just before she left Manhattan for Aleford, marriage, and motherhood. There had been slumps here in Aleford. For now she could weather the storm without a bailout. Have Faith was still running the café at the Ganley, a local art museum, and it provided a nice, steady income. Before she took the job, Faith had checked out the fare offered by the previous purveyor. The lettuce in her salad was black and slimy; the canned tuna in the tuna salad reminiscent of the botulism-loaded cans from the Spanish-American War. The brownies looked like cow chips. The café attracted more visitors to the museum, once word got out that food poisoning was no longer a risk.

Lost in thought and pastry, Faith was startled when the door opened. It was Niki Constantine, Faith's longtime assistant. A year and a half ago Niki had married Phillip Theodopoulos in an extravaganza that made *My Big Fat Greek Wedding* look like an elopement. Niki had grown up in nearby Watertown, during which time her mother had made her expectations clear to her only daughter. College, okay, but an engagement ring from a nice Greek boy by graduation; a June wedding; first grandchild a year later: "We don't want people counting on their fingers." Niki had rebelled, starting with culinary school instead of Mount Ida College, and then refusing to date any male remotely Greek in heritage, instead parading boyfriends who ranged from Lowell bikers to a Buddhist old enough to be her father, maybe grandfather. And then despite her best intentions, she had fallen hard for the man of her mother's dreams—Yale undergrad, Harvard MBA, handsome, family oriented (he had pictures of his parents, sibs, *and* their kids in his wallet), plus he was Greek. First generation. Throughout, Faith had watched from the sidelines, listening to Niki's descriptions and laughing. In addition to being the best assistant she could have wished for, especially when it came to desserts, Niki was also the funniest friend Faith had.

Niki wasn't smiling today.

"I thought you and Phil were driving down to see his parents in Hartford."

Just as Niki had found herself drawn inexorably into the vortex that was her mother's idea of a real wedding—Niki's gown had had so many crinolines she'd told Faith she felt like one of those dolls her aunt Dimitra crocheted skirts for to hide the toilet paper roll—she'd also been pulled into Phil's family, although she found that she enjoyed being an aunt to his numerous nephews and nieces. The fact that his mother made the best baklava in the world and always for Niki didn't hurt, either.

"Phil needed to go golfing—and I wasn't in the mood to read *If You Give a Mouse a Cookie* forty times in a row."

"Sit down, and as soon as I finish this, *I'll* give you a cookie. You look tired. Out late clubbing? Make some coffee. I wouldn't mind a cup."

Niki had refused to give up her lifestyle as a freewheeling twenty-seven-year-old and Phil was happy to go along.

When Niki didn't respond—unheard of—and instead slumped into a chair without removing her jacket, Faith hastily wrapped the packets of dough, crossed the room to the freezer, and set them inside. With all that butter, they had to go in immediately. She stood in front of her friend and said, "How about *I* make the coffee and *you* tell me what's going on."

Niki sat up a little straighter.

"No coffee."

Faith began to get very worried. Niki loved coffee, delightedly bringing ever more unusual blends to Faith's attention—the latest was Malabar Monsooned from India, its special taste indeed acquired from exposure to monsoons. Niki wasn't just a connoisseur. The stuff ran in her veins, and she joked that one of her ancestors' ships must have gone radically off course, ending up in Scandinavia instead of Macedonia.

Pulling a chair close to Niki's, Faith sat down and took Niki's hand.

"Tell me what's going on," she said quietly.

"Oh Faith," Niki said, bursting into tears. "I'm pregnant!"

"But that's wonderful!"

Niki had been regaling Faith and Pix for months with the various folk remedies her mother and aunts had advised to speed conception. Niki had told them she was sure plain old trying would eventually work, and meanwhile it wasn't "trying" at all, but more fun than should be legal—her words.

Faith added, "This is the news you've been waiting for . . ." before her voice trailed off. The woman sobbing in front of her wasn't shedding tears of joy. There must be something wrong with the baby. But it was so soon. She couldn't be far along. Faith would have noticed and Niki wouldn't have been able to keep it to herself, although she had told both Faith and Pix that no one was to tell Mrs. Constantine until Niki was at least eight months along. Niki didn't want to be wrapped in cotton wool and subjected to endless advice about what to eat, what not to look at—her mother had already advised against any movie scarier than *The Sound of Music* lest it affect her future grandchild's psyche.

"Is it the baby? Did they find something—"

Niki interrupted, rubbing her eyes with her hands in what looked like an angry gesture.

"No, I'm sure nothing's wrong. I haven't been to the doctor. Just did the test at home because I missed my period—and I'm never late. But you know me. Healthy as a horse. Phil, too, so the baby should be doing fine. That's not it."

She started to cry again. Faith got a box of tissues from under the counter. The only other time she could remember seeing Niki in tears was when the Constantines' dog died, a chocolate Lab they'd had all Niki's life. She swore that his coat was what inspired her to turn to truffles and the other sweets she loved to create.

Suddenly what Niki had said when she arrived came back to Faith, "Phil needed to go golfing." The ground was still hard and it was cold. Phil enjoyed the occasional round, but he wasn't a fanatic. Why did he "need" to golf today? In his corporate world, there was only one reason Faith could think of—networking. Big-time.

"Is something going on at work for Phil?"

Niki blew her nose.

"Just that he lost his job yesterday."

"Damn!"

There wasn't anything else to say. Faith put her arms around Niki. She was crying harder. This should have been one of the happiest days of her life. Phil had been steadily working his way up the ladder, but he'd only been with this firm for three years. There were a lot of occupied rungs above his.

Niki took another tissue and wiped her eyes.

"Yup. Handed him a carton and took back the key to the men's room. He started dialing as soon as he walked out into Post Office Square, and the only nibble he's gotten is this golf game with someone who knows someone who was at Yale with him."

The days when job hunting consisted of scanning the want ads in the *Boston Globe* and mailing out résumés were totally foreign to Phil and Niki's generation. Now it was all about networking, the golf kind, and the Internet kind.

"He's lined up interviews with some headhunters. The most immediate problem is his parachute. It wasn't golden. More like cheesecloth. A month's pay and three months' health insurance."

There it was. Health insurance, the policy had covered Niki, too, and now it was good for only three more months.

"But surely he'll find something before it runs out."

Niki shook her head. "He has friends who have been out of work for much longer than that. We have some savings and he can cash in his 401(k) . . ."

"Don't even think about it. I'll cover you and Phil, as an employee spouse, here," Faith said.

"You have no idea how much money that's going to cost you, especially with my preexisting condition."

"Expecting a baby isn't like cancer or heart disease. I'll talk to Ralph and we'll get it ready to go immediately in case you need it. And that's final." Faith could see that Niki was getting ready to argue some more. On Monday morning she'd call Ralph, her insurance agent, who handled Have Faith's business coverage, and tell him what was going on.

"Coffee now? I've got decaf beans," Faith offered, mindful of avoiding caffeine during pregnancy.

"I don't think so," Niki said, graphically gesturing—finger pointed down her throat. "That's how I first knew. About a week ago the smell started making me want to barf. I haven't actually been losing lunch, but feel like it a lot. Weird." Niki seemed to be considering the situation.

"Okay, how about a glass of milk and some cookies, then?"

Niki's responses—verbal and physical—meant she was edging back toward her normal self and Faith was relieved. Phil would find a job in due course and meanwhile Niki could enjoy her pregnancy, although there was an oxymoron in there someplace if Faith's experiences were anything to go by. Mostly she recalled having to pee constantly and panicking when she wasn't near a bathroom. Pix had told her it was one of the main reasons for joining a club in Boston. You could go downtown when pregnant without fear.

"And once little beanbag or whatever nauseatingly cute name you guys come up with for him or her in utero arrives, we're all set up here for you to bring the baby to work," Faith said.

When she had purchased Yankee Doodle Dandy Dining, the catering firm that had previously occupied the space, she had completely remodeled the facility. During the process, she created an area where her kids could safely play from the time they were toddlers well into elementary school. Amy still liked to come hang out when her busy schedule permitted it.

"I haven't thought that far ahead," Niki said, "but not having to pay for day care will save a lot. It also gives me an excuse to keep my mother from taking over."

Niki's mother indeed was a force of nature, but Faith liked and admired her, even while she understood how hard it was for Niki to have such a controlling individual hovering over her life. "Smother Love" might have been coined for Mrs. Constantine. Which was why Faith doubted Niki could keep her condition secret. However, Niki's brother was engaged and this could possibly deflect attention from Niki for a while, as his fiancée was only half Greek and her future mother-in-law was busy teaching her how to make all her future husband's favorite dishes. The situation had caused Niki to mention recently that there really *were* gods up there on Mount Olympus.

"Phil must be over the moon," Faith said, relaxing into their usual companionable mode.

Niki dipped her molasses sugar cookie into her milk and took a bite.

"I haven't told him yet," she mumbled.

The mode switched back.

"You haven't told him! Niki, eventually he's going to notice the patter of little feet."

"I know, I know. The stick only turned blue yesterday, and yes, I was really, really happy. Then he called with his news, and by the time he got home, I'd decided this was not the time to lay it on the guy that he'd better be out there hustling up some bread because there was going to be an extra place at the table for a bunch of years. Besides, I have a job, which brings me to the reason I came by. Oh hell, I came to tell you, you know that, but I also came to ask you a favor."

"Anything," Faith said.

"First, I don't want you to tell anyone I'm pregnant."

"Not even Pix?"

"Especially not Pix."

Ursula and now Niki. What was up with this? Poor Pix. Life was getting even stranger than usual.

"You know she can't keep a secret. The first time she saw Phil, she wouldn't be able to look him in the eye, would get all red, and he'd know something was going on."

"Sweetie! Pix is away for almost two more weeks. You can't keep this from him that long."

"I'll keep it from him as long as I want." Niki jutted her chin out, all traces of tears gone. "I don't want him to be distracted. He has enough on his plate without piling on a helping of father-hood." Niki seemed to be favoring meal metaphors.

"Okay." Faith backed off. Niki didn't need Faith adding to her stress. "Anything else?"

"It's a biggie. And if you think it will affect the business at all, you *have* to say so straight-out."

Faith was mystified. Niki continued. "Could I use the kitchen here when we're not doing a job? I thought maybe I could set up a dessert-catering Web site to bring in more money. Get Mom to spread the word about my cheesecakes at her bingo nights."

Niki's cheesecakes *were* truly delectable. Poetry even. Besides the traditional New York and strawberry-covered cakes in a variety of sizes, Niki also did praline, Amaretto, chocolate macadamia, and a new to-die-for pomegranate with a raspberry liqueur glaze. She was working on one for spring featuring Madagascar vanilla beans and toasted coconut.

"You didn't even have to ask—and don't worry about hurting business. Our customers almost always want full-service catering for dessert buffets—servers and people to clean up. This will be fun. I'll help."

"No you won't. I'll get Tricia. She wants to learn more about desserts. And of course I'll use my own ingredients."

"Look, it will all work out. You know me. I'm not Little Mary Sunshine, but we'll get through this. And now, just for a little minute, can we shout for joy? You and Phil will be such wonderful parents."

"You're going to make me cry again. I'm doing that a lot lately. Better than throwing up, though."

Faith decided not to tell her that this would in all likelihood start soon. Hair-trigger emotions first, sore nipples, and then morning sickness, which often stretched into the afternoon in Faith's case. Plus, it seemed she had just recovered when the infant she'd produced started what the books termed with scientific precision "projectile vomiting."

"I *am* happy," Niki said. "Very, very happy."

"Me, too." Faith smiled. "How about we call your business 'Little Mary Cheesecake'?"

"Don't push it, boss," Niki said. "I'm more the Suzy Creamcheese type."

*   *   *

It was close to five o'clock by the time Faith got home and she was surprised to see that Tom's car was gone. Where could her family be? But there were lights on in the parsonage kitchen. It was a mystery.

Faith went in the back door and found her daughter making chocolate chip cookies.

"Don't worry, I wasn't going to turn on the oven until you came home, Mom," Amy said.

Faith gave her conscientious little girl a hug, praying that she stayed that way, especially during her teen years.

"Where is everybody else? Dad's car is gone."

"He had to go to some meeting. He left you a note, and Ben's doing homework in Dad's study."

After a series of incidents last fall, Ben's computer was now out of his room and in a more public part of the house. Faith and Tom had followed the suggestion of many educators that with this simple act, they could control their child's behavior without constantly looking over his or her shoulder. Just the presence of an adult helped kids think twice—or more—about their conversations in cyberspace, particularly ones about other kids. You might think you're chatting to one or two others, but in reality it could be one or two billion, a fact few kids absorbed fully.

What kind of meeting could be held on a Saturday night? Faith wondered. That time was sacrosanct for the clergy who were preparing for a Sunday service. Presumably they were getting in an even holier mood than usual, and perhaps adding a comma or two to the following day's sermon. In reality there might be ministers who wrote their sermons early in the week, but Faith didn't know any and her husband was definitely not in that club. Most Saturday nights Tom Fairchild was frantically rewriting what he had decided before was just fine.

His note was written on the dry-erase family bulletin board.

"Sherman Munroe has called an emergency meeting of the vestry. No idea why. Back soon, I hope. Love, Tom."

Sherman—and don't ever call him "Sherm"—was one of Faith's least favorite parishioners. He was a relatively new arrival to Aleford. He'd lived in town for only five years, but as he was fond of saying, "My people started the place." There were some Munroes in the Old Burial Ground, so they *had* been around at the time of the town's incorporation, but as for starting anything, if they had, they hadn't stuck around to finish—the ones aboveground, that is. One and all had absented themselves until Sherman turned up after retiring from, according to him, a highly lucrative manufacturing business in Pennsylvania. Millicent Revere McKinley, whose frontal lobe was a veritable Rolodex of Alefordiana, conceded that he was descended from "those early Munroes," her tone suggesting that some other Munroes would have been preferable. She had followed it up with a few tart sentences expressing her opinion about locating businesses not simply out of state, but out of Aleford.

By taking on jobs no one else wanted to do, Sherman soon became a player at First Parish and a thorn in Tom's side. Everything that had occurred before Mr. Munroe's arrival had been done "bass ackward"—a phrase Faith particularly despised, along with "connect the dots." And now that he was on the vestry, things were even worse. Faith speculated about what emergency Sherman had dreamed up. Dissatisfaction with the brand of coffee being used for coffee hour? A reiteration of his ongoing objection to the haphazard way Sherman thought the sexton placed the prayer books and hymnals in the pews?

Faith had been looking forward to telling Tom about her conversation with Ursula and all of Niki's news. Like Ursula, Niki had recognized that the don't-tell rule excluded spouses and conceded that Faith would have to let Tom know she was pregnant.

Yet, most of all, Faith was annoyed about the stress this Munroe jerk was causing Tom. She was tempted to call his cell and tell him to come home for dinner. It was bad for him to skip meals. His postpancreatitis care had specifically included this warning. Someone occasionally brought cookies to the vestry meetings, but you couldn't count on it. And the meeting better not go late. Tom needed his sleep.

Faith was working herself into a very righteous snit when she heard the car pull in. Amy's cookies were in one oven, giving the house a delicious smell, and Faith had optimistically popped the country ham and potato au gratin made with a Gruyère-laden béchamel sauce in the other. She had broccoli crowns, the stems saved for soup, in a pot ready to steam at the last minute. Ben had set the table—it was his turn—and it looked as if the night would be salvaged.

The moment she saw her husband's face, she told Amy to go join Ben and read while he worked. Faith would watch the cookies, and dinner might be a while.

She didn't have to ask what was wrong. The words came rushing from Tom's mouth like an avalanche, each one pushing the next forward with deadly force.

"The independent audit we authorized has uncovered a shortfall. A large shortfall. Over ten thousand dollars is missing. Missing from the Minister's Discretionary Fund."

Faith was having trouble taking it in. She stood for a moment with the casserole she'd removed from the oven in her hands. "The Minister's Discretionary Fund?"

Tom sat down heavily, still in his coat.

"Yes, the Discretionary Fund."

Faith knew what it was. She'd just been repeating his words, hoping somehow she had heard him wrong. She hadn't.

The Minister's Discretionary Fund. Money that the Reverend Thomas Preston Fairchild alone had access to and for which he was solely accountable.

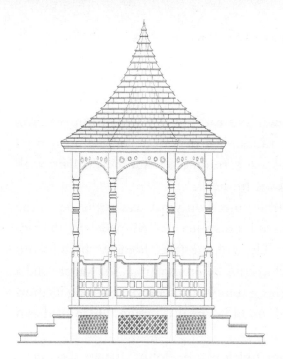

CHAPTER 3

Normally Faith liked the Sunday morning service, which was a good thing since she seemed to have been destined to sit through endless numbers of them starting in early childhood. Unlike First Parish, her father's church didn't have child care until relatively recently, so her mother had had to tote Faith and Hope with her, settling in the last pew on the right with books, puzzles, and boxes of animal crackers to keep her children occupied and quiet. It must have been nice for Jane Sibley when her daughters were finally old enough for Sunday school and she could enjoy the service without worrying about crumbs on the pew cushions. Faith's first Sunday after arriving in Aleford as a new bride, she had instinctively zeroed in on the same pew, only to be escorted to the front left by the Senior Warden. "This is where the minister's wife *always* sits."

Today she was glad she couldn't see the faces behind her, although she imagined any number of eyes were boring holes in her back as she prayed for the hour to go quickly. What had happened at last night's meeting should be only from the vestry to God's ear, but more likely it was from the vestry to Aleford's.

She wanted to get Tom back home. He'd been up and out of

the house before she'd had breakfast on the table, grabbing an apple cinnamon muffin she had just taken from the oven and resisting her plea to sit down and eat. She'd watched him striding over to the church, his unfastened dark robe billowing behind him. He reminded her of that cartoon character in *Li'l Abner* with a permanent rain cloud over his head.

She struggled to keep her mind on what was going on in the pulpit. The New Testament lesson. Sherman Munroe was the lector this morning. His ruddy, vulpine face shone with righteous well-being and he licked his lips before starting. She suppressed a shudder. It was like watching some sort of animal stalking its prey. Tom, in contrast, was pale and his face was drawn. He looked as if he needed to lie down.

"The Gospel lesson for today is from John, chapter six, verses four through fifteen."

Sherman read well. It was the familiar story of the loaves and the fishes. Tom was using this reading as the reference point for his sermon. Late last night he'd given it to her to read—something he rarely did. They had been pretending to watch television—a DVD of the British comedy series *The Vicar of Dibley*. When he hadn't laughed even once—it was the Easter Bunny episode— she'd suggested bed. He'd switched off the set and asked if she'd "look over" what he'd written for the morning. She'd poured herself a glass of merlot and made him a steaming mug of cocoa. She knew he'd wanted to make sure there was nothing in the sermon's references to the miracle—multiplying much from little—that could be misconstrued. Of course there wasn't and this reassurance seemed to be what he needed to finally fall asleep. She lay wide awake, shaken by what this accusation, not even made directly yet, was already doing to her husband.

The sermon touched upon the question of what it is that sustains us—those material and nonmaterial things that feed our lives. What goes into our individual loaves and fishes, and how we can use our faith to nourish not just ourselves but others—making those five barley loaves fill twelve, and even more, baskets. Tom was an able and often eloquent preacher. There were people in church every Sunday, not members either of First Parish or the denomination, who came solely for the sermons, which was fine with him. That his words could inspire, comfort, provoke thought, or simply interest someone was gratifying. It was one of the things he'd hoped his ministry might accomplish over the years. His own brand of loaves and fishes.

Today, though, Faith feared his words would be minimized by a delivery that was not up to his usual. He had stumbled during the Call to Worship and again when reading the General Thanksgiving. She only hoped he could get through the entire service.

Sherman was done and stepped down, resuming his seat across the aisle from Faith. Front row right. He glanced her way and lifted an eyebrow.

She hated him.

It had been his idea to hire an independent CPA who specialized in nonprofits to do the annual financial review. It had always been done in house prior to this year. She found herself wondering why he had not merely suggested it, but insisted on it. "Good business practice" was his oft-repeated rationale. But a church wasn't a business! During those discussions, Tom had come home from vestry meetings alternately furious and exhausted. "It's a total waste of money! What does the man think? That Mr. Brown has a Swiss bank account?" Mr. Brown was the sexton.

Sherman prevailed. It wasn't hard to see why he'd been such a successful CEO and now here were the results.

Faith directed her gaze to the early spring flowers—jonquils, tulips, and daffodils in pale yellows and ivories—that graced the altar in memory of Ursula's late husband, who had died at this time years before Faith had come to Aleford. She was sorry neither Ursula nor Pix could see them. Especially Pix, she thought, feeling a bit selfish. A terrible time to be away. Sam Miller, one of Boston's most esteemed lawyers, would make quick work of this mess. Well, he'd be back in less than a week and surely nothing would happen that fast. She thought about that raised eyebrow and the smug look on Sherman's face as he left the pulpit. Maybe Tom should call Sam. But it would spoil the family's happy time meeting the new in-laws. No, better to wait, unless things took a turn for the worse. The whole business was preposterous. Her emotions seesawed between extreme anger and extreme fear. In her anger mode, she wanted to leap across the aisle and smack that self-satisfied smile off Sherman's face. The fear mode was keeping her seated. She had no doubt the man was a formidable enemy. He'd be charging her with assault and battery as soon as her hand had left a mark.

Charges. Embezzlement was a crime. It all came down to that. Last night Tom had tried out a number of scenarios to account for the missing money and none of them worked. It all came down to him.

Sherman. Was it mere coincidence that the discrepancy turned up this year after his push for the independent audit? Could he possibly be involved in some way? A move on his part to discredit—and get rid of—the minister?

She began going over everything once more, her mind only partially on Prayers for the People.

Each year the church allocated a certain amount for the Discretionary Fund to be used as the minister saw fit. At the end of the fiscal year, the minister reported what had been dispersed and how much was left to be rolled over. The only other church record kept was a list in the minister's files of the amounts, but the list did not include to whom funds had been given or for what.

Faith had a pretty good idea of some of the recipients. A phone call would come; Tom would take off for a hospital, sometimes even a police station. Money for medicine and medical emergencies not covered by insurance, a family member who needed bail, a mortgage payment to avoid foreclosure, and money for the basics of life—fuel and even warm clothing during the bitterly cold months, food always. Some of the money came back; some didn't. All the transactions were completely confidential.

Besides the church's contribution, individuals made gifts to the fund in memory of a loved one or in celebration of an event. The Discretionary Fund account was separate from all other church accounts at the bank. Only Tom could sign the checks or use the PIN-protected ATM card.

He had no idea what could account for the huge gap between what he reported and what the bank reported as the total in the account for the last fiscal year. At the meeting, the vestry had asked him to go back over his lists of dispersements for five years. More if he was so inclined. They hoped he would be able to report to them in two weeks. It was Sherman who had suggested the deadline. "So this thing doesn't drag on too long."

She stood up for the hymn. *"O star of truth, down shining / Thro' clouds of doubt and fear."* The music filled the church valiantly, and tunefully—except for the inevitable warbling, off-key sopranos. *"Though angry foes may threaten"*—Faith's eyes shifted across the aisle. Sherman was adding his alto, that moist red mouth shaped in a perfect oval. Sundays meant three-piece suits from Brooks with a club tie. The few times she'd encountered him on a weekday, he hadn't strayed far from the fold—khaki pants with knifepoint creases, V-neck sweaters, and casual shirts all with the logo, a plump sheep dangling from a ribbon, the emblem of the Knights of the Golden Fleece, adopted for his store by the first Mr. Brooks in 1818. Sherman Munroe: a wolf in sheep's clothing?

"I must not faithless be." Behind her the organ music swelled as it brought the hymn to a close.

"Faithless." Not a problem. She sat down and turned her face up toward her husband's as he started his sermon.

She stopped thinking about the rumors that she had earlier imagined building up steam among those seated behind her, ready to envelop Faith and her family.

She stopped thinking about the odious man across the aisle.

She stopped thinking about Ursula and her story; about Niki and her problems; Pix and her insecurities.

She simply listened.

Pix was feeling loopy. She wasn't used to champagne at breakfast, but the resort was renowned for its champagne brunch, so champagne it was. Mimosas. And the food. She was a little drunk on that, too, starting with dinner last night—crab cakes the size of baseballs for starters followed by chateaubriand and ending with Turtle pie for dessert. The chocolate-pecan variety, not box or snapping ones.

Next to her, Sam was making quick work of eggs Benedict with smoked salmon instead of ham and Dan had asked for seconds on his brioche French toast with caramelized bananas, in addition to all sorts of other delicious things. He'd given his mother a bite and she could taste walnuts plus something else, a hint of rum? She'd opted for her favorite—two eggs over easy—but here served with Timms Mill cheese grits and a local hickory-smoked sausage. She loved breakfast food, but usually her meal consisted of hastily consumed yogurt, some fruit, and toast.

The men were all heading for the golf course and the women were due at the spa for a full day of manicures, pedicures, facials, and massages. Pix kept her nails short, and the last time they'd seen polish was for Sam's sister's big anniversary party last fall. They were clean, though. She'd never had a massage and wished she could ask Faith what to expect. She assumed she'd have to get fully or partially undressed and she'd hate to make a mistake.

What if you were supposed to take only some things off and she was in the buff? At this thought she realized the champagne had definitely gone to her head. A massage mistake? She'd just do whatever Samantha did. Samantha would know. Her glass had been refilled by an unseen hand and she almost drained it before she remembered the alcoholic content of what she was starting to believe was the best orange juice she'd ever had. Fizzy.

The bride and groom—or was that the bride- and groom-to-be?—looked so happy. They'd both ordered huevos rancheros. Obviously they were meant for each other.

She looked at her watch. Twelve-thirty. Faith might be home from church if she'd cut her appearance at coffee hour short as she occasionally gave herself permission to do.

"Will you excuse me a moment? Please don't get up," she said.

Southern men had such beautiful manners and it had instantly rubbed off on her own husband and sons as soon as they'd arrived at the resort. Doors were opened, chairs pulled out, and when she or any of the other women rose, they all rose as one. A girl could get used to this stuff, Pix thought.

Heading for the ladies' room, she ducked instead into an un-occupied hallway leading away from the main dining room and pulled out her phone. Bless Samantha and her insistence on the family calling plan when she'd left for college. Pix couldn't imagine what she'd done before she had a cell phone. She'd already talked to Dora twice since arriving and was reassured that Mother was doing fine. Faith had called after her visit yesterday to report the same. And it was Faith she speed-dialed now.

But she didn't want to talk about Ursula. Or what one wears for a massage.

The parsonage answering machine picked up. Drat. Faith must still be at church.

"Hi, um, it's me. Or I, whichever." Pix hated leaving messages.

She always felt self-conscious. "Anyway, give me a call when you get a chance. Everything's okay. Just, well, call me." She realized she'd been whispering. Very Deep Throat.

She returned to the table after going into the ladies' room and washing her hands. To do otherwise would have been dishonest, and there wasn't a deceitful bone in Pix's body. Although, as Faith had told her soon after they realized they were going to be best friends not just forever, but since they lived next door, for every day, "You couldn't tell a lie to save your face, just the rest of the world's."

The men stood up. Dan pulled out his mother's chair, first picking up the napkin the waiter had refolded and handing it to her.

Yes, a girl could get used to all this, but it could also get to be a little weird. "Weird" didn't even begin to cover it. She knew the champagne was muddling her thoughts. There were a lot to muddle.

Outside, the view looked as if the South Carolina Tourist Board had ordered it up. The sea and sky had been painted with one brush, a brush dipped in shimmering aquamarine. There wasn't a single cloud in the sky. Instead it seemed they'd all descended in a blinding white layer on the smooth curve of the beach at the foot of the lawn that stretched out from the resort's veranda, which was adorned with a long, beckoning row of rocking chairs. Pix thought about the dreary landscape she'd left, when? Just yesterday? Driving past palms and flowering shrubs from the airport, she had relaxed for the first time since the doctor had called with the news about her mother. The Harbour Town Lighthouse, striped like a fat candy cane, looked like a child's sweet. The Cohens had booked it for a sunset reception for the last night. Friends and family were driving from Charleston and other places to officially toast the betrothed couple. Pix was sure the view would be spectacular. The weather was cooperating and the forecast promised not a drop of rain. She sighed when she thought about all the preparations that were going into this wedding celebration. Maybe Samantha would elope.

The Millers had arrived before the Cohens, and Pix had stretched out on the chaise on their own private patio while everyone else had hit the beach. She wished Faith could see the room— a bed that must be larger than a king with a tentlike canopy and plenty of comfy, overstuffed armchairs piled with bright pillows. The bath was the size of one of her kid's bedrooms, complete with a rain forest shower and a whirlpool, both of which she intended to try as often as possible. But first she had closed her eyes just for a minute. . . .

There had been a scramble to get dressed and down to dinner. All her dread at meeting her future in-laws had returned and fortunately Samantha had stopped by, since Pix had completely forgotten to change her flats for heels.

Miles away from last night and at the brunch table, Pix absentmindedly drained the rest of her mimosa.

"Surely you aren't going to ignore the chef's famous sticky buns, Pix? You're in pecan country now," said Mrs. Cohen. No, it was "Cissy." They were all on a first-name basis as soon as they'd greeted each other. Apparently "Sister" was a common nickname in households like Mrs. Cohen's where she'd been the only girl growing up with two brothers. And her given name was Cynthia. It certainly wasn't any more unusual than "Pix." She had been tiny at birth, and Pix's father had referred to his new baby girl as his little pixie, a name promptly adopted by everyone and soon shortened to Pix. It no longer applied by the time she was two, and by the time she was fifteen and grazing the six-foot mark, it was ludicrous, but it had stuck. Given that Ursula had named her daughter Myrtle after both a favorite aunt and the ground cover with tiny purple blossoms, Pix had opted for the lesser of two evils, jealous of the Debbies and Margies in her class.

"Another mimosa to go with the bun?" asked Dr. Cohen, ever

solicitous. His bedside manner was faultless. Pix put her hand firmly over her glass at the thought. At all her thoughts.

"No, thank you, Steve, I'll pass," she said, aware that she was speaking very distinctly. Loopy, yes, she was loopy and it was starting to give her the giggles.

Stephen Cohen, M.D. Her son's father-in-law-to-be. She glanced at her watch. She should have left the message on Faith's cell instead of the parsonage phone.

Stephen Cohen.

Steve. Her Steve.

Most Sundays, whether by prior invitation or as a result of an impulse on Tom's or Faith's part, the Fairchilds had guests at their Sunday dinner table. Happily, thought Faith, today was an exception. The other exception was staying at coffee hour until the bitter end. And if the coffee was anything to go by, the bitter dregs. She'd sent Amy home with Ben as soon as Sunday school had let out, ushering them through the side door and watching them cross the cemetery until they disappeared into the parsonage through the back door. Ignoring their disappointment at having to forgo the tomato juice and Ritz crackers offered up for First Parish's smaller fry (she had not managed to make even the slightest change in coffee hour from this to the choice of Triscuits and orange cheese or Vanilla Wafers for the grown-ups), she resolutely stood by her man and smiled until her mouth hurt.

At last, Tom and she walked out into the fresh air. She took his hand.

"For the moment, two choices. After some lunch, we can sit down and start trying to figure this all out. Or we can go off somewhere with the kids and try to forget it for a few hours. Which one?"

"Door number two," Tom said, pulling her closer to his side

as they made their way between the rows of headstones with their lugubrious epitaphs. She always walked quickly by "As you pass by / And cast an eye / As you are now / So once was I" and slowed to consider what "She did what she could" might have meant to the survivor who commissioned it carved on the plain slate devoid of the angels or ghoulish figures so popular with those who practiced the art of gravestone rubbing. Faith did have a favorite epitaph, a more modern one. Her father had sent it to her after a parishioner had come across it on a trip: "Here lies an Atheist / All dressed up / And no place to go."

They'd reached the parsonage and stopped before going in.

"In any case," Tom said, "until I talk to the bank, all our speculation is just that. I need to compare my records to theirs."

"Okay, where to?" Faith was relieved that Tom had picked what she thought was the better course of action. She intended to get to the bottom of all this, but she needed more information. The first thought that had crossed her mind after Tom's announcement was that somehow the theft had occurred when Tom was ill. It was where she planned to start, anyway. She was already making a list in her mind. Who had taken over what?

"It's a good day for kites. Crane Beach?" he suggested. "Bring Frisbees, too?"

Crane Beach was a wonderful nature preserve up on the North Shore in Ipswich. The kites would soar with terns and other seabirds. As for the Frisbees, it would be a fun challenge tossing them in the wind and keeping them from the waves.

"Perfect. I'll pack snacks while you and the kids have some of the borscht I took out of the freezer last night. We just need to heat it up. There's still some of that dark rye to go with it."

Faith had made vats of borscht last August with the succulent beets from the garden of her Sanpere neighbor Edith Watts. Faith's secret was using red onions and adding a red bell pepper [see recipe, p. 247]. The color of the soup was glorious and she'd swirl some low-fat sour cream on top in the spiderweb pattern the kids loved. The Fairchilds had altered their diet somewhat since Tom's illness and Faith found there were things, like regular sour cream, that could be replaced with low fat or low sodium without a loss in flavor. Not butter, though. Real butter. She was with Julia on that one.

She noticed the light on the message machine was blinking and she was tempted to ignore it. Her clerical training was too strong, however, and she pushed the button. Being a man or woman of the cloth meant you were *always* on call.

It was Pix and she sounded as if she were phoning from the bottom of a well. Faith increased the volume and played the message again. It was typical Pix Miller. Much hemming and hawing and no information. This one was unusually cryptic, though. Faith knew Ursula was fine and Pix had made a point of saying that everything at Sea Pines was okay when she'd called after her arrival. Probably a sudden need for wardrobe advice. Except Samantha was there. Faith took out her cell and called.

"Hi, I just got your message. What's up?"

"Everything's great and this place is really lovely—the views, the room, and you would love the food. We just finished a fabulous brunch."

"You're with people, right?"

"Absolutely. And the guys are all about to hit the links, what ho, while we womenfolk get massages, the works."

Pix was sounding like a cross between P. G. Wodehouse and Zane Grey. "The links, what ho"? "Womenfolk"?

"Mimosas at brunch?" Faith asked.

Pix was an even cheaper date than Tom when it came to booze and had been known to get slightly tipsy on her mother's rum cake.

"Yes, several."

"Well, you certainly sound cheery. Now, maybe I can guess why you're calling. The massage? I don't think you've ever had one, have you?"

"That's right, and yes, Samantha is going with us."

"So that's not it."

"Nope."

"Is it bigger than a breadbox?"

Entertaining as the conversation was, Faith wanted to get going.

Pix lowered her voice. "Much, much bigger."

"Ah, a person. And he or she is there, so call me when you can talk. We're off to Crane Beach to fly kites."

"Keep an eye out for a snow owl. They might still be there."

"Of course," Faith assured her friend, although this had been most definitely the furthest thought from her mind. But it was the kind of thing Tom got excited about. Bird-watching. A New England trait inbred along with a love of Indian pudding and touch football. She made a mental note to tuck some binoculars and the Sibley bird guide in the canvas tote she'd packed.

"Coming," Pix called to her unseen companions. "I've got to go, but . . . well, I'll call later."

"Have fun, sweetie," Faith said, "and I hope they keep the champagne flowing. You deserve it."

Although the weather was fine and a pale sun shone, the sky and sea at Ipswich were a single shade of gray, almost indistinguishable from the color of the sand as the tide ebbed. The children's kites joined others, rising and falling in brilliant streaks. Tom and Faith walked along the tidemark toward a rocky outcropping in the direction of Castle Hill, a magnificent early-twentieth-century estate open in the warmer months for tours and concerts. Faith had catered events there and it was an exquisite setting, especially at night, the house sitting high on a bluff above the sea, with long views of the North Shore coastline.

Crane Beach was no Sanibel, but soon Faith's pockets were filled with tiny whelk shells and bits of beach glass.

There had been no sign of any snow owls, but plenty of the terns, gulls, and plovers. Tom had the binoculars around his neck.

After determinedly talking about everything except that which was uppermost in their minds, Tom finally said, "Okay. I've gone over and over the past year, all the money I've given out—it's not hard to recall things that are emergencies like this—and I keep coming up with the figure I gave them. No more, no less. Well, we won't discuss it now."

Faith stopped and faced him, forcing him to a standstill also. "It's like a sore in your mouth. You want to keep your tongue from touching it, but you always do. And it's always still there. I think we *should* be discussing this whenever we feel like it and especially as soon as you get back from the bank tomorrow morning."

"Someone there may be able to shed some light on the whole thing, I hope, but we'll have to wait to talk it over. It's one of my days at the VA hospital," Tom said. He took his wife's hand and they turned around, walking slowly back toward Ben and Amy, eyes still trained on the sand the way people do when they walk on a beach.

Faith had forgotten about the VA. Tom was one of the volunteer chaplains there.

"It could be someone at the bank. And he or she could be dipping into more accounts than just yours," Faith said.

Tom shook his head. "I suppose it's possible, but somehow I don't think that's it. Everyone's been there for ages and—well—they know their clients."

Hawthorne Bank and Trust did have branches in several localities, but was scarcely on a scale with Bank of America. There was a bowl of Tootsie Pops on the counter in front of the two teller windows and the bank sent you a birthday card each year signed by everyone at the branch. You were greeted by name. But Faith wasn't so sanguine. It didn't mean the individuals who worked there were immune to corporate greed, although there had been no signs of any bailouts, which seemed to be the signature of this sort of activity these days.

And as for knowing their clients, that might be why Tom's account had been selected. Tom, well respected in the community, a safe target. Or simply because of the nature of the account. This wasn't the first time that Faith had marveled at her husband's innate trust of his fellow man and woman. As for herself, she planned to stop by and start a conversation about vacation destinations. See who'd been on a cruise lately or planning one of those expensive tours of Egypt. The Boston Museum of Fine Arts had mounted a blockbuster Egyptian exhibit, "The Secrets of the Tomb," and suddenly half the population of Massachusetts seemed to be heading for the Nile and the rest were reading or rereading Alan Moorehead.

"The big question is whether the money was taken in cash from the ATM or in checks," Faith said.

"I've been thinking that, too. I get a copy of any checks cashed with my statements and they're all in a binder locked in one of the file cabinets in my office. When I need to distribute some cash, I go to the machine, but there's a record of that, of course, and I save the slips in the same binder attached to the appropriate statement."

"Tom, when is the last time you went over the statements?"

He looked up—and then down. "I've been meaning to . . ." His voice took on a defensive quality. "So much piled up when I was sick and there's never been a problem with the account. In the past I used to go over them for the end-of-the-year report and maybe a few times in between."

"And it wasn't something you could delegate to the parish assistant."

"No."

Soon after Tom's arrival, the parish secretary had been renamed the parish administrative assistant. For many years the post had been ably filled by Rhoda Dawson, who moonlighted on her days off as Madame Rhoda, Psychic Reader. Where was she now when they needed her? Faith wished ruefully. The last she'd heard Rhoda had moved to Sedona and had branched out into aura photography. The post was then filled by Pat Collins for several years. Last winter she'd joyously announced her engagement. She got married soon after and accompanied her military spouse to his new posting at Fort Drum in New York. This year's Christmas card had brought news of a baby due in July. Neither woman would have had access to the particulars of the fund, but somehow Faith's instinct told her that they'd know what had happened—or it wouldn't have happened in the first place. Maybe.

Most men are very bad with change and her husband was no exception. Tom grumbled even as he toasted Pat at the party the Fairchilds threw for the couple. An ad was placed and the Aleford grapevine alerted. Tom hated all the candidates. They weren't Rhoda or Pat. Finally a friend at the Harvard Divinity School, where Tom had taught during a sabbatical several years ago, told him about Albert Trumbull.

Albert had been in one of Tom's classes and he'd liked the young man—bright and headed for a parish ministry. They'd kept in touch for a while after Tom left. The last Tom had heard Albert had decided to get a doctor of theology degree. And then, he'd abruptly applied for a leave. He'd been looking for a job other than at CVS while he tried to decide what his calling really was.

Tom had gotten in touch with him immediately. No better place to be while you decided whether you wanted to be in a parish than actually in a parish. Albert had arrived and stayed.

"Albert is going to be very upset about all this," Tom said.

"Should you call him when we get home? Give him a heads-up? He's bound to hear the moment he comes to work tomorrow." Faith didn't know the young man very well. He lived in Cambridge and had continued to attend Memorial Church in Cambridge with the minister the Reverend Peter Gomes, limiting his First Parish contact to workdays.

"You're right. I hate to do it by phone, though."

"Tell him what's going on briefly and have him come in early. You can head over to the Minuteman Café to drown your sorrows in coffee and buttermilk pancakes. You'll need plenty of sustenance before you go to the bank."

Tom slung his arm over his wife's shoulders. He was feeling better and he could tell from her suggestion that she was, too. When Faith's thoughts turned in their natural direction—food—he always knew she was okay. A mix-up of some sort. That's all this would turn out to be. He was beginning to think it was a good thing Sherman had brought in the outside CPA and this had come to the vestry's attention. Keep church business on the up and up. It would all get straightened out tomorrow.

They were both reluctant to end the day and sat watching the kids.

Faith had told Tom a little of what Ursula had related the day before and they talked some more about it, both agreeing that Faith should try to spend as much time as possible with her while Pix was away. Wherever the story was going, it was obviously of great importance to Ursula, and it could only help her recovery to have a sympathetic listener. Tom had been as surprised as Faith to hear that Ursula was not an only child. She had often mentioned her parents to Tom, as well as cousins she'd been close to, all of them gone now, but never a brother.

Their conversation turned to Niki.

"I'm worried about her," Tom said. "I wish she'd tell Phil right away. Okay, it's not the best time to break the news, but the longer she waits the worse he's going to feel when he does find out. If it were me, I'd be upset that my wife didn't think I could handle it all. And this isn't macho stuff. Partners, best friends, plus all those words that get said at the altar. You don't keep secrets from each other."

Faith had a very fleeting moment of remorse, remembering secrets she had kept from Tom, mostly having to do with dead bodies, but never secrets about things like a future visit from the stork.

"Absolutely, honey," she said.

The next morning Amy missed her bus again, and after dropping her off at school, Faith arrived at work feeling annoyed with her daughter. This was happening more and more frequently. Amy seemed to have no concept of time, and Faith hated playing the heavy, telling her to hurry up over and over again each morning.

The Ganley Museum Café was closed, like the museum, on Mondays, but Faith wanted to make up two soups—squash with apples and mulligatawny—for tomorrow. Other than the Ganley, the only obligation the catering firm had until the weekend was a dessert buffet for a library fund-raiser. Have Faith was doing it at cost. Libraries were a special passion of Faith's starting in childhood with her neighborhood branch in Manhattan and continuing to the present with Aleford's superlative library. Cutbacks both on the state and town level meant that the library had taken a hit, hence the pressing need for fund-raisers of all sorts. The tickets for the event Thursday night included desserts, beverages, and the opportunity to mingle with a number of local authors who would be signing their books—a portion of the sales would go to the library, too. Exposure for the writers, money for the library—win, win. And it wouldn't hurt Have Faith, either. They'd been prominently featured in the advertising. Niki was planning to feature several trays of rich butter cookies shaped like volumes and brightly iced with the titles of well-known books, including those by the attending authors. She was also doing several kinds of cakes that would look like fanned-out pages.

Niki was at the counter surrounded by springform pans. She greeted Faith with a grin.

"Never let it be said that my mother shirks from any opportunity to help her children. And said help has resulted in a multitude of orders for cheesecakes. Saturday night was Ladies' Night at bingo. I don't even want to think about how she got these orders, but I understand threat of the evil eye may have been involved."

Faith was relieved to hear the old Niki, and her lighthearted tone must also mean she'd told Phil the news.

"I'm sure Phil was overjoyed about being a dad. What did he say? And any nibbles from the networking golf? That's not the right word, but I don't know what else to use. Divots?"

"Turns out the guy is about to lose *his* job and he was hoping Phil had nibbles, divots, or whatever, for him."

"Oh dear," Faith said, hanging up her jacket.

"And I haven't told Phil yet," Niki mumbled.

"Oh dear," Faith said again. She pulled a stool over to the counter and sat down.

"You don't understand," Niki said. No mumbling now. She spoke defiantly. "A Greek man's whole identity is based on his work, his being able to take care of his family. At the moment, Phil only has a wife—an employed wife—so, not so much pressure. I'm not going to burden him with this until he at least has a viable offer."

"Not to be pessimistic, but you're the one who said how bad the job market in the Boston area is right now for MBAs. It could be a while. And what happens when he finds out that you've kept it from him all that time?" Faith recalled what Tom had said. "You're supposed to be partners—for better or worse. How will he feel when he discovers you've been going solo?"

"I don't know and I'm not thinking about it now! I'm just going to make and deliver these cakes!" Tears were streaming down Niki's cheeks. "Damn. Can you get me a Kleenex? I don't want salt dripping in the batter."

Faith pulled a carton from under the counter and moved the bowl away.

"I cry all the time when Phil isn't around," Niki admitted.

"Hormones," Faith said, stirring. It *was* hormones, but it was also Faith's words. She'd made her friend cry. "Look, you do what you think is best. I shouldn't be pressuring you. You know what's right for the two of you. Maybe it's a Greek thing, maybe not—"

Niki interrupted her. "Forget 'best.' I have no idea what I'm doing, boss. And don't shut up. Besides being creepily unnatural for you, I need to hear the other side. You could be right. You're probably right. Oh, I don't know."

"Go wash your face and I'll help you finish the cheesecakes and then we can get the Ganley stuff for tomorrow squared away. I'm spending the afternoon with Ursula."

"How is she doing?"

"Much better, and I'm hoping by the time Pix comes back, she'll be on her feet again."

"Pix at Hilton Head. It sounds like some kind of book. You know, like *The Bobbsey Twins at the Seashore*. My mother bought the whole series at some rummage sale when she first got here. She thought it was what American girls should read. I'm surprised I'm not named Nan or Flossie."

"I talked to Pix on the phone yesterday. She'd left one of her cryptic messages on the answering machine. I still don't know what it's all about. She couldn't talk and was going to call back, but so far no word from the South except that she'd been drinking mimosas, was going to have her first massage, and had encountered something larger than a breadbox, most likely a person, that she wanted to tell me about."

"Mimosas," Niki said wistfully. "No booze for the next eight or so months. You hear that, kid? Mommy's already sacrificing." She paused. "Omigod, I sound just like my mother."

It's a great deal to ask, Ursula Lyman Rowe said to herself as she waited for Faith Fairchild to arrive. She thought of the envelope tucked under the cushion of the window seat opposite her bed. She fancied she could see its shape outlined in the William Morris fabric slipcovering, and if she stared at it long enough she might make the paper rise, burning its way through the linen to the surface.

There's no turning back now, though. She knew Faith. She wouldn't let Ursula stop the story. She knew it was something important. Yet, what she didn't know was that at the end she'd have to make a decision herself.

Ursula sat up straighter. Tomorrow she'd insist that Dora let her sit up in her chair. The overstuffed armchair that Arnold had lugged home from an auction downtown. "A perfect reading chair," he'd said. And so it had been, by oneself or to a child curled comfortably on one's lap.

She was feeling better. Saturday night she had slept straight through until morning, not needing Dora to help her to the bathroom and especially not awakening unable to return to sleep—her mind filled with upsetting images.

She heard light steps in the hall. Faith had come.

"Hello, dear. It's so good of you to give up your time this way." Faith bent over to kiss Ursula's cheek.

"It's a pleasure," she said, and meant it. She'd been looking forward to stepping back into Ursula's long-ago world all day, and not simply as a distraction from the preoccupations of this one. Tom had called to tell her briefly there wasn't much to tell. He'd go over it with her later.

"Open up my top dresser drawer," Ursula said. "At the bottom of my handkerchief box, there's a folder with a photograph. Would you bring it here, please?"

Faith did as she was asked. The box was square and covered in quilted satin that must have once been a brighter rose. A long narrow box that matched it was on the other side of the drawer. Gloves.

She lifted the lid and then carefully removed the stack of embroidered Irish linen handkerchiefs Ursula kept there, along with one of the sachets she and Pix made each summer from the lavender they grew in their herb garden at The Pines on Sanpere. Underneath was the flat cardboard folder with the name of a Boston photography studio in fancy script across the front. Faith took it out, replaced everything, closed the drawer, and walked back over to Ursula.

"Open it up," she said.

Inside was a sepia oval portrait of a man. Just his face. His hair was carefully parted in the middle and he was staring straight at the camera. Although he wasn't smiling—it looked to be a graduation shot or some other momentous occasion—the curve at the corners of his mouth and a glint in his eye suggested that the moment after the shutter snapped, he'd jump up laughing. There was a subtle energy in the face. He was very handsome—and very young.

"That's Theo," Ursula said.

Her next words took Faith completely by surprise.

"Have you ever been to Martha's Vineyard?"

Bewildered at Ursula's sudden change in topic, Faith answered, "Yes, I've been to Martha's Vineyard, but I don't know it well."

Fleeting images of freshly painted white clapboard, bright red geraniums in hanging baskets, wicker porch furniture, American flags, and a genuine Coney Island carousel where she once snatched the brass ring passed through her mind, as well as the Vineyard's "Hollywood East" reputation.

"That's where it happened. On Martha's Vineyard. In a gazebo."

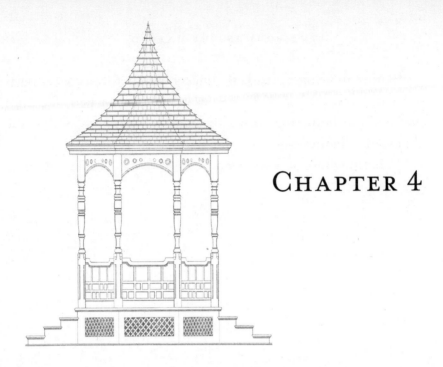

CHAPTER 4

Ursula pulled her arms out from beneath the light throw Dora had spread over her and folded her hands together. She was stretched out on the chaise. The signal was clear. She was ready to pick up her tale.

"There was a catastrophic winter storm on Sanpere in 1929. Trees came down all over the island and it took many months to repair the damage, and even so just the worst of it. There were several large tamaracks near our house, and with their shallow roots, I imagine they must have been the first to go, stoving in the entire back roof. A big pine took care of much of the front. Father was able to arrange for a temporary fix to keep the weather out, but for the rest he had to wait his turn. As long as he was going to have to do such major repairs, he decided to enlarge the kitchen and add two more bedrooms over it plus a new bath that Mother had been wanting for ages. I was excited about the plans until I heard it meant we wouldn't be able to be there for the summer."

Faith nodded in commiseration. The idea of Sanpere in the summer without Ursula and her family was akin to the swallows giving Capistrano a miss in March.

"Father rented a very large house on Martha's Vineyard that one of his friends from the Somerset Club owned. The man and his wife were taking their daughter, who was just out, to England. No doubt her mama wanted to capture a title for the family. People did in those days."

"Consuelo Vanderbilt," Faith commented.

"Oh yes, the poor Duchess of Marlborough. Her life could have been written by Edith Wharton. In any case, the house on the Vineyard was much grander than either of our houses and I began to feel very guilty at how much I was enjoying the summer."

Ursula's family belonged to the Teddy Roosevelt school of rustication, Faith reflected. Plunges into the frigid deep at dawn, hearty hikes, plain food—as much simple living as money could buy.

"The cottage—that's what the owner called it—was in Oak Bluffs at the end of a long dirt road. It was set overlooking the water with open fields on one side and forest on the other. There were stairs down to the beach and the water was quite warm. I can still smell the beach roses, the same *Rosa rugosas* we have in Maine, but the scent was stronger, or perhaps that's a trick of memory. Along the front of the gray-shingled house, there were rows of hydrangeas with blooms the size of beach balls—quite impossible, but again that's how I see them in my mind's eye. Behind the house there was a massive garden with vegetables as well as flowers. The gardener told me it had been planted before construction was finished so it would look as if it had always been there. The house must have been about twenty years old and there were wide porches and verandas that went around it—we sat out there for tea and often in the evenings. I'm sure the whole thing would now be judged an architectural monstrosity with all sorts of conflicting styles—Arts and Crafts eyebrow windows, Gothic turrets, a Federalist widow's walk—but I adored it. My room was in one of those turrets and at night I could hear the sea and the faint rustle of eelgrass in the soft wind. The weather was perfect that summer. No storms. Blue skies and just the right amount of wind every day. The sailors were in heaven."

She reached for her water glass.

Faith said, "Let me get some fresh water for you, or would you like juice?"

"Water is fine."

"I'm not tiring you, am I?"

"Not at all, Faith dear. I haven't felt this well in weeks."

After she drank some water, Ursula continued. She was talking a bit more quickly now, as if she wanted to get to a certain point before stopping for the day. The almost dreamlike reminiscence gave way to narrative. Faith was pulled in once more. Ursula's description had been so vivid that Faith could clearly visualize the house and surrounding landscape.

"Mother liked it that Father was able to be with us more than he could when we spent the summer in Sanpere. He would often take a Monday to make a long weekend, spent a week in July and planned another in August. Despite the drive and the ferry, it was easier to get to the Vineyard than to The Pines. There was always someone coming or going. With so much space, Mother indulged her love of company. Her sister, my aunt Myrtle, visited a few times with my cousins, who were between Theo and me in age. The two sisters were very close. The flu epidemic in 1918 had taken their parents and their two younger brothers. We used to skip rope to 'I had a little bird / Its name was Enza / I opened the window / And in-flu-enza.' We had no idea what it meant and that millions had died, including our relatives. Mother never said anything. People didn't—at least in our family. Illness was never mentioned. I discovered what happened when I was older and living out in Aleford."

Faith was only too aware of this early-twentieth-century pandemic. The H1N1 swine flu had been the same strain as "the

Spanish Flu" or "la Grippe" and there had been some tense weeks before the vaccine was available for the Fairchild children when a cough or slight fever was anxiously watched.

"Other friends of Mother's from the Fragment Society would arrive, and of course my parents knew many people from town who summered on the island."

"Town." Faith was amused at Ursula's Brahmin reference. "Town" always meant "Boston"—as if no other existed.

"Life on Martha's Vineyard was much more social than life on Sanpere. There were Theo's Harvard friends coming for the weekend or dropping in from their parents' places on the island. Father wasn't so keen on all of them. He didn't care for Charles Winthrop, who was older and in a rather fast set at the college, or a girl named Violet Hammond. She wasn't at Harvard, only men in those days. Father did like Schuyler Jessup, who was a great pal of Theo's. Scooter—he was always called that—was often around and usually brought a girl named Babs Dickson, whose parents were friends of Father and Mother's, with him. They later married. She was one of those athletic young women who always seemed to have a tennis racquet or a golf club in her hand. She wasn't in college, but some sort of finishing school. I have no idea what she could have been doing there in those days. Certainly not learning to embroider and curtsy. Her father thought college courses put too great a strain on a woman's mind. Such nonsense. What did he think? Her brain would suddenly explode? He didn't seem to mind her straining her body, and I remember thinking how beautifully she moved—very feline, and with all this pent-up energy.

"The weekends Father stayed in town, the group would always come down. At night they'd roll up the rugs in the living room and dance. Mother didn't mind. And all day long they kept the Victrola going. Rudy Vallee, Bix Beiderbecke, Louis Armstrong. There was a piano, too. Someone always seemed to be playing it.

Scooter was the best. He had a very pleasant voice. Whenever I hear certain Cole Porter songs, they take me back to that summer."

Ursula gazed across the room at the large window. Faith had the feeling that it had become a kind of screen and Ursula was watching these figures from her childhood cavort across the sunlight.

"Theo had passed his English literature course on the condition that he write several papers over the summer. But he had failed mathematics, so would have to repeat it. Father hired a tutor, a serious young man who had just graduated and was entering the law school in the fall. He was from the Midwest, an only child, and neither parent was living, so he had to make his own way in the world—a scholarship student, which was rare in those days. He'd been the teaching assistant in Theo's medieval history class, and Father was convinced that their study sessions were the reason Theo had passed, and he was no doubt right. Theo called him 'the Professor' and soon everyone, even Father, did. I remember the first time I saw him. He had the most beautiful eyes I had ever seen—brown with tiny flecks of gold."

This brought a smile to Faith's face. A crush. Growing up, she'd had many herself.

"There weren't any children my age, and except for the people I've mentioned, no one was living at the house that summer besides the servants, although those who were local went home at night. I didn't mind. There was the whole outdoors to play in and my books to read indoors, and out. I also learned a new language—Martha's Vineyard Sign Language. I thought it was great fun. There was an extremely high percentage of hereditary deafness on the island dating back to the eighteenth century, peaking in the mid-nineteenth, but still quite prevalent, especially in Chilmark, well into the twentieth. The gardener was deaf, as were several of the kitchen help. One of them, who was very young and very pretty, made rather a pet of me. I learned to sign by watching the servants talk—all of the ones from the island used it, even the ones who weren't deaf. When I became adept, which was rather quickly—children pick up these things so much more easily than adults—I discovered that they liked my mother, feared my father, and thought Theo and his friends were very funny.

"I thought all the grown-ups were endlessly fascinating and I became very clever at finding places where I could observe them undetected. Under the piano in the living room was a good place. And then there was my own special place—not so much a place from which to watch people, but a kind of fort I'd made for myself underneath the rhododendrons next to a gazebo. It was quite an elaborate one that the owners had had constructed in the woods—more like a summerhouse or folly—a screened-in octagon with a wide bench around the sides. When I first happened upon it, I thought it belonged in something like Frances Hodgson Burnett's *The Secret Garden,* but upon reflection I decided it was more suited to Grimm. It was set away from the main house, deep in the woods down a dark, narrow path, nothing like a garden gazebo. It became my favorite spot. That hiding place by the gazebo . . ."

"You just don't trust me, Father! Dash it! The Professor's a good chap and I'm all for helping him out, but I don't need a tutor down at the Vineyard this summer. I'm more than capable of writing the papers myself, and as for the math, I would have passed the exam if I had felt better." Theo stopped short. He didn't want to go into the reason for the monstrous headache that had caused the numbers to swim before his eyes and the feeling that he might retch at any moment, which kept him from putting down what little he did know on the paper before him. It had been foolish to go off

with Charles, but it was only going to be for a quick bite at Jim's Place in the Square, and then Violet had appeared with a friend. It would have been rude not to ask them to a show in town and supper afterward.

Violet. Theo tried to concentrate on what his father was saying. It should have been easy. The old man was shouting. But he kept seeing Violet's face—that impossibly alabaster skin, ruby lips, flashing sapphire eyes. He wished he were a poet. Maybe he'd give it a try. "Thine eyes like pools of melted sky." Not bad. Not bad at all.

"Theo! Have you heard one word of what I've been saying?"

"Of course, sir. You think I'm a 'wastrel' and need a watchdog. I give in. I'll let the Professor keep my nose to the grindstone."

Theo had absorbed enough from his English courses to know he had muddled any number of metaphors. He found himself trying hard not to smile. His father was right. He wasn't taking all this seriously. Slacker fellows than he was had graduated. It had been important to protest at the start, but Theo knew this was one he couldn't win so there was no need to drag the unpleasantness out.

Theodore Artemus Lyman—he'd given his son a different middle name, Speedwell, which seemed enormously ironic at the moment—sighed heavily and got up. "See that you do. I'll be getting weekly reports, and those papers must be submitted to the college by the end of July."

"Don't worry, Father. It's going to be a wonderful summer."

"That's what I'm afraid of," Mr. Lyman muttered as his feckless son escaped out the door.

Ursula crouched lower behind one of the tall blue and white Japanese porcelain jars that stood in the hallway on either side of the library door. Soon she wouldn't be able to fit into the space between the jar and the wall—it was getting to be a tight fit—and one of her favorite hiding places would be gone. You could hear everything that was said in the library, especially if the door hadn't been closed all the way as today. She loved the jars, with their misty scenes of landscapes that came straight from one of Andrew Lang's fairy-tale collections. She leaned her cheek against the jar's cool surface and closed her eyes, gently tapping the rim. She imagined that the soft, clear note was a temple gong and shadowy figures were moving in a rapid wave toward a shrine.

She leaned back against the wall and opened her eyes, in no hurry to move. School was over for the year and the house was in an uproar of cleaning and packing. Most of the rooms would be shut, the furniture draped like so many ghosts. Father would dine at his club and only use his library, one sitting room, and his bed and dressing rooms.

Poor Theo! It was a shame that he'd have to spend his summer studying, but Ursula was glad the Professor would be with them. When she had been introduced to him, she'd immediately asked him if he liked birds, and instead of answering "Only songbirds, kiddo," as Scooter had, the Professor had replied, "All birds or specifically shore, meadow, or woodlands?" He wouldn't be working with Theo every minute, and she'd already packed the Leitz binoculars she'd asked for and received for her birthday plus her little life-list notebook bound in bright red Moroccan leather, hoping he would join her when she searched for new sightings to add.

She was worried about what the storm on Sanpere had done to her things—her bedroom was in the back of the house, which had received the worst damage. Was her fern collection safe? She'd spent hours neatly pressing, labeling, and gluing them into a scrapbook. And what about the abandoned birds' nests she'd found and arranged on a shelf in her room? For all she knew they could be in a sodden heap in the middle of the floor. It was exciting to go to a new place, but she wished they could go to Sanpere for just a little while, even if they had to stay elsewhere. Her father had promised a full account of her things. He was going up in August to check on the work. She sighed. It was a long time to wait.

What was this summer going to be like? In her mind the two events—the damage to the Sanpere house and Theo's disastrous grades—had somehow merged together as the reason why they had to go to this new island. It might not make sense, but it was how she felt.

Why couldn't Theo just do his schoolwork and then go have fun afterward! That was why he kept failing. All that fun. He needed more serious friends, although Scooter was awfully nice. But a friend who would keep him from his weaknesses. A friend like the Professor.

Father had just said that Theo must get it through his head that he would have to make his own way in the world. Theo had laughed and said that was exactly what he intended to do—enter the business world like his father. He'd quoted former President Coolidge, "The business of America is business." Ursula knew this was one thing father and son agreed on—and on what a great man the new President, Herbert Hoover, was. Father had replied, "That's all very well, but you have to be a college man, son. You have to be a Harvard man, like all the Lyman men." Theo had answered that he knew that, although from the amount of money his barber on Dunster Street was making on the stock market, maybe college wasn't so important these days. In the next breath, he'd said he was kidding and his father had laughed. Told him to get some tips. "He shaves some pretty wealthy faces and my broker's is one of them, I'll have you know."

Ursula had hoped the talking-to would end on this cheerful note. Maybe Theo would have time to take her to the new Marx brothers movie, but Father got agitated about Theo's grades again and her brother rushed by her so fast she couldn't wiggle out in time to stop him.

She hoped he could wiggle out of the trouble he was in and make it a good summer. He just had to. Suddenly Ursula felt trapped by the big vase and struggled to slip out. Tossing her hair back over her shoulders and away from her flushed face, she decided she was too old for this kind of behavior and wished she could get back the talismans she'd placed in the jars that even now she could barely reach—a pearl button she'd found on the street, a British sixpence, the ticket from the first symphony concert she'd attended, and all those lines of poetry she'd written on tiny scraps of paper—offerings to oblivion. It would be impossible to retrieve them now without tipping the vases over.

The front door banged shut. Theo was gone. Her eyes filled with tears.

Pix looked at her nails. She vaguely remembered that it was supposed to mean something if you looked at them with your fingers stretched out or curled into the palm—like wearing your circle pin on the correct side of your blouse collar. Somehow the manicurist had transformed them into perfect pink shells—and the same with her toes. She really should have them done more often.

And now she knew why people loved getting massages. She'd been so relaxed she'd dozed off. And that facial! Last night as she carefully applied her makeup—mouth and eyes—the glowing face in the mirror looked five, no ten, years younger. She felt positively sybaritic. And not at all like herself. Well, there was a reason for that . . .

She picked up her phone and, conscious of her nails, carefully dialed Faith.

"I was just going to call you! Your mother is doing so well. We had a nice, long visit this afternoon, and when I left Dora said she was going to get her up longer tomorrow and into her big chair after they do their constitutionals in the hallway. How was the massage? And the in-laws?"

"It's been wonderful. Cissy is the planner and she seems to have thought of everything. Yesterday was fun—and the massage was terrific. We'd all been together almost constantly since we arrived, and she was sensitive enough to tell everyone that for last night, we'd all go our own ways."

"Smart lady. This bodes well for the future, especially when it comes to sharing grandchildren. What did you and Sam do?"

"Absolutely nothing. Long walk on the beach and then a room service dinner on the patio we have right outside our room."

"This doesn't sound like the Sam and Pix Miller I know. Are you sure you didn't squeeze in something educational or strenuous?" Faith laughed. "Sounds romantic, however, so perhaps there was some exercise after all? I know you're blushing, Pix."

Pix was.

Faith continued. "But what was it you wanted to tell me? Your mysterious bigger-than-a-breadbox item."

"Oh Faith, you know that line from *Casablanca* when Bogart says, 'Of all the gin joints in all the towns in all the world, she walks into mine'?"

"Of course."

"Well, of all the weddings in all the towns in all the world, Dr. Stephen Cohen has walked into mine."

"What on earth are you talking about? Don't tell me you know him?"

"It was when we were in college, and yes, I know him."

"But isn't that a nice coincidence? A sign that this match was meant to be? One of those serendipitous cosmic coincidences? Unless he was and is a total jerk."

"No, the opposite, in fact. But Faith, I *knew* him."

"Are we talking about 'know' as in, say, the biblical usage?"

Pix raised her voice, "Oh honey, yes, I'm all ready to go. Just checking on Mother with Faith. Everything's fine."

"Sam came in?"

"Yes—and yes to your other question. Gotta run, talk to you later."

Faith closed her phone and looked out the window. Barring a blizzard, the daffodils would be in bloom for Easter, less than three weeks away. She found herself unable to alter her gaze, or move her body away from the spot where she'd been standing while she was on the phone. Cliché that it was, truly life was way stranger than fiction. No one could have made this up. Myrtle, aka Pix, Rowe Miller, her best friend and next-door neighbor and currently starring as the mother of the groom in a swanky resort in Hilton Head, South Carolina, had, in her distant past, slept with the father of the bride.

Riveting as both Ursula's saga and Pix's still to be revealed were, Faith turned her thoughts to assembling a chicken dish, a variation of coq au vin, for dinner before picking up Ben from his clarinet lesson—thank heavens it wasn't something large like a tuba or loud like drums—and Amy from a friend's, where she was working on a science project. Faith sometimes thought all she'd ever remember about her children's school years were science projects. They seemed to pop up with alarming frequency and require an endless amount of time. Fortunately the papier-mâché model of the inner ear was being constructed at someone else's house this time. Faith was still finding Popsicle sticks from the scale model of a cyclotron that Ben made in fifth grade. Could that be right? Maybe she was confusing it with the scale model of the Alamo for history. She was in no hurry to see her children grow up and go off on their own, but she greeted each vacation from school and school-related tasks as a reprieve, with summer the best of all.

When Faith returned with kids, Tom was home ahead of them, and from the bleak smile he gave them as they came through the back door, she knew the news from the bank hadn't been good. She hustled the kids off to do homework and put the chicken in the oven. It was comfort food. The Fairchilds liked dark meat, so she had used the whole legs, adding carrots, onions, parsnips, and some garlic before dousing it with red wine and seasoning it with fresh sage and a small amount of salt and pepper. Covered, it baked in the oven for an hour before she took the foil off to brown it [see recipe, p. 248]. She was serving it tonight with potatoes she'd steamed, sautéed in oil and butter, before liberally sprinkling it with more sage.

"There's no question," Tom said. "The money was taken out of the account at intervals over about nine months or so using an ATM, and all from the one at the Aleford branch. Five hundred dollars is the limit that can be withdrawn in one day and that was the amount of each transaction. Twenty in all. The last one was made the night before we left for Maine in December."

"Merde!" She reverted to the strong French epithet she'd adopted when the kids were little, but old enough to understand, and mimic, the English ones. She had been hoping that the withdrawals would have occurred when Tom was verifiably somewhere else. "And the others? None when you were in the hospital?"

Tom shook his head. "Several when I was recuperating at home, but I was up and about. It's not a long walk to the bank."

Faith sighed. The parsonage, like the church, bordered the Aleford green, as did several old houses plus the historic tavern where the minutemen may have bolstered their courage by hoisting a few that April morning. Main Street snaked around the side and kept going straight through the town. With good binoculars, you could see the bank at, memorably enough, 1776 Main.

"When did the withdrawals start? That should tell us something."

"Just about a year ago. I have all the dates."

"Have there been any new employees at the bank during this time? It seems to me there was a new teller that winter."

"No new tellers, just several from other branches who filled in when someone was sick or had another reason for missing work. And they'd have no way of knowing my PIN. I'm the only one. No other changes in the additional employees, either."

"What about checking the tape from the surveillance camera?"
Again Tom shook his head.

"Mice chewed the wires. They didn't discover it until January. Nothing had recorded since the previous year."

This was a perennial hazard in rural Aleford. The Ganley Museum's cameras were always being attacked by rodents with a taste for what Faith imagined was a well-aged blend of plastic and metal—provocative with a hint of fruitiness.

Her husband looked exhausted and Faith decided the rest of this conversation could wait while he stretched out on the couch before dinner. He could watch the news. That would put things into perspective.

"Why don't you catch *The News Hour* while I finish dinner? We're not going to solve this now."

But we will, she added to herself.

Both kids somehow seemed to have developed their own versions of the Vulcan Mind Meld at too early an age, and during dinner Faith kept up a steady stream of conversation about Ursula's childhood reminiscences in order to keep Ben and Amy from figuring out that something was terribly wrong. It had been an effort at first, but soon they were all talking about what it must have been like in the predigital age. And then they got on to the Great Depression. Ben was filled with facts and figures.

"Thirteen million people lost their jobs. And they had these places called 'Hoovervilles,' after the President, where homeless people lived in cardboard cartons and slept under blankets made out of newspapers. They called them 'Hoover Blankets.' The day all the banks failed was called 'Black Tuesday,' but my history teacher said it isn't true that a lot of the rich guys who'd lost all their money jumped out their office windows. Maybe just a couple. She also said that even though a lot of those rich people did lose all their money, a lot held on to it and made even more."

Faith was impressed, both with her son and his teacher. Amy's mouth had dropped open.

"They only had newspapers for blankets! Why didn't the rich people buy them real ones?"

Tom and Faith looked at each other. One of those unanswerable questions, then as now.

"Well, sweetheart, they weren't thinking straight," Tom said.

"Or kindly," Amy added emphatically.

As Ursula, whom Faith had come to regard as a kind of Yankee Sheherazade, told her tale, the parallels between the summer of 1929 and the current economic situation were eerily similar—the ever-widening gap between rich and poor with the middle swallowed up in the process.

After dinner, Ben retreated to work on a story he was doing for extra credit in English. Bless the compelling practice teacher, Faith thought, and slightly uneasily added, and hormones. Amy was taking a shower at her mother's insistence. Eliminating her daughter's morning one might help her make the bus on time.

Tom had gone into his study only to emerge fifteen minutes later to make a cup of tea for himself.

"Want one?'

"No, thanks," Faith said. "But I'll keep you company with some milk and broken library books I brought home from work."

Understandably Tom looked puzzled.

"Cookies Niki's making for the fund-raiser," Faith explained.

Before the water molecules boiled, Tom's did. He was up and pacing around the room.

"I go back and forth. Resign—or not? Replace the missing funds . . ."

Faith gasped. Ten thousand dollars was a rather large chunk of change. And resign? This couldn't be happening . . .

"Except," Tom said, "both could be taken as an admission of guilt."

The little bird on the kettle was whistling. Faith made the tea.

"Tom, no one in the parish possibly believes you took the money. Maybe they think there was a careless error, but not malicious intent."

"Tell that to Sherman Munroe. The way he looked at me in church yesterday you'd think I was keeping a mistress in a fancy condo at the Ritz."

Tom's notions of what things cost were delightfully naïve. Faith had always paid for her own clothes and gifts for her husband from a separate account that she'd had since before her marriage, setting it up again when she moved to Aleford. Faith had curbed her youthful label fetish over the years, but still, if Tom had known what the deceptively simple little black dress Faith had worn to a recent party cost, he'd faint.

"The missing money might cover two nights. You and your mistress will have to scale down."

Tom reached for a cookie.

Faith reached for a pad of paper and a pencil.

"You're not going to get anything done tonight on your sermon, so let's make a start on finding out who's really responsible. Eventually this will lead to the money, and although I'm sure it's long gone, whoever it is will have to replace it—and then some." Faith was thinking jail time.

"You're right. I can't concentrate on anything else."

"Walk me through the whole thing. Where do you keep the Discretionary Fund records, the list of amounts? And where do you keep the checkbook and ATM card? Here or at the church?"

"They're all together in a file in my office at the church. Together with the bank statements, which are in a binder. The ATM card is slipped under the plastic thing that separates the checks from deposit slips in the checkbook wallet."

"And everything is sitting there in one of your file drawers, clearly labeled? Easy for anyone to access when you're not there?"

"Not so easy. It's one of the locked file cabinets and you'd have to know which one, plus have the key."

"Okay." Faith felt they were getting somewhere. "You keep the file cabinet keys on your ring with the keys to your office, the church, and the house?"

Tom looked down. "I'm afraid I keep those keys in one of my desk drawers."

"Unlocked?"

"Unlocked."

He looked guilty as sin. Faith got up and hugged him from behind, resting her chin on his head. He always smelled so good. A clean, slightly citrus soapy smell and something ineffable that was Tom.

"Obviously, this is a problem that goes with the turf. Trusting humankind." She wouldn't have him any other way, but it was going to hurt him now.

She began to think out loud. "Still, although this widens the field of suspects"—adding to herself, The entire congregation plus passersby—"we should focus on people who have been in and out of your office in the past year with some frequency. People who would know where you kept the checkbook and card, as well as the keys."

She sat back down and picked up the pencil.

Tom looked better. He reached for another cookie—the white lettering on the chocolate icing read, *The Hunch*. Faith took it as an omen.

"Albert, although I can't imagine—"

Faith interrupted him. "Yes you can. Think Dorothy Sayers, 'Suspect everyone.'" She wrote down, "Albert Trumbull, parish administrative assistant."

"All right. Next. James came on board as associate minister a year and a half ago when Walter retired."

For most of his career in the ministry, Walter Pratt had divided his time between First Parish and teaching at Andover Newton. He'd never wanted to assume the top job, telling Tom he was "content to watch from the sidelines." This was a false description of his active involvement. When Walter died suddenly of a massive coronary, Tom had taken it not only as a personal loss, but a loss of part of the parish's history. More than once since Saturday's meeting with the vestry, he'd wished Walter were by his side still.

Faith wrote down, "James Holden, associate minister."

Quickly Tom ticked off, "Lily Sinclair, our Div School intern—she arrived about a year ago, as I recall, and left in the beginning of this January for her last semester. Eloise Gardner, education director. I suppose we have to include the sexton, Eli Brown, he's in and out of my office. And the vestry. Some have a more visible presence than others."

"Sherman, for example."

"Sherman, for example," Tom agreed grimly.

It wasn't a long list, except for the vestry, which was composed of five individuals elected by the congregation plus the senior and junior wardens. Faith put those names on the bottom of the sheet. Meetings weren't held in Tom's office, so she'd ask him at another time to take a look and see if any of the names, other than Sherman's, popped up as people who'd been around more than the others.

She took his mug and made him another cup of tea.

Action was obviously the antidote for this poisonous situation. Yet, Tom couldn't be directly involved. Which left . . .

"Anyone working directly with you probably knows you keep keys in your desk drawers. Or if they don't, it would be the first place anyone would look. I think the next step is getting to know Albert, James, Lily, Eloise, and even Mr. Brown"—the sexton was pushing eighty and was usually called "Mr. Brown," as a sign of respect, Faith supposed—"a whole lot better. I'll start digging."

If it weren't for that fact that this was her beloved who was involved, she'd be greeting the prospect with pleasure. Incurably curious, she had already started to speculate on what might be under the rocks she turned over.

Pix knew she looked good even before her appreciative husband gave a low whistle when she came out to the patio where he was reading the morning paper. They'd had a leisurely breakfast before she went to get dressed. Faith had nixed Pix's dubious collection of jeans, many of them hand-me-downs from her boys once they shot up, all of them worn at the knees from gardening. The jeans she put on today were new and fit like a second skin, making her long, shapely legs look even more so. She was wearing a royal-blue tank top with a large, oversized broadly striped shirt in blue and white, the tails tied around her still slim waist. Kind of like Sandra Dee in one of those Tammy movies, Pix had thought when Faith demonstrated the way she believed the outfit worked best.

There was a wonderful place in Brooklin, Maine—Blossom Studio—that made glass beads, which were transformed into exquisite forms of jewelry. Sam had given her a simple gold neck wire with a large frosted Nile-green bead. She'd put that on at the last minute, and some makeup.

She'd only been away from Aleford for three days, but it felt like a month, a very pleasant month.

The Cohens had been coming to Hilton Head since Rebecca was born and Pix recognized kindred spirits in their desire to show off the place they loved. It was the way she felt taking guests around Sanpere for the first time. Today Stephen and Cissy had arranged an ecotour by boat with a captain knowledgeable not only about the Low Country's natural life but its history as well. The boat was large enough for all of them, but small enough to get close to the osprey, herons, ibis, egrets, and perhaps, away from the inlets and marshlands, dolphins. They'd be on the ocean heading for a picnic lunch on Daufuskie Island, one of South Carolina's Gullah Sea Islands.

Walking toward Sam, she'd flashed back to another time many, many years earlier when she'd emerged dressed and ready to go. She'd known she looked good that time, too, and the man—a young man, not long out of his teens—had whistled, too.

"Wow," he'd said. "I thought you were going to be a dog. Brian never said, I mean, excuse me, this is coming out all wrong, sugar. Let me start over." She'd been instantly charmed by his soft Southern accent, laughed, and taken his arm. His comment didn't sound all wrong to her, not at all.

When her roommate at Brown had first suggested Pix come with her for Green Key Weekend at Dartmouth, Pix had refused. Mindy was from Savannah, and she'd met Brian when she'd gone home for the holidays. They'd been seeing each other since—or rather "keeping company."

"You can't sit and pine for that Sam Miller all weekend. It was time you two went your separate ways. I mean, you've known him your whole life, right? Isn't that kind of like incest? Besides, why should you be the one to mope around the dorm when he's the one who gave you that sad old line about needing some space? I swear, any man that says that to me is going to see some space— outer space."

Pix hadn't been able to contradict her. Everything she'd said was true.

"You need a real man, not one of these ice-cold Yankees. Brian's roommate, Steve, sounds perfect for you. Real outdoorsy. He said to bring your skis. He's premed. You'd never starve as a doctor's wife."

"Whoa," Pix had said. "If I do go, and I'm not saying I will, isn't it a little too soon to be planning a trip down the aisle?"

"It's never too soon for that, darlin.'"

Considering that Mindy was Phi Beta Kappa and applying to

law schools, she wasn't just going for her MRS degree. But she had told Pix the beginning of their sophomore year when they'd started rooming together that although she planned to have a career, a successful one, there was nothing more important in life than being a good wife and mother.

From the Class Notes, Pix knew that Mindy had achieved all three of her goals, or so it seemed on paper. After graduation, they hadn't stayed in touch.

Several of the girls on her floor had raised an eyebrow when she mentioned she was going to Green Key at Dartmouth—one said something vague about testosterone and be prepared to run— but the more Pix had thought about it the more she'd decided Mindy was right. Sam Miller wasn't the only fish in the sea. And the more she'd gone over their last conversation when he'd said he wanted some space, wanted to see other people, the madder she got. Yes, they had known each other a long time—not their whole lives, just since middle school. But so what?

Walking toward her Dartmouth date, who was not short, as she'd feared, and very good-looking, she'd been glad she'd gone.

Just as this Hilton Head time was starting to pass in a rapid blur, that weekend had been a blur—except a blur of parties with lots of dancing. There was always plenty of some kind of delicious fruit punch at the fraternity houses, and she'd been amused by traditions like the raucous "chariot" races with fraternity members serving as the chariot horses, charging across the college green while onlookers pelted them with water balloons and eggs.

She never did go skiing, and by Sunday, she'd convinced herself that Steve, not Sam, was the real love of her life. She had a vague recollection of explaining this at length to Mindy Saturday night while sipping a lot of that yummy punch. She'd awakened with a start, and a headache, late Sunday morning in Steve's room, in Steve's bed.

They'd talked on the phone a few times and he was supposed

to come down to Providence when Brian did. And then she was supposed to go to Hanover for some spring skiing. They never saw each other again and it was a pleasant memory of the kinds of things one does in youth and never again. Pix avoided all and any kinds of punch for many years.

The following summer she was home in Aleford running the tennis program at a local day camp. Early one evening—one of those perfect summer evenings when the light is so long it makes everything look like a stage set—Sam Miller knocked on her door, got down on one knee, held up a ring, and said, "I've been a complete idiot. First forgive me, and then marry me."

Which they did right after graduation the following June at First Parish with the reception at Longfellow's Wayside Inn.

When she'd seen Stephen Saturday she'd recognized him immediately, despite a receding, and gray, hairline. Mark had always referred to his future father-in-law as "Rebecca's father" or "Dr. Cohen." Steve had been premed when Pix knew him, but the country was filled with doctors with that last name. It had simply never occurred to her that the two were one and the same. Yes, her Steve—well, not really hers—was from the South, but in that insular way of her fellow Northeasterners, she tended to think of Dixie as one large cup.

She'd also been afraid she might have been mistaken. Context is everything, and she'd been finding as she grew older that more and more frequently people were looking familiar. She'd thought she saw her mother's dear Norwegian friend on the subway a month ago. It seemed an impossibility, but she was still about to greet her when she realized it wasn't Marit at all. Context. People greeted her and she knew she knew them, but from where? PTA days? Volunteering at Rosie's Place? Sanpere?

Yet, it had only taken a few seconds to be absolutely sure who Stephen Cohen was, and had been.

"I want to call Faith about Mother, since we'll be gone all day and I doubt our cell phones will work on the water. Would you go down in case they're already waiting? I won't be long."

Sam gave her a kiss, and then another.

"You want to blow this off? Just you and me today?"

Pix smiled. She supposed she was having what people called a "second honeymoon"—with at least one man.

"That would be terribly rude, but I'll take a rain check."

As soon as he was out the door, she called Faith, who was at work but said she had a moment to chat.

"Now, tell me everything, Ms. Miller. To think, you have a past I know nothing about! You sly little minx!"

Pix told her everything.

Faith reacted with enthusiasm. "I'm glad you kicked up your heels a little—that time and whenever else in your flaming youth. Clearly Sam was the one, but you needed to find out you could be the one for somebody else, too."

"It was all a long time ago," Pix said, "and I'm pretty sure those Dartmouth boys were pouring every known kind of alcohol into the punch bowl, but it happened and I'm not sorry. Not about that weekend."

"Then what?"

"Oh Faith," Pix cried. "He doesn't remember me!"

CHAPTER 5

Down East, Faith had occasionally heard someone described as being "sick with secrets," and while she didn't think she had reached that point, she definitely felt she was suffering from a surfeit of them as she sat next to Ursula in the early afternoon on Wednesday. There was the missing money at First Parish, which Faith hoped Ursula would not hear about, knowing how upset the former Senior Warden would be. And then there was Niki, whom Ursula knew. The older woman would most certainly think the news of a wife's pregnancy should be shared with her husband. However, these paled in comparison to the situation Ursula's daughter found herself in—a situation to be kept from her mother at all costs.

Faith had spoken to Pix the day before at greater length and had tried, in vain, to convince her that she had not aged beyond recognition since college. Yes, her hair was a bit shorter, but it showed no silver threads among the bronze. Nor had she gained weight, and if any cottage-cheese cellulite existed, it wasn't apparent, even in a bathing suit. A few crow's-feet at the eyes, but the rest of her face was smooth. Faith only hoped she would look as good as Pix did some years hence. Of course for Faith, there was always a Plan

B involving a discreet "vacation." Pix had not and never would resort to cosmetic surgery. When the wrinkles appeared, as they would, she'd be one of those people who say they've earned them. Faith would be one of those people who say they've earned erasing them—the result not Joan Rivers or Nancy Reagan, but merely a slightly younger version of her own self.

"Okay, maybe he doesn't recognize me physically, but he should remember my name. It's not as if there could have been a lot of other people named Pix in his life, and especially not that weekend."

From what Faith had heard about the wild Green Key weekends of yore, there would have been a plethora of Muffys, Bunnys, and yes, Pixes from the Seven Sisters, Ivies, and other schools in attendance. But she was also sure this wasn't why Dr. Cohen didn't remember her friend's name. Faith had no doubt as to the reason.

"It's a guy thing. Think about it. Remembering names, especially female names, is not in their DNA. I've caught Tom stumbling over them more than once. Do admit, you've seen this with Sam—and your sons."

"Well . . . yes," Pix had said, "and my father could never keep people straight, female and male. Mother used to whisper in his ear at parties, she told me, so she wouldn't be embarrassed when he forgot that the next-door neighbors were Sally and Bob, not Susie and Bill."

"Okay, feel better now?"

There had been a long pause.

"So, I guess I was just a one-night stand?"

Faith had had to go through it all over again and at the end Pix had still sounded forlorn.

Before she'd hung up, Faith told Pix, "Don't you dare let this put a damper on everything. Tonight I want you in that strapless number we bought. I guarantee that Stephen Cohen and every other Y chromosome in the place will never forget you in that."

Pix had sworn her to secrecy and Faith would never violate the trust, but she wished she could tell someone, Niki in particular. Faith could discuss the situation with her, and yes, have a giggle. The person she had absolutely no desire to tell was the woman next to her now. Parents didn't need to know everything. As she thought this she realized, however, she wasn't anywhere near this point with her kids.

This was going to be the third installment of Ursula's tale, and as each chapter was revealed, she seemed to gain strength and look better. "Sick with secrets." The phrase came back to Faith again. Was this what had been ailing Ursula?

"You are good to come and listen so patiently, Faith dear. I'm sure you have all sorts of better things to do," Ursula said.

"Please don't think this—and there's no rush. Things are very slow at work and I have plenty of time. Being with you is exactly where I want to be," Faith said, meaning every word and then some. Faith felt honored at having been chosen to hear whatever it was Ursula needed to reveal—and it transported her away from her other worries.

"Throughout life," Ursula began slowly, "there are times when you read about a terrible tragedy and want to turn time back for an instant. When you want to keep someone from getting on a plane or opening a door. Or you may even want to turn time back many years, granting someone a happier childhood instead of the one that led to misery and worse—that sort of thing. You say to yourself, 'What if?' Since that summer, my turning-back-time 'what if' has been, 'What if Father hadn't gone to Sanpere that August weekend?'"

Faith nodded. She knew the feeling well—and it worked in the other direction, as well. Times you didn't want to change. What if she hadn't accepted the catering job at the wedding reception where she'd met Tom? Their paths would never have crossed otherwise.

"As I mentioned, the house in Maine was undergoing major construction. In those days, getting to the island took much longer than five hours and involved train and steamboat travel. Father had hoped to get away from work at the end of July, but there were already rumblings of the crisis that would occur on Black Tuesday and he had to stay in town. He never discussed business with me and all I knew then was that Father was 'very occupied with work.' Again, if he had been able to go earlier, would it have changed what happened?"

Ursula looked steadily out the window for a few moments before continuing.

"I rather think not. Naturally Theo thought this would be the perfect time to have the house party he'd been talking about all summer and my mother agreed. He would have picked any time Father was gone for a long stretch. Unlike Father, who thought their music was an assault to the ears and their dress the same to the eyes, Mother liked having the young people around. She seemed very old to me, but she was only just forty. And, in any case, she never denied Theo anything. It was Father who didn't spare the rod—not literally, but definitely figuratively. I know the Professor didn't think the party was a very good idea. At the time I thought it was because Theo still had so much math to study if he was going to pass the course in the fall. Later I learned there were other reasons.

"Some of the guests were at their family houses on the island, but Scooter Jessup, Babs Dickson, Charles Winthrop, and Violet Hammond were all staying with us. I think those young women were the most beautiful creatures I've ever seen. I was completely captivated by them—the way they talked, and especially by the way they looked. Years later when I read Fitzgerald's *Gatsby,* there was a line that has stayed with me about Daisy Buchanan and Jordan Baker weighing down their white summer dresses 'like silver idols' against the breeze a fan was making. When I read it I was back in the living room of the house on the Vineyard watching from a corner as the music played and the breeze from an open window caused those sheer white linen dresses to ripple ever so slightly."

Ursula was back in the room now, too, and from her description Faith could clearly see the images of the women. Bobbed hair, Clara Bow mouths, and rolled stockings. Flappers. Those "silver idols."

"Violet Hammond was the most beautiful of all. She truly did have violet eyes. How could her parents have known the name they chose was going to be so apt? I've never heard of babies with such dramatic-colored eyes and I've never seen such eyes again, except in an Elizabeth Taylor movie. But not on a person I knew. The men were all mad for her. She had a very beautiful voice, too. Husky, not high-pitched, and she spoke softly. Years later I wondered whether this was so people, especially men, would have to lean in closer to hear her.

"And she wore a very distinctive perfume. She said she had it made up for her in Paris. It wasn't floral. Nothing as mundane as lilacs or roses. Sandalwood, or some other exotic Far Eastern scent."

"She *does* sound lovely," Faith murmured.

"Oh yes, exquisite. Her people were from Chicago. She'd been sent to Boston to live with a cousin of her mother's. I don't think I ever knew why, although I have an idea that she was taking a painting course at the Museum of Fine Arts. She was just out of school—I think it may have been Miss Porter's or Dobbs—and she'd been a famous beauty there, too, very popular with the boys at Yale. The cousin lived on Beacon Street across from the Common, and I don't think Violet received much supervision from her. Mother never said anything directly, but she made it clear that the Hammonds were not, well, people she'd care to know. I heard her talking to her sister, Myrtle, about them. The 'Chicago Hammonds' as opposed to 'our Hammonds.' It wasn't about money. Even though Violet had gone to an expensive private boarding school, it was my impression the family wasn't very wealthy. She never appeared in the same outfit twice, but I think that's why I have the idea she was doing something artistic—she was very clever with scarves and such. With Mother it wasn't about money—money wasn't important to her. Breeding was. This sounds terribly snobbish. It was terribly snobbish."

Ursula reached for the glass of water on the table next to her and drank.

"Are you hungry?" Faith asked. Ursula's hands were so thin. When she brought the glass to her lips, Faith fancied she could see the bones under her thin skin like an X-ray against the sunlight from the window. "I brought some of the currant scones you like, and the last of the strawberry preserves we put up in July." The strawberries in Ursula's garden at The Pines were the stuff of legend.

"Thank you, no. But could you stay a bit longer?"

"Until five. Tom is working at home today." Faith didn't offer any further explanation. After trying to write his sermon in the shadow of his file cabinets at the church yesterday, he had decided to give the parsonage study, neutral territory, a try today.

"As I said, everything hinged on Father's absence, and then Mother had to leave, too. The second 'What if?' but one that wouldn't have mattered if Father hadn't been so far away—and impossible to reach. No cell phones. Not even a landline at The Pines until many years later. She must have sent him a telegram. I wasn't told. She had received a telegram, though, early that morning. Aunt Myrtle had been rushed to the Massachusetts General Hospital for emergency surgery. Appendicitis. It was a much more perilous diagnosis in those days than now and Mother left for Boston at once, leaving the housekeeper in charge—and the Professor. Although he was only a year or two older than the others, he seemed like an adult. The others were still children, intent on having a good time above all else. Mother did suggest that perhaps the young people staying at the house might want to leave, but Theo said he thought 'Aunt Myrt' would be upset to know that her illness had caused anyone an inconvenience."

Selfish, foolish, or just very immature? Faith wondered to herself about Theo. Ursula obviously had adored him—and did still.

It was as if she had read Faith's mind, or perhaps her last words had triggered the defense.

"He wasn't a bad person, Faith. Not at all. Generous to a fault, especially with his friends. But I'm afraid he was weak, easily influenced, and not terribly interested in what Father and the Professor both had mapped out for him as a course of study. In the ordinary way of things, he would have squeaked through Harvard and done very well in business, perhaps with Father. People liked and trusted him. Although the years that followed weren't good for most of his generation."

"Those Depression years for young men in their twenties weren't much different from recent times," Faith said. "The highest unemployment is in that group."

Ursula nodded. She was glad her elder grandson was gainfully employed and concerned about Dan, the younger, soon to finish college.

"In any case, Mother left in a rush, reassured me that Aunt Myrtle would be fine, but said I should still add an extra prayer for her before I went to bed. Selfish child that I was—although at that age, sickness and death have little reality—I confess what was really worrying me was not my aunt, but whether I'd be able to go to Illumination Night. Do you know what this is, Faith?"

Faith did, having had the great good fortune to be on the Vineyard some years ago on the second Wednesday in August. She hadn't known about the Grand Illumination previously. For her, a grand illumination meant the lighting of the tree at Rockefeller Center at Christmastime.

"It was magical," she said. "I'll never forget the moment when all those strings of Japanese lanterns were lighted on the cottages, which are pretty colorful by themselves."

Faith had immediately coveted one of the little Victorian Carpenter Gothic–style houses. She'd learned the two rooms up and two rooms down with front porches trimmed with froths of lacy gingerbread scrollwork had replaced the tents pitched earlier in the nineteenth century by attendees at the Methodist camp meetings that became popular during the Revival.

The houses were painted in bright peach, rose, turquoise, and yellows with contrasting trim. When she'd expressed her desire, her friend had told her that the houses were passed down from one generation to the next, and even if one did go on sale, it was by word of mouth and gone moments later. This part of the Vineyard was also the setting for one of Faith's favorite books, *The Wedding* by Dorothy West, a member of the Harlem Renaissance. West had been coming to Oak Bluffs since childhood, her family part of the early African American summer colony who had made Oak Bluffs with its famed Inkwell Beach an ongoing destination.

Illumination Night had obviously captured Ursula's imagination, too.

"By the summer I was there, Illumination Night was an old tradition and I'd been hearing about it for weeks, especially from the servants. By this time I'd become adept at the Vineyard sign language and considered Mary Smith, who worked in the kitchen, a new friend. She wasn't much older than I was and was walking out with the gardener. I think I mentioned this the other day."

Faith nodded. Ursula had mentioned the young woman, but not her name.

"The lanterns sounded like something out of a fairy tale—

Mary told me that originally they were plain ones until a Japanese family opened a gift shop in Oak Bluffs in the 1870s when there was such a rage for Asian art. After that the lanterns had to be from Japan or China.

"And I thought the little houses were playhouses when I first saw them and used to beg to be taken to see them. Mother had a friend who owned one and I loved to sit on her tiny porch in a rocker that was small, too. There were always people strolling by and stopping to say hello. I'm afraid I wasn't missing Sanpere at those times, although at others I wanted intensely to be there.

"The huge tabernacle in the middle of the campground looked like a rustic palace. I had never been inside and this was another reason why I had been counting the days until Illumination Night. As soon as we heard about it, Mother promised she would take me and I think she was excited to go, too."

Faith remembered the Tabernacle. It was interdenominational now, and Illumination Night, as well as the other summer events held there, was run by the Camp Ground Association. They should try to take the kids this year, although August meant Maine. Even Ben, who had recently adopted a world-weary air more reminiscent of Garbo than a seventh grader, would be impressed. The lanterns were what turned a summer band concert, albeit an extremely large one, into a unique experience. The lantern collection went with the houses—if they changed hands—and some were over a hundred years old, painted by artists or an owner's children and grandchildren. Many were still illuminated with candles. At dusk, someone who had been appointed, a terrific honor, lit the signal lantern at the Tabernacle and immediately hundreds of others festooned on the surrounding houses glowed. At eleven, they were extinguished, and church chimes filled the now quiet night, signaling the end of another Illumination Night.

Faith had even gotten into the old-time sing-along at the Tabernacle, especially when they sang "East Side, West Side, All

Around the Town." The band concert that followed the sing-along had been heavy on Sousa. It had all suggested a simpler, carefree time, although as Faith listened to Ursula she doubted such a moment had ever existed even in "The Good Old Summertime."

"The weather that day was unseasonably warm, especially for Martha's Vineyard," Ursula said. "Perhaps that had something to do with it, too."

"You're all a bunch of slugs. Big fat oozing slugs!" Babs said. She was carrying her tennis racquet and dressed for the courts.

"Darling girl. It's too hot for tennis. Too hot for anything, except a dip in the ocean. What about it?" Theo looked around the living room at the group that had assumed a variety of languid poses, none more drooping, or aesthetic, than Violet's. She was stretched out on one of the cushioned wicker chaises. Her shapely legs and ankles, down to her bare feet—she'd kicked off her shoes—were nicely displayed.

"Too salty, and Babs, even your devoted Scooter isn't going to bake on that clay court. Run along and practice that divine backhand of yours." Violet's slightly sarcastic tone turned the compliment truly into a backhanded one.

Babs flushed, walked over to Scooter, who'd been idly playing the piano, and grabbed his hand.

"I suppose a walk on the beach won't kill you? You can borrow one of Violet's sunshades if you don't want to freckle."

"Hey, don't have a conniption, honeybun. Everything's jake. If you want to play tennis, I'll play. Violet isn't my mouthpiece."

"You're a doll." Babs planted a big kiss on the top of his head. "But it is hot. Let's walk now and play later."

"I thought it was 'Let's play now and pay later,'" Theo quipped.

"That's only you, Lyman," Charles Winthrop called out. He was looking at the ocean through a brass spyglass. "And speaking of paying, I believe you owe me several simoleons from last night. Damn, not a single sail. Nothing's moving. I'd hoped to get out to-day. Dickie Cabot said to come over if the wind was right and we'd head out. Nice little boat they have."

"If you call a yacht that sleeps eight with quarters for the crew little, then I'd agree. And Charlie, there are ladies present." Theo sounded peeved and seized on Winthrop's oath. He also considered it devilishly poor taste to mention the money he owed after several late nights of cards with a few fellows who'd dropped by. Charles wasn't the only one he'd lost to and it was partly the cause of a head-ache that was getting worse not better as the day wore on. The other cause was too much gin.

"Stop it, both of you," Violet said, swinging her legs to the floor and stretching like a cat. "Order some lemonade, Theo, and we can play mah-jongg in the shade on the porch. It must be cooler there."

Theo walked to the door and pressed a button to the left of it. Mrs. Miles, the housekeeper, soon appeared and he asked her if she could please bring some cold lemonade to the porch.

"Yes, Mr. Lyman," she said.

She was barely out the door when Violet gave a throaty laugh. "She has a beau, your Mrs. Miles."

"Really, Violet, the servants' affairs are of no concern to us. Leave the poor woman alone," Babs said.

"It's really very sweet," Violet continued, taking no notice. "He appears every night after dinner and lurks in the shrubbery until she's finished and then they disappear in the direction of the beach. A bit gritty for nooky, I'd say."

"And you should know," Babs said softly to Scooter.

"I heard that," Violet said, not in the least bothered. "Better to be the bees' knees than a Mrs. Grundy."

"Meow," Scooter said, and got up from the piano. "Are we taking that walk or not?"

"Taking it," Babs said. "See you in the funny papers."

Mrs. Miles returned with a tray. Ursula was at her heels. She'd been in the kitchen talking to Mary.

"Would you like the lemonade in here or on the porch, Mr. Lyman?"

"The porch will be fine. Let me get the door."

"The Professor would like you to meet him in the library, Theo," Ursula said. "I saw him in the hall and told him I'd tell you. And don't forget, you promised you'd take me tonight since Mother can't."

"What does he want now?" Theo ignored the rest of what Ursula had said.

"Go and swallow your medicine like a good boy. I don't want my Theo flunking out." Violet walked over and slipped her arm through his. "We'll be thinking of something fun for tonight's party. Charades?"

Theo brightened immediately. "Which reminds me, I've got to see a man about a dog in Edgartown as soon as I can get away from Herr Professor."

"Remember, Baby likes champagne, Daddy," Violet said as she squeezed his arm.

Ursula thought this sounded pretty stupid. Theo wasn't anywhere near old enough to be Violet's father. She knew it was slang—which her mother had forbidden her to use—but shouldn't even slang make some sense?

Violet dropped Theo's arm, and Ursula grabbed the other one, tugging on it slightly.

"You promised! And we don't have to stay too long. Just see the lanterns lighted and hear some of the music."

Theo shook her off and walked toward the door.

"Later, squirt. I've got a date with an isosceles triangle."

She followed him out and down the hall into the library. It was smaller than the living and dining rooms, but bigger than its counterpart at the Lymans' Boston house. A large fireplace dominated one wall. The rest were lined with bookshelves that came halfway up the walls. Above and on top of them, the owner displayed his weaponry collection. There were elaborately etched swords, some in embossed silver scabbards that looked as if young Arthur had pulled them from the stone. In addition there were several very frightening-looking spiked maces and crossbows. Another wall was devoted to American weapons starting with the muskets the colonists used against the British, up through the Spencer carbines of the Civil War. The last wall was filled with African and South American spears. They were arranged like the spokes of a wheel with an enormous moose head as the hub. Ursula had spent hours in the library, reading and contemplating the décor. The moose looked slightly surprised to find himself surrounded by such foreign objects, she thought. There was a leopard skin spread out in front of the fireplace over the Oriental carpet that almost covered the entire floor, leaving only an edge of gleaming wood to show that the quality of what was beneath equaled what was on top. The leopard was headless. Doubtless, she imagined, if the house's owner had killed it, he would have displayed that head with the spears. He must have killed the moose and decided it would have to do. A large library table was covered with richly illustrated books on the history of weaponry—and a number of guns ranging from a tiny pearl-handled revolver to the kind of gun Tom Mix carried in the movies. She'd learned many interesting new words from the books and it certainly was a very different kind of hobby from any of hers— the ferns and birds' nests in Maine, postcards in Boston. Her father collected stamps, which took up considerably less room.

"Sorry to drag you away from your friends, Theo, but we don't have a great deal of time left and there's still so much to get through." The Professor sounded tired, Ursula thought.

"Well, let's get to it, then," Theo said and then seemed to regret

his tone. "You've been cooped up here all morning in this heat."
When he wasn't tutoring Theo, the Professor was editing his senior
thesis, which he hoped to publish. "How about some cold lemonade?
Ursula, run out to the porch and get us both a glass."

"Thanks, I am feeling warm, so a glass of something cold
would be very nice. Meanwhile, shall we start on page fifty in the
text?"

Ursula was only too happy to fetch the drinks. As she left she
thought, Page 50? That's all? The text was a thick one. Maybe
they were reviewing. If not, Theo would never be through the book
by the end of the summer.

When she returned the two men were in deep conversation, but
it wasn't about mathematics. She knew it was wrong to eavesdrop,
but could she help it if she had to slow down so she wouldn't spill
on the carpet?

"Don't be sore, Theo. I'm your friend first and tutor second.
You know that. Think of this as advice from one friend to another.
It's just that with both your parents gone and word about this party
all over the island, I'm afraid things are going to get out of hand.
Can't you call it off and have dinner with the people staying in the
house? Maybe ask one or two other couples? Roll up the rug after-
ward?" He was leaning forward, smiling persuasively, and Ursula
wondered how her brother could possibly resist giving in.

Theo was on the opposite side of the desk, slouched in a leather
chair. He was cleaning his nails with a sharply pointed stiletto—
Ursula had asked her father what it was and he'd told her. He'd also
told her not to touch it and would be appalled at the use to which
Theo was putting it. The gold handle was elaborately enameled in
emerald green. The house's owner used it as a letter opener and it
rested on a special little tray.

"Sorry, can't do it. I'd look like a chump. Vi, I mean the girls,
would be very cut up. They're looking forward to putting on their
glad rags. Not much chance here."

There was a brief silence.

"Best get to work, then."

Ursula almost burst into tears. How could Theo disappoint his friend—his wise tutor, wise counselor—this way?

She gulped and said, "Here are the drinks. I could get some cookies from the kitchen if you want. Cook baked this morning."

"That's very kind of you, Ursula, but I'm all set with this. Thank you." The Professor took the glass from her hand. Theo took the other glass.

"They light the lanterns at dusk, Theo. We could be back for your party in plenty of time."

Her brother was seldom cross with her, so Ursula was surprised at the vehemence of his next words.

"Can't you see we're working here? Now get going—and stop pestering me about a bunch of lanterns!"

Ursula started to answer back, but the look on his face stopped her. He was scowling. A rare sight.

"Illumination Night? It's tonight?" asked the Professor.

"Yes," Ursula said, her voice shaking slightly, "and with Mother gone there's no one to take me. Mrs. Miles was supposed to be off today, but said she'd stay since Mother had to leave. Mary is only working until just before dark, and I'd ask her, except I know she's going with . . . with someone else, and Theo said—"

"What I said was 'get going'!"

"I'll take you," the Professor said. "I've heard about Illumination Night for years."

"Don't you want to go to the party?" Ursula asked.

"No, I don't care to attend."

Daylight savings time had started earlier in the month, an event Faith always greeted with great joy. It might be freezing outside, and snow up to the windowsill, but there was light! Although it was close to five o'clock, sunshine was flooding Ursula's bedroom, giving the illusion of a balmy summer day.

"You must be getting tired," Faith said.

"No, happily I'm not." Ursula reached for Faith's hand. "Is there any way you could stay another hour? I hate to keep you from your family, but I really don't feel fatigued and I'd like to tell you some more of my story."

The tale was reaching its climax and perhaps its end, as well. Faith had sensed it all afternoon. She didn't want to leave.

"Let me give Tom a call. I'm sure it will be fine."

"I'll ring the bell for Dora. Some of Millicent's restorative calf's foot jelly for me, and tea for you instead, I think." Ursula smiled mischievously, knowing full well Faith's opinion of all things Millicent. She rang the little brass hand bell shaped like a lady with a wide hoop skirt, a gift from Samantha, who had found it in an antiques shop. It was always placed nearby.

Tom told her to stay as long as she wanted, and soon they were settled back with not only the tea and jelly but also some cucumber and cress sandwiches. Dora was well-known for her British-style cooking, particularly nursery comfort foods like jam roly-poly and rice pudding.

Ursula picked up where she had left off.

"Theo's guests were beginning to arrive as we left for the campground. Most of the women were quite dressed up for the Vineyard. Violet, who was acting as hostess, was wearing one of those long white satin backless dresses that movie stars like Carole Lombard and Jean Harlow had made so popular. She had a long rope of pearls, not real I'm sure, that she'd tied at her neck so they hung down her back. Her skin was almost as white as the necklace and as smooth. Babs was wearing a long gown, too. It struck me because I'd never seen her dressed up before and hadn't realized that she was quite lovely, too. It was sapphire blue and cut quite decorously compared to Violet's dress. The men who were staying at the house were all in dinner jackets, which must have been terribly uncomfortable. The heat hadn't broken."

Ursula slipped out from her hiding place beneath the piano and went into the dining room. Theo had had food delivered from some restaurant and the table was covered with platters of all sorts of delicious-looking things. She took a plate and started to reach for some lobster salad, stuffed back in the red shell, but realized that she was too excited to eat anything except some toast that had been placed next to a mound of caviar. She was momentarily tempted by the shiny black roe—she'd had it once and it tasted like the sea— but she decided to stick to the toast.

She heard the Professor's voice calling her name and then he was at her side.

"Time to get going?"

"Oh yes, please."

They left the crowded room and slipped into the kitchen, leaving through the back door into the still night. The last noise from the house that Ursula heard was a champagne cork popping and a woman starting to sing 'Yes Sir, That's My Baby.'

She had put on her best frock. Rose-colored silk. A dropped waist with a pleated skirt. Her mother would not have approved. Ursula had felt a twinge of guilt when she'd slipped it over her head—but only a twinge, and that soon disappeared.

If Mother wasn't back tomorrow, perhaps the Professor would take her to the carousel—the Flying Horses—in Oak Bluffs. Mother had heard that they were originally at Coney Island, a place Mother called 'a vulgar amusement park,' but she hadn't expressly forbidden Ursula from going.

She darted a glance at her companion. He was a grown-up, but not terribly old. Only twenty.

"Have you been enjoying your summer? I understand it's quite different from the place you normally go in Maine,"

Ursula started talking and soon she felt as if she had never before talked to anyone so understanding. He wasn't at all condescending and she moved from a description of Sanpere Island to her desire to explore Boston, and the whole world—her eagerness to grow up.

Blessedly, he didn't tell her not to be in a rush, but spoke of his own hope to travel once he had finished law school.

"Perhaps I'll be able to find a job that won't start until the fall, allowing me a summer to roam. I've a yen to go to the Lake District, Wordsworth country."

And Beatrix Potter's, Ursula almost said, before deciding mentioning Peter Rabbit's creator might seem childish.

A few minutes later she realized she could have mentioned Peter, or anything else. The Professor was interested in everything she was interested in—his bird list was twice as long as hers!

He found seats for them near the front. The Tabernacle did not disappoint. They sang lustily, joining the others raising their voices, the notes reverberating into the twilight as the sun's last rays struck the stained-glass panels below the wooden tented ceiling. Through the open sides, Ursula could just make out the unlit lanterns strung on every porch, swaying slightly, waiting for the signal. She thought the Tabernacle was indeed a holy place, and very far removed from King's Chapel.

The music was over too soon, but outside there were the lanterns, illuminated now—hundreds of them. They ate peppermint ice cream—"The color of your pretty dress," he said—and wandered about looking at the glowing orbs.

"I'm afraid we should be getting back," he said.

Ursula looked at her watch. Theo had given her a Gruen wristwatch for Christmas. Mother had told her not to take it to the Vineyard because she might get sand in it, but she'd packed it anyway, loath to leave one of her most precious possessions behind. Tonight she'd happily tightened the black grosgrain ribbon strap and thought she'd much rather have it than the pearls and other jewelry the women were wearing.

She'd only stayed up this late—it was just after ten o'clock—on New Year's Eve. The Professor was right, regrettably. It was time to go.

As they neared the house Ursula could see there were cars all over the drive and even some on the lawn. Father would be terribly upset, she thought. They had been hearing the music from quite far away and now, close to the house, it was very loud.

"Let's slip in the kitchen way again and I think you'd better go straight to bed. I'll be in the library if you should need me." He looked a bit anxious and Ursula knew he was concerned that the party showed no signs of winding down. Then he smiled at her. "It's been a lovely evening. Good night."

"Thank you for taking me. It was perfect."

Mary was helping the people who'd brought the food, but Ursula didn't see Mrs. Miles. Mary signed that she would be leaving soon for the Illumination and wasn't it wonderful? Ursula signed back that it was better than anything she had ever seen and, feeling a sudden shyness, raced up the back stairs, realizing when she got to the top that she hadn't said "good night" back to the Professor. She started to turn around, but he'd be gone. It didn't matter. She'd say "good night" to him twice tomorrow night to make up for it. Perhaps she'd tell him why.

As Ursula went into her room, she felt as if she were floating, like one of the lanterns. She changed, said her prayers, and got into bed. It was impossible to sleep. Her room in the turret was stifling even with the windows open. And the noise. Not just the music, but people were in the pool, directly below, splashing and shriek-ing. There seemed to be a constant stream of cars coming and going. Finally she decided to retreat to her place in the woods.

Her place by the gazebo.

She took a blanket with her and made a cozy nest beneath the rhododendrons. There wasn't anyone in the gazebo. She'd been afraid there might be some couples there, but it was empty, although someone had strung up some Japanese lanterns like the ones in the campground and lighted them. The noise from the house was muted.

She felt quite drowsy, but fought sleep to enjoy the novelty of sleeping outdoors. She could see the sky through the branches. It was a clear night and the stars were bright. For a time, Ursula amused herself by picking out the various constellations. Theodore Artemus Lyman was an avid amateur astronomer and had taught his children all the names.

I wonder whether the Professor is a stargazer, too . . . she thought fuzzily. The night air was cool at last. She slept.

Ursula hadn't been asleep long when she was awakened by the sound of loud voices nearby. Two men were arguing in the gazebo. She couldn't see them through the thick foliage, but she could hear them clearly. One was Theo; she wasn't sure who the other was. Theo was slurring his words. She'd let him into the house in Boston one night very late and he'd sounded the same. She'd had to help him up the stairs to his room. He was very unsteady. The next day he'd told her he'd never mix champagne and whiskey again, but it sounded as if he had tonight. The other voice was similar. How silly these men were to get drunk and quarrel, Ursula thought.

"I've got to have the money now. I told you they won't wait. They want the money tomorrow first thing! You said you'd have it tonight! I'm done for if my father finds out!"

"Can't do it, old chum. Jus' tell 'em."

"Snap out of it, Theo! I'm telling you I'm in a jam. They won't give me any more time. They've threatened to hurt me—and they will."

"No money here. Not on this little old island."

"Get it from somebody. What about your tutor?"

"Poor as a church mouse. Hey, that's funny."

Theo started to laugh and stopped abruptly.

"Whadya have to smack me for? Thought we were friends. Let's go back to the house. Need another drink. Want to see Violet. Violet with the violet eyes."

"Look here, I'll smack you again if it will bring you to your senses. You owe me the money fair and square. You knew we were playing for high stakes. Had to impress Violet, didn't you. Well, she wasn't. She thinks you're a sap."

"Watch what you're saying! I'm no sap. I'm gonna go ask her. Ask her what she thinks of you, too!"

Ursula ducked farther back into the bushes. She was starting to get frightened. Maybe she should run to the house and get the Professor. Theo, oh Theo, why did you have to get yourself in such messes! She had ten dollars left from her summer spending money. He was welcome to it and then this person would leave him alone.

"You're not going anywhere."

"Who's gonna stop me?"

"Me, that's who!"

"Come on, les go have a drink, buddy. Stop fighting. Make up. Friends. You're my friend, right?"

Theo's voice had lost its belligerent tone and Ursula was relieved. She heard a few thumping noises—they were crossing the wooden floor of the gazebo—followed by the sounds of running feet.

It was all right, then. They'd gone back to the house. She decided to stay where she was. It was so quiet and peaceful. A beautiful night.

It seemed as if she had barely fallen asleep again when she heard a woman's screams. She got up and ran out from under the bushes into the clearing. There were two people standing up in the gazebo. The lanterns were still lighted and the woman who was screaming was Violet. The other person was a man. His back was to Ursula and she assumed it was Theo. People were streaming out from the house—the path was visible from where she stood—and there was a great deal of commotion. She could hear cars starting up. A great many cars. Violet kept screaming and screaming. Ursula wanted her to stop. Why couldn't someone make her stop?

The gazebo looked bigger than it did in the daytime. She walked over toward the door. It was wide open. Someone tried to pull her away, but she kept going. The ground felt cold and hard beneath her bare feet and she started to shiver.

The other man wasn't Theo. Theo was lying on the floor. He was on his back and his eyes were closed. He's fallen asleep here, Ursula thought. Why is Violet screaming? And why hasn't he woken up with all the noise?

She went in and walked over to him, kneeling down to shake his shoulder. It was then that she saw the blood on his starched white shirtfront. It was so red. There wasn't much, but it was very red. Once he'd cut himself shaving and come to breakfast with a bit of tissue on his face; blood was still seeping through. Father made him leave. It was so very red, Theo's blood. Running through his body. So very alive that morning.

But she knew he wasn't alive now. He was dead. Knew the moment she'd knelt down. That's why Violet was screaming. But why was the Professor standing over him with the stiletto from the library in his hand? The blade was glistening red. The same color as Theo's blood. Nothing made sense.

The Professor's face looked very different from the way it had looked earlier that night. She put her hand on Theo's face, his lovely face. It was still warm. She took one of his hands in her other hand and held tight. And then Ursula laid her head down on his chest; she couldn't hear his heart beating at all. Violet had finally stopped screaming. Ursula had heard a slap, like in the movies. She didn't want to leave her brother surrounded by all these people, all these strangers, and she told the Professor to make everyone else leave. To leave the two of them alone with Theo. After she spoke, no one moved for a moment, or said anything, and then Charles Winthrop, Scooter Jessup, and some other men grabbed the Professor.

"Everyone heard your argument tonight," Charles said. "And now you've killed him, Arnold Rowe. Someone call the police."

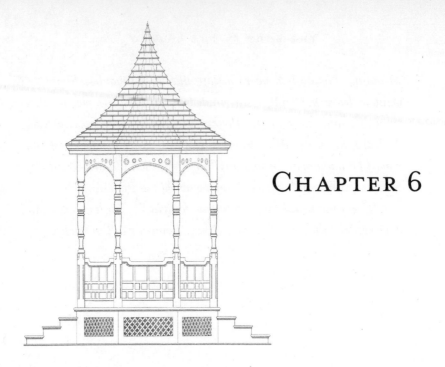

CHAPTER 6

Arnold Rowe?

The Arnold Rowe that Ursula Lyman married?

The Arnold Rowe who was the father of Pix Rowe Miller?

As Faith walked home, she took little note of the soft spring dusk with its swelling branches silhouetted against the diminishing daylight. She arrived at her own door without remembering the steps that had taken her there. It seemed as though one minute she'd been sitting in shock next to Ursula and a minute later here she was taking her keys from her jacket pocket.

She did recall a scene in between. Dora had come into the room—almost as if Ursula's startling revelation had been a cue. She'd seemed to take in the situation with one swift glance and said in a firm nanny's-here-to-take-charge tone, "Now, we've had a lovely long visit with Mrs. Fairchild, but it's time for a bit of a rest."

Then she'd walked closer and seen the tears that had filled Ursula's eyes as she was describing the tragic scene she'd witnessed. She spoke even more sternly. "I'm sure it's all been very nice, but I think we'll take it easy tomorrow. I'm sure Mrs. Fairchild could come back Friday or Saturday."

Faith had felt chastened, although at the same time she thought *she* hadn't done anything. But who had? What had happened in the short time that young Ursula had been asleep? And an even more pressing question: What had happened in the days, months, and years following? It was absurd to think that somehow Ursula had met another man with the same name and married him.

She'd leaned over and kissed Ursula's soft cheek before leaving.

"I'm fine," Ursula had murmured. "Dora's a benevolent despot, thank goodness, and if you could come back later this week, I'll continue."

"I'm afraid this is too upsetting for you." Faith had been and still was concerned. Surely the tale had reached its climax and, hence, the end.

Ursula had shaken her head emphatically. "No, please. We have to finish. I need your help. . . ."

At that point Dora's efficient manner propelled Faith out of the room, down the stairs, and onto the sidewalk before Ursula could say another word.

There it was again. The mention of needing help. But for what? Faith was mystified. The crime had occurred some eighty-odd years ago when Ursula was in her early teens. Still considered a child in that era, even more so because of her privileged and protected upbringing. Things were so different now. The other day when Faith had picked Ben up at school, there had been a group of girls—total fashionistas—waiting in front for rides. Some had adopted the Japanese schoolgirl look, complete with eyeliner to make their eyes appear as large as the waifs in manga. Others were going for Miley Cyrus as Hannah Montana with skimpy tees and plenty of pink glitter. Their cell phones seemed welded to their hands like some sort of new life-form appendages, and their pocketbooks were the size of steamer trunks. They didn't carry knapsacks. What they did carry in common was an air of supreme self-confidence and independence. Faith wanted to believe that below the surface there was at least a little angst, but she wouldn't bet on it. No one would ever describe these girls as children, and the fact that their counterparts were gracing the pages of *Vogue* and other fashion magazines at this tender age reinforced the image. An image she hoped she could help Amy avoid while guiding her through the rocky shoals known as adolescence. Even the geek girls—in their own tight group as far away from the others as possible—had their iPhones attached and requisite suburban goth garb. Faith thought of Ursula curled up asleep next to the gazebo as the horrific events of that night progressed. Today's girl—wearing an oversized T-shirt instead of a long white cotton nightdress—would have called 911, tweeted, and posted on Facebook in a matter of seconds.

She looked at her watch. It was six-thirty, and stepping into the parsonage she was greeted with the scent of oregano. It signaled Tom's standby meal and one he was always happy to have an excuse to order: a large pizza with extra sauce, roasted peppers, Italian sausage, heavy on the oregano, from his friend Harry at Country Pizza, Aleford's one and only concession to fast food, and vastly superior.

"We're in the kitchen, Mom," Amy called out.

It was a happy scene. Faith got a plate and cutlery, and sat down, pleased to note that Tom, or one of the kids, had also made a big salad. What she wasn't pleased to note was the line on Tom's forehead that always surfaced when he was troubled.

"How's Ursula?" he asked.

"When I got there she was sitting up in that big chair by the window and dressed." Faith had been delighted to see Ursula in her habitual Liberty-print blouse and poplin skirt from Orvis. "Steady improvement these last days—by the time Pix comes home, she may even be out dividing her hostas or delving into some other planting chore." Faith was a little sketchy about gardening schedules. Tom was the one who got his hands dirty, and when he was pressed for time, Pix pitched in, saying there wasn't enough to do in her backyard, which was an out-and-out lie, since at the height of the season it resembled an outpost of White Flower Farm or Wayside Gardens. Faith's knowledge of seasonal blooms was strictly governed by what appeared in the beds in Central Park or on the wide median strip down Park Avenue.

"It's a busy week for me with the library fund-raiser tomorrow night and the Tillies on Friday," she said. "I'm not sure when I'm going to be able to visit her again. We'll see what Saturday looks like."

This was one of those times when Faith wished early on she'd adopted the European custom of feeding the children first and whisking them off to bed, or homework at this stage. The weight of what Ursula had just told her was palpable and she needed to share it with Tom. She also needed to know what was causing his telltale furrow. The phone rang and he jumped up. "I'll take it in my study." Not a good sign.

It could be one of Tom's groupies asking him to arbitrate on the crucial debate over the kind of flowers the Sunday school children should receive on Easter—pots of pansies or bulb plants?—or a parishioner complaining about last Sunday's choice of hymns. Faith was hoping it was this type of call, ordinarily ones that caused her to wish Tom had opted for a different line of work, used-car salesman, insurance agent, tap dancer, anything but the clergy. Tonight she'd take the interruptions as a sign that all was still right with the world at First Parish. They wouldn't be calling him if they thought he'd had his hand in the till, or rather collection plate. What she feared, however, was that it was one of the vestry, notably Sherman, with more bad news.

The kids were finished eating. "Put your dishes in the sink. I'll clean up, so you can get a start on your homework. And Amy,

please put out what you plan to wear tomorrow—it's going to be
a sunny day. No more missing the bus because you're busy trying
on outfits."

"That's not fair, Mom. I don't do that. Much," Amy protested,
and left the room in a huff, unusual for her. Faith feared it was a
portent of things to come.

Ben was lingering at the sink. "She really doesn't do that. Did
you ever think she might be missing the bus on purpose?"

Faith whirled around and looked her son straight in the eye.

"Benjamin Fairchild, what do you know about this? What's
going on with Amy and the bus?"

Ben shrugged. "I think you should ask her. Much better for
parents and kids to have direct communication."

Faith resisted the impulse to shake him. When had her son
morphed into Dr. Phil?

"I intend to do that right away." She dried her hands and went
upstairs. Tom was still on the phone.

She knocked on her daughter's door before going in.

Amy was sitting at her desk reading.

"What's up, Mom?"

Her little face looked calm and happy. Maybe Ben was wrong.

"Sweetheart, is there some reason you don't *want* to take the
bus? Something going on during the ride?"

One look at her daughter's face told Faith there was. It crumpled and Amy didn't even try to stifle the sobs that erupted with
the suddenness of a summer's afternoon thunderstorm.

"Is it those girls? The ones on the playground? Are they on
your bus? Let's sit down over here." Faith awkwardly edged over
to the bed, holding her daughter, feeling like a hermit crab. As
they sat down, Amy buried her head in her mother's shoulder.

The sobs subsided; she hiccupped, raised her head, and nodded. Faith realized Ben was standing in the doorway.

"Josh's brother is on the same bus and he told Josh and Josh told me, but Amy didn't want you to know. I guess she thought you could just keep driving her in the morning, and you usually pick her up after school for dumb ballet or something."

"I told you not to tell, Ben!" Amy shouted at this convenient surrogate target.

"I didn't; she guessed. Kind of," he said, and started to walk away.

"Wait a minute," Faith said. "What else did Josh say?" She was pretty sure she wasn't going to get very coherent answers from Amy for a while.

"Just that they're these girls who think they're very hot. Like they date and stuff already."

"In third grade!" Faith was truly shocked.

"Well, not date date, but you know, go hang around where older guys are—sixth graders—and text stuff."

Faith had heard all too much about the craze for "sexting" among teens—sending suggestive photos, some pretty innocent, of girls at a slumber party egging each other on; others not innocent at all.

"Stuff like what?"

Ben gave her a look that told her he knew exactly what she was talking about. After the incidents last fall involving cyberbullying, her son's expertise in and knowledge of all things microchip was a given.

"Not that stuff. Stupid stuff like pictures of their dogs and cats wearing sunglasses and underwear. Supposed to be cool, but really lame."

Having dealt with the side issue—upsetting and weird as the image of pets in panties or what-have-you was—Faith got back to the matter at hand.

"Okay, so these girls who think they're so great, what are they doing to Amy?"

"Mom, I really have to do my homework. Amy will tell you.

Just give her a moment." And he was gone. That avatar who had replaced her son—whom she'd previously thought was clueless about social interactions—was a guy after all. She was going to have to rearrange these thoughts from now on. Ben had quite suddenly become very savvy. Faith gave Amy a moment.

"These girls are teasing you. Only you?"

Amy nodded.

"Do you know why?"

Amy took a deep breath. "None of my friends are on my bus. It's just me. On the playground, there are more of us."

Simple math.

"And what are they saying?"

"I don't know. Well, like I smell bad and lately something else." Amy's voice dropped.

Faith waited.

"They keep saying that they watched me salute the flag in assembly and that I need a bra."

"Mean girls" didn't even begin to come close. Amy was as flat as a board, concave in fact, and here they were suggesting she was feeling herself up! Faith was ready to get names and get even. She tried to remember the yoga-breathing thing for calming down that her friend Patsy had taught her.

"A lot of girls in my class have bras, Mom."

"If you want, we can go to Macy's tomorrow after school."

Amy brightened considerably.

"But," Faith continued, "I'm not sure this will solve the bus problem."

"I could let them see a strap," Amy suggested.

Faith knew these girls even if her sweet daughter didn't. "They'll find something else, I'm afraid. How about tomorrow morning sit in the front seat right behind the driver?"

"I can try, but usually Stacy Schwartz is there and I don't really know her. She's in fourth grade."

"Sit with her," Faith said. Stacy was probably seeking protection, too. "And I'll think about this some more." Plus she'd call the school again.

"But we can still go to Macy's?"

"We can still go to Macy's."

Leaving her children to their labors and thankful, as always, that she had left this sort of thing far behind, Faith went downstairs to finish cleaning up in the kitchen. The door to the study was closed. She put her ear to it and Tom was still on the phone. She hadn't heard the phone ring, so it was the same call. While she hoped it was not a serious matter—death, disease—she also hoped for a minor crisis, one that had absolutely nothing to do with the Minister's Discretionary Fund.

As she wiped the counter, she heard the study door open. Tom came into the kitchen.

"That was Sam. I left a message for him earlier to give me a call, asking him to call as soon he got back to Aleford."

Faith was relieved. Sam must have had to come back early for some reason and now he could help deal with all this. The Hilton Head group had been due to split up tomorrow morning, with the ladies heading to Charleston for the bridal shower; the rest returning to jobs and school.

Faith's respite from worry was short-lived.

"Sam isn't going to be back in Aleford until the middle of next week at the earliest," Tom said. "He has to go to California to depose a number of people involved in the class action suit the firm has been working on since last fall. He's the only one not in court right now."

"So this means . . . ?"

"This means I told him everything that's been going on, and as soon as he's back—unless by one of God's miracles it's all been cleared up—he'll go over everything. I've retained him as my lawyer, Faith. He advised I do so and I thought it was a good idea."

Ever since Tom had broken the news, Faith had been avoiding the harsh reality of the situation he was in. The word "lawyer" brought it into sharp focus. She moved closer to her husband and put her arms around him.

"Sam will take care of it," she said. "This is what he does. He'll see something everyone, even the bank, has missed. What else did he say?"

"He pretty much asked me the same questions you did—who had access to the file, the keys. He also wondered if I'd been aware of anyone standing behind me when I used the ATM. Apparently there's this thing called 'shoulder surfing'—stealing someone's PIN by looking over his or her shoulder when they enter it. There are other ways, too, but he didn't go into them. I'm trying to think back, but it's hard. That ATM area at the bank is pretty small and sometimes people are filling out deposit slips while you're using the machine or just waiting their turns. I've done it myself."

She should have thought of this! Someone hacking into Tom's account! Several years ago when Faith had taught a cooking for dummies course during the project week at Mansfield Academy, a local prep school, she'd met Zach Cummings, a computer whiz— although there must be some other techie term that was more precise, and colorful. Since then they'd stayed in touch. While she'd been at Mansfield she became involved in a murder investigation. Zach, innocent of any wrongdoing, had been pulled into the chaos. He was at MIT now and she'd e-mail him tonight. She felt hopeful again, and also a bit as if she were riding one of those Martha's Vineyard carousel horses—up, down, up, down, all in the space of a few seconds. Yes, a hacker. This had to be it. The unknown stranger. The equivalent of a tramp passing through town—or rather in or near town since all the withdrawals were from the same ATM. Tom was merely unlucky. Very unlucky. It was like having your credit card number stolen by a server in a restaurant or someone who identified the card's numbers from the touch-tones when you used it in a public place like an airport. The ATM didn't make any noise, or did it?

Tom mentioned "God's miracles." Well, sometimes God needed a little help.

"Let's go sit in the living room," Tom said. "Kids doing home-work?"

"Yes, presumably reading English assignments, although Ben is so eager to make a good impression on the practice teacher, he's probably composing a sonnet for extra credit."

Throughout the evening, despite all the other distractions, Ursula had been very much in Faith's thoughts. She told Tom about Theo's death and Arnold Rowe's presence.

"I never met him," Tom said. "He'd passed away before I came to First Parish, but everything I've heard about Arnold Rowe has always made me sorry I didn't know him. Not just from Ursula and Pix, but others here and on Sanpere."

"I wish I had, too. But Tom, if there had been any hint of scandal, don't you think we'd have heard?"

This had been puzzling Faith.

"Not necessarily. It was so long ago and didn't happen in town. I knew Ursula was born in Boston and had roots there, but it was always my impression that she'd grown up here. Arnold, too. I had no idea she was in her teens, or maybe it was even later, when she moved to Aleford. And we don't know about her husband. As for Sanpere, there are no secrets on the island, that's for sure, but once you cross the bridge—or in those days got on the steamer—well, what happens in Vegas stays in Vegas."

Faith nodded in agreement. "I've thought of all this, but how and why did their parents keep Theo's death—his whole life, in fact—and Arnold Rowe's possible involvement, from Pix and her brother, Arnold junior? You hear a lot of family secrets, but isn't this a little extreme?" Faith often lamented the fact that Tom's calling necessitated the keeping of such secrets. Secrets she'd love to know.

"You'd be surprised," Tom said. "Without going into specifics"—Oh, do just this once, please do! Faith said to herself—"I've had people tell me that they've just discovered a parent was married before, and with issue, that they had a sibling who died, and yes, an aunt or uncle they never knew existed. One parishioner answered a knock on the door to face her father's duplicate. Her father had been dead for some years, so you can imagine the shock it gave her. It wasn't a twin, but a brother two years younger who had been estranged from the rest of the family since he had run off as a teenager. He was never mentioned. There was no way his niece would have known of his existence. What was even stranger was that without ever having any contact with his older brother all those years, he'd adopted the same mannerisms, haircut, style of dress, even the frames of his glasses were identical. For some reason this struck her the most. She kept saying, 'He was wearing my father's glasses!'"

Family secrets. Tom was right. She could think of some examples, too. And something else could have played a part.

"In this case, don't you think it's generational, as well? Parents didn't tell their children everything the way they tend to now."

"I imagine when Ursula relates the rest of her story, this may be clearer. Certainly I didn't know much about the lives of my parents and the rest of the family—or their friends—when I was growing up. The two spheres—adulthood and childhood—touched at mealtimes and a few other points, not the continuous hovering that goes on now."

"Helicopter parents," Faith said.

"Exactly, and I hope we're somewhere in between. Too many secrets isn't a good thing."

Faith knew Tom was thinking about last fall. No, too many secrets wasn't a good thing at all.

She thought of Niki, about Pix, Ursula of course, and someone out there who knew where the missing money was.

Sick with secrets.

Across town Ursula Lyman Rowe was in bed, but not asleep. It wasn't the moonlight streaming through the window that was disturbing her slumber. It was what was below, under the cushion.

There had been a second letter in today's mail. Dora had brought it in after Faith left. The long white envelope was mixed in with get well cards and several bills. Ursula opened it first.

There weren't any clippings this time. Just a single sheet of the same paper with a single sentence in the same hand.

You saw the knife in his hand.

Faith loved the Aleford library. She loved all libraries, starting with the earliest she could remember, the Sixty-seventh Street branch of the New York Public Library. It was one of those endowed by Andrew Carnegie. While the Aleford library had not had Babb, Cook, and Willard, Beaux Arts architects, as the Sixty-seventh Street library had, it was still a gem. Constructed in the early 1920s, the original fieldstone building had been expanded and renovated several times, most recently the children's room. An anonymous donor had provided the funds for much-needed new furniture, fresh paint, and a wondrous entryway from the main library that transformed a previous small dark corridor into a bright, exotic jungle. The two walls had been mirrored, creating the illusion that the flat rows of lush green plywood foliage placed in front extended for acres. The librarians had fun periodically changing the cutouts of parrots and other creatures that peeped from behind the leaves.

Tonight's fund-raiser was taking advantage of most of the library's square footage. Have Faith had set up enough dessert stations so people would be able to nibble at will and not have to stand in line, or jostle each other. Coffee was in reference and there were flutes of prosecco at the circulation desk. Aleford was a dry town and likely to remain so—a package store, a "packy," in *our* Aleford!—but dispensation was granted for special events at venues like the library and the Ganley Museum. The Minuteman Café, the café at the Ganley, Country Pizza, and the deli counter at the Shop 'n Save were the only places for food not prepared by individual Alefordians. If you wanted booze with your meal, you had to drive to Concord or Waltham. Lincoln, Aleford's other abutter, was dry, too, although Faith had heard rumblings about a new restaurant with a liquor license. She'd like to have been a fly on the wall at *that* town meeting. Whenever the matter came up in Aleford, the picture of inebriated diners careening through the streets of town—diners from "away"—was painted with such broad strokes that those in favor of lifting the ban never stood a chance. The fact that the glass-recycling container at the Transfer Station, the dump, was the size of a boxcar and filled with a far greater number of empty wine and whiskey bottles than jelly jars did not enter into the discussion. Faith would have loved a nice little bistro in town where one could meet friends, have steak frites, and a glass of *vin*. Not in her lifetime, or rather Millicent's.

She spied Millicent coming in the front door. She was on the board of the Friends of the Library and involved in tonight's arrangements. She was carrying a large punch bowl.

"Some of my grandmother Revere's gunpowder punch—minus the pinch of gunpowder, of course. I'll put the bowl where you tell me and perhaps one of your helpers can get the punch cups and the containers of punch from my car? I know there's coffee, but people might like something with a little kick. There's ginger beer in it."

She looked at Faith with such patently false disingenuousness that Faith couldn't help laughing. They both knew the punch was intended not simply to compete with the prosecco, but obliterate it. Gunpowder, indeed.

"All right, Millicent. We'll put it out alongside the wine and you can dispense it. I'll send Scott Phelan out to your car. Where is it?"

"In the back, but I'll need to mingle. I'll line up some of the Friends to help ladle."

There was no need to describe Millicent's car to Scott. It was famous. He worked in a garage and body shop in nearby Byford. Every time he saw Millicent at a function while working for Faith he said the same thing: If there were more people like Millicent, he'd be out of a job. He also said he'd give anything for the car. She had purchased the Rambler in 1963 and drove it so rarely—she could walk most places—that it still looked as if it just came off the showroom floor. Not a scratch, not a dent—nothing to fix. Mint.

As Faith helped Millicent set up, she seized the opportunity to pump her in what she hoped would be a subtle way first about Arnold Rowe and then about Tom.

"It's a shame Ursula can't be here tonight. She's such a fan of David Hackett Fischer's." The noted historian would be giving a brief talk and introducing the other invited authors.

"We *all* are," Millicent corrected her. His book *Paul Revere's Ride,* signed to her, took pride of place next to Millicent's family Bible.

"I understand Ursula's husband was quite the history buff also." Faith felt fairly safe in her assertion. If you lived in Aleford, willingly or not, you were a history buff.

"Oh yes, Arnold was quite a scholar."

"I'm sorry I never got the chance to meet him. From what I've heard he was very interesting."

Millicent snorted. She was the only person Faith knew, other than certain teenage boys, who made this sound in public. Millicent could get away with it; the boys not.

"If by interesting you mean endlessly gazing at stars, collecting rocks, counting birds, and reading Plato in the original Greek, then yes, Arnold Rowe was interesting. Other than that a rather dull man; Ursula was the one with sparkle. Arnold was nice, but the kind of person nothing much ever happened to. Good in a husband, I suppose. Steady."

Faith felt as if Millicent had handed her Arnold gift-wrapped. If Millicent had an inkling that there was anything dark in his past, she would not have told Faith about it, but she *would* have dangled a multitude of tantalizing hints in front of her. Millicent's Arnold Rowe sounded very respectable, and maybe not too much fun at parties. Faith decided to continue to press her luck.

"Hard for Ursula to have been widowed so long and I don't believe she has brothers and sisters."

Millicent didn't like it when people knew things she knew. "Yes, she was an only child—as was Arnold." So there.

"I didn't know that," Faith said. It was important to keep Millicent happy.

Scott brought the cups and libations and for a while she was busy helping Millicent transfer the contents of several plastic liter bottles into the bowl and floating on top the orange and lemon slices Millicent had brought in an ancient Tupperware container.

"You must try a little." Millicent beamed.

Faith had sampled the brew on other occasions and it wasn't bad. While not revealing all of grandmother's secret ingredients, Millicent had given Faith the basic recipe some years ago. Roughly two-to-one ginger beer to orange juice with grated nutmeg, cinnamon sticks, lemon zest, and possibly the secret ingredient was a dash of clove since Faith could definitely taste it and Millicent never mentioned it. In an earlier day, a pinch of gunpowder *was* added, which would have imparted an odd flavor—and could not have been good for you. Faith had the idea that the whole thing had originated in England to celebrate Guy Fawkes's failed attempt to blow up Parliament. In which case, the British—used to vegetables boiled into mush and other treats—would no doubt have welcomed the gunpowder's kick.

"Delicious. Very refreshing. We should serve this for the parents at church at our end-of-the-year Sunday school picnic. It's been quite a year at First Parish."

Faith cast her rod.

And got back a very rusted, very dented tin can.

Millicent looked her in the eye. "I suppose that's what some people would call an understatement. I hope the Reverend will be here tonight. The important thing is to keep going."

It was ludicrous to think that Millicent—all Aleford, and even most of Middlesex County—hadn't heard about Thomas Fairchild, embezzler.

Many miles south, but in the same time zone, Pix Miller was standing outside at the top of the Harbour Town lighthouse looking at the sunset. She was holding a glass of champagne. When she thought back on this stay at Hilton Head, glasses of champagne would figure prominently.

It was their last night and she was sorry. Each day had been a perfect blend of time together and time alone, time alone with Sam. She'd seen dolphins, birds of all sorts, and spectacular sunsets. The one that was stretched out in fiery golds and pinks sinking into the sea in front of her now was the most gorgeous. Or it could be the champagne. A girl could get used to this. She'd been running that phrase through her mind a lot this week, too.

Mother was fine. Better than fine judging from Faith's and Dora's daily reports. During the first enthusiastic description of how much Ursula had improved virtually the moment she left town, Pix had been slightly miffed. More than slightly. Why hadn't Mother shown this kind of progress when her daughter was there? But then Hilton Head, her hosts, having Sam and her children around, and maybe the whole Southern charm thing began to smooth away the rough edges. She had been dreading being in Charleston, shopping, and being on her own without Sam. It was one thing to be on familiar turf like Sanpere and quite another to be someplace completely new. Now she was looking forward to it. And anyway, Samantha would be there.

And Stephen.

The fly in the ointment.

He had not indicated by even the merest flicker of an eye that he recalled Miss Rowe. Maybe Faith was right. Maybe it was a guy thing. She hadn't told Faith that Sam never forgot a name or face, but he was a lawyer. Different wiring?

The music from the party drifted out. The Cohens had hired a DJ and he was playing everything from the Beatles to Black Eyed Peas.

"Having a good time, Mom?"

It was the groom. She gave him a hug.

"Heavenly, darling. You picked a wonderful girl and a wonderful family."

"Don't I know it—and she thinks the same about us."

Pix grabbed the moment. "Dr. Cohen, I mean Stephen, looks so familiar. Could we have met him before, do you think? Has he said anything?"

Pix blushed. This was not prodding. This was stepping in it.

"Met you and Dad before? I think he would have said something, and I don't know where. They go to New York City once or twice a year for the museums and opera, but unless you sat next to them at a performance, I wouldn't think your paths have crossed."

There it was.

"Your father doesn't like opera."

"You don't, either, you just think you should," Mark teased her. She decided to change the subject.

"I'll be making all the final arrangements for the rehearsal dinner when I get to Charleston. I know the groom doesn't have much to do, but are you all set?"

"Done and done. Picking up the rings next week, and I've ordered silver penknives engraved with each of their initials for the ushers. I got Dan a Swiss Army watch that does a ton of things, including the ability to set multiple alarms—wish I'd had that in college. I'm having something engraved on the back of that, too."

Much to Pix's delight, Mark had selected his young brother as his best man.

"He'll love it."

"Let's see what else? I set up spreadsheets so the Cohens could keep track of the RSVPs and separate ones for Becca and me for thank-you notes. My bride says electronic ones are out and is writing them by hand. Plus you've seen the Web site, right?"

It was all a little much—spreadsheets? Were the vows going to be in the form of a PowerPoint presentation? Pix was glad Rebecca was old-fashioned enough to nix e-thank-yous.

"You haven't, have you? Oh Mom, you are such a Luddite! Anyway, it's not too cutesy. Just one picture of us and the rest info."

Sam came up on Pix's other side. He was chewing.

"You have got to go inside and have some of this food. I thought nothing could top last night, but this is something else again!"

The night before, acting on Faith's advice and with the resort's help, the Millers had hosted a Low Country boil on the beach for their soon-to-be in-laws. Pix had been dubious—a pot full of what sounded like wildly disparate ingredients: shrimp in their shells, smoked sausage, new potatoes, small rounds of corn on the cob, whole onions, and Old Bay seasoning plus water—but it had been fantastic. Faith had told her it was also called "Frogmore stew," a South Carolina staple named after the place where it originated, no frogs involved.

"I'm supposed to make notes for Faith about what's being served. She wants to add a Southern station to her catering offerings."

"Take my iPhone, Mom. You can snap some pictures and text her the descriptions," Mark said.

The twenty-first century. Not too shabby. She realized she was echoing her kids' highest words of praise.

"Give me that thing and show me what to push."

Mark laughed. "Love you, Mom."

"Love you, too, sweetie."

Soon Pix had captured, and sampled, the buffet: a bountiful raw bar; Charleston crab cakes; shrimp with cheese grits—Boursin, the server told her and she dutifully noted it for Faith—slices of roast pork with apples and dates; wild rice; biscuits with shavings of country ham; salad dressed with Vidalia onion vinaigrette; and the desserts! Pecan pie and Key lime pie, red velvet cupcakes, flourless chocolate cake with praline sauce, pineapple upside-down cake with rum sauce—Pix had resolutely stuck with champagne, but rum seemed to be flowing not just in the food, but in the mojitos—and an ambrosial layer cake new to Pix, hummingbird cake. Cissy Cohen urged a piece on her as she was taking the photo. "Nobody knows who invented it or where the name came from. It just appeared in the late nineteen sixties, and since then, you can't have a dessert table without it. My mother says it's called 'hummingbird cake' because it's as sweet as the nectar the birds like to drink, but I've also heard that it's called this since it makes you 'hum with delight.' Take a bite."

Pix did, and the combination of crushed pineapple, chopped ripe bananas, and chopped pecans—were they the official nut of

South Carolina?—in the rich cake topped and layered with cream cheese frosting didn't make her want to hum. It made her want to sing out loud. Dessert was Pix's favorite form of food. She had the LIFE IS SHORT; EAT DESSERT FIRST pillow to prove it.

"You need some more champagne." Stephen Cohen was carrying a bottle of Mumm's.

"'Need' may not be the correct word, but it is lovely. Thank you so much for tonight—and the whole time here. It's been perfect."

"Well, we plan on having many more of these good times," he said, looking into her eyes.

Recklessly Pix grabbed a fork and tapped the side of her glass. People had been making toasts all evening. She raised her glass as the room grew quiet.

"Many thanks to Stephen and Cissy, our hosts, and"—she faced Mark and Rebecca—"to you especially, but to everyone, 'May the best day of your past be the worst day of your future.'"

Past? What had she said? Had she gotten the quote right? She knew it was something about the past and future. She'd left out the middle about the present, though. Or maybe there wasn't a middle part. Stephen poured her some more champagne and kissed her cheek. Cissy patted her arm and said they were going to have so much fun in Charleston.

"Hear, hear!" someone cried out, and everyone clapped.

Sam appeared at her side.

"Very nice, dear."

Samantha appeared on her other side with a plate.

"I think you need to eat something, Mom," she said, laughing.

Faith brought the last of Niki's book cookies out and refilled the platters. They had been a big hit. Tom had arrived just after the talk and now he was speaking with the library director, making his apologies for being late. Faith could tell what he was saying by the look on his face. His face was an open book, appropriately enough for the evening's venue. Always had been and she hoped always would be. It was impossible for him to dissemble. Tonight, however, she wished he looked less like he'd lost his best friend and more like a man without a care in the world. No, maybe a little care, as befits a man of the cloth, but definitely a man without anything on his conscience—or money stashed in an offshore account.

He came over to her and picked up a cookie, *Crime and Punishment*. She snatched it back. "Try this one with the chocolate frosting," she said, handing him *The Hound of the Baskervilles* after skipping over *Gone with the Wind*. "Everything okay?" It wasn't like Tom to be late. Yankee that he was, if they were invited for seven o'clock, he'd stand on the doorstep a minute before and push the doorbell on the dot. New Yorker that Faith was, she'd first of all never invite guests that early, and next, plan on the earliest arriving thirty minutes late.

"Sam called. He was on his way to a big do the Cohens are throwing, but he wanted to caution me not to talk to anyone, not the vestry, no one, about any of this until he's back and can be present."

"That sounds like a very sensible idea," Faith said, knowing full well that her husband didn't view it that way at all. To him, it was an admission that he had something to hide that he could speak only with a lawyer present.

"I suppose."

"Anyway, you can talk to me. A wife can't testify against her husband, or for," she added hastily, as a look of alarm crossed Tom's so very expressive face. "I'm sure it won't come to any sort of court action," she bumbled on, cursing her runaway mouth.

"I'd better find out when we're supposed to make the pitch.

Soon, I'd imagine, before people start to leave," Tom said, ashen-faced after his wife's remark.

The library board of trustees was composed of some town elected members plus all the "standing clergy." For Faith the phrase always conjured up images of some people sitting surrounded by others in robes standing over them. Weeks ago, the library director had asked Tom and Father Hayes to speak about the current, and omnipresent, fiscal crisis and hopefully coax a few checkbooks from pockets.

Court action, wives immune from testimony—what was she thinking of! Tom disappeared into the crowd and Faith saw Sherman Munroe give him one of his smarmy looks. She was sure this was a man whose face never betrayed him, just assumed whatever nasty pose he wished. It was all she could do to keep herself from seizing the bowl and dumping gunpowder punch over his head.

"Another success, boss. Looks like there won't be a single crumb left. Tricia will be disappointed." Scott began to clear away the serving platters that were empty.

"I made up a plate of goodies for you to take home."

"Thanks—and hey, I hope Niki gets one. Now that she's eating for two."

"Did she tell you she was pregnant?" Faith was surprised.

"Nah, but I've been through it twice, and remember, I'm one of five; Trish is one of seven, so somebody's always got a bun in the oven. I guess by now I've got some kind of babydar."

"Well, she isn't telling anyone, not even Phil—he lost his job, in case you didn't hear—so whatever you do, *don't* let her know that you know."

Scott shook his head. "Might not be a good time, but secrets from your old man? A big no-no. Trish pulled that, I'd be madder than hell."

Niki picked that moment to appear.

"Could you empty the coffee urn, Scott? I, well, I—"

Faith broke in. "I need you to help me scout the library for anything left around. I wouldn't want the librarians to find a dirty coffee cup shelved with New Books."

She wanted to help Niki out. She also didn't want the smell of the coffee to provoke sudden, uncontrolled evening sickness— much worse to discover on the shelves than a cup.

Scott winked at her.

Secrets. Too many secrets.

Have Faith's next event was less than twenty-four hours later, but the scene was markedly different. Occupants of the White House came and went. Hemlines rose and fell. Tides ebbed and flowed. Moons waxed and waned. But the Tiller Club remained unchanged. The Tillies, as they always referred to themselves, had first seen the light of day as a group of sixteen sailing buddies who'd grown up in places like Pride's Crossing, Hamilton, and Manchester-by-the-Sea on the Massachusetts North Shore. Despite boarding school and later college, they always managed to be home during the summer and spend every waking moment on the water. At age sixteen, they'd decided to formalize the bond with the club, adopting a crest with crossed tillers rampant on an azure shield topped by the prow of a ship emblazoned with "Carpe Tela"—"Seize the Tiller"—their boyish motto. The first of the club's bylaws defined the process for adding new members. One carefully vetted Tillie of their same age would be added each year. Niki, then Ms. Constantine, had been with Faith at the first Tillie dinner, and throughout the evening it was this bit of Tillie trivia Niki kept coming back to in astonishment. "So," she'd kept saying, "when they're all ninety-nine—and these WASP sailing types live forever—they're going to have to beat the bushes, or rather troll the briny deep, for someone named Chandler or Phelps who's still capable of steering straight at that age?" It had boggled Faith's mind, as well. So far—the Tillies were now forty—there had been no problem finding suitable candidates.

The Tillies took their social gatherings almost as seriously as their sailing. Most, in fact, combined the two, with cruises up the Maine coast to Northeast Harbor in the summer and to the Bahamas in the winter, during which there was much traveling between yachts for a "gam," which mimicked earlier whaling-ship visits back and forth solely in the amount of alcohol consumed by the captains. Ahab would not have had the Wheat Thins with WisPride and Goldfish crackers thoughtfully provided by the wives, although there may have been hardtack to go with the grog.

Tonight's Spring Fling, the Tillies' concession to the club's slightly diminished funds, was a mere blip, the chairman assured Faith. A year hence, at most two, would find the traditional fall game dinners and summer clambakes firmly reinstated.

Faith was familiar with the yacht club in Marblehead. It was where the fall dinner had been held each year. The club didn't provide meals in the off-season, which was why the Tillies had needed a caterer, but it was possible to hire the club's waitstaff and Faith had always done so. Tonight she had pared that down, bringing both Scott and Tricia, whom she could depend on. Besides, the Phelans needed all the extra hours they could get with business at the body shop off. Scott was already busy tending bar—the Tillies may have opted for chicken instead of beef, but they weren't about to stint on alcohol. No silly drinks like Cosmos or Blue Martinis were bringing a more pronounced flush to cheeks ruddy from days squinting at the sun. It was strictly a scotch, bourbon, and possibly gin and tonic crowd with good clarets at dinner.

Servers were passing hors d'oeuvres: tiny duck beggar's purses, blood-orange-glazed shrimp on bamboo skewers, mini Cuban sandwiches, goat cheese gougères, and tuna tartare on potato crisps. No lobster, no smoked oysters or caviar, but she'd also set out platters with an assortment of roasted peppers, sausage slices, stuffed grape leaves, cubes of smoked gouda and jalapeño jack cheese, with plenty of bread sticks and crackers. She'd learned early on that the Tillies might have obediently eaten their veggies in the nursery, hence all those strong bones and good teeth, yet they didn't want to see anything resembling a crudité now. She'd mentioned Brussels sprouts sautéed in walnut oil and topped with toasted walnuts as an accompaniment for one of the game dinners, and the then chairman had looked as horrified as if she'd worn high heels on the teak deck of his Herreshoff.

The room was filling up and it was warm enough for some of the guests to sit out on the porch that stretched across the back of the club, facing the water. Each Tillie was allowed to bring one guest, and from the increasing volume of conversation, it appeared tonight was full muster—another happy Tillie dinner. As she crossed the large living room, Faith realized that the "cottage" on Martha's Vineyard that Ursula had been describing must have resembled the club, a late-Victorian wood-shingled structure with a decorous amount of trim. The floors were covered by good, and appropriately worn, Orientals. The fireplace that dominated one end of the room was massive. Genre seascapes in dire need of cleaning and photos of notable yachts and crews hung in between the trophy cases that lined the walls. The furniture tended toward comfortable leather sofas and oversized wing chairs.

The next two hours passed quickly as Faith and Niki hustled to get the food out. As Tricia and the waitstaff from the club served the traditional chocolate cake and coffee, Scott helped pack up the food and used dinnerware. He and Tricia were having babysitter problems and had to be home sooner than usual. They'd take the van. Faith and Niki could manage the rest, loading Faith's car.

"Sit down," Faith told Niki. "They're going to move on to

their cigars and brandy. Things are starting to wind down, but they haven't inducted this year's member, which always takes a while."

Tillie events were rigorously choreographed. At the height of the evening, ribald toasts were made and they threw their napkins, tied into knots, at one another, dislodging their wives' headbands and causing their bow ties to run downhill. By the end of the evening they'd calmed down and took the swearing in of the newest Tillie seriously.

"I'm not tired," Niki said. "And you're the last person I expected to treat me as if I were made of glass. Another reason not to tell Mom—or Phil."

"You've been on your feet all night, missy. And I believe I have, in the past when you were not enceinte, told you to sit down when I thought you were tired."

"Okay, okay, maybe I'm a little sensitive."

Faith started to tell her it was hormones and then thought better of it. She also decided not to bring up the conversation they'd had in this very kitchen several years ago about communicating with one's spouse. Faith had hit a rocky patch in her marriage where she and Tom, especially Tom, were deliberately passing like ships in the night—the image appropriate to tonight's venue jumped back into her head. Each tentative start to discussing their problems that Faith placed in Tom's path had been ignored. It was Niki who'd set her straight, saying in essence that if Faith had wanted meaningful communication she was looking to the wrong gender. The phrase "we need to talk" was viewed completely differently by men and women, sending each in a diametrically opposed direction. Women to a side-by-side conversational exchange; men out the door for parts unknown.

It had been a big help, that talk. Niki and she had laughed—and cried a bit. Not long after, Faith and Tom weathered the storm. Tonight Faith wished she could remind Niki about the way Faith's taking the initiative, albeit obliquely, had solved the Fairchilds' problems.

"I know what you're thinking," Niki said.

"No you don't."

"Oh yes I do. This kitchen always brings it back and don't you dare throw my words in my face."

"I think you're doing it for me," Faith said.

For a moment she thought Niki was going to explode—she had inherited her mother's famous temper—and then she started laughing.

"I guess I am, but Faith, I'm not telling him. Not yet."

The sound of a utensil on a glass calling for quiet came from the next room.

"Come on, let's peek," Niki said, going to the door.

There was no need. The chairman was coming through it.

"Please join us as we wrap up the evening. As usual you've given us a splendid time and we all want to thank you before it ends."

Faith took off her apron, Niki followed suit, and they went into the dining room. The lights had been turned up.

"The membership committee head is going to introduce our new member and then I'd like to publicly thank you," the chairman whispered.

Faith smiled back at him, as she did at whoever was chairman each time the thank-you was proposed. If the script ever changed, she'd know that hell had frozen over.

"No surprises," Niki said softly into Faith's other ear as the newest Tillie stood up. "This isn't going to be the year they induct an African American, Jewish, Native American woman apparently."

But it *was* a surprise. When the newest Tillie stood up, Faith knew the name before it was announced.

The Reverend James Holden, First Parish's associate minister.

"I know James," she said to the chairman, so startled that she forgot to lower her voice.

"Good man, Holden. Great sailor. And damn lucky. Just bought the prettiest little Bristol thirty-three I've seen in a dog's age. Stole it from some poor guy declaring bankruptcy for only ten thou."

Ten thou, Faith thought. Ten thousand dollars.

James Holden was making a pretty little acceptance speech—and Faith could hardly wait to ask him where he'd come across all the pretty little pennies he'd used to buy the pretty little boat.

She wished she could jump up and corner him right now. After all, "Time and tide wait for no man"—or woman.

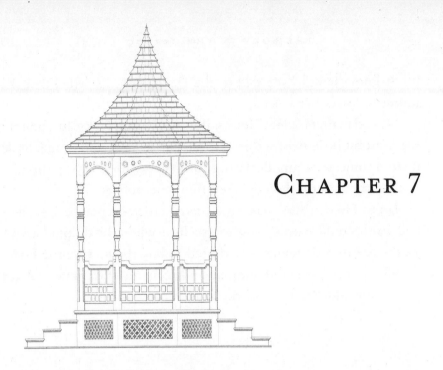

CHAPTER 7

"Afterward I was very ill for a long time," Ursula said, her words in concert with the steady downpour outside the window. The rain had started as Faith drove home from Marblehead the night before, building to a window-rattling thunderstorm in the early hours of the morning. Soccer practice had been canceled and both kids had quickly filled the unexpectedly free day with various activities with friends. Tom was rewriting his sermon yet again, and after checking with Dora, Faith had come to see Ursula, who was sitting up, looked well, and picked up the threads of her tale almost as soon as Faith entered the room.

"Scientists say you can't contract illnesses from shock, although a shock can make you feel ill, but I developed a serious case of scarlet fever. I had, most probably, contracted it days earlier on the Vineyard, but the symptoms were overlooked. I freckled in the sun and my high color had also been ascribed to too much exposure—and excitement. Before she left for Boston, Mother cautioned me to wear my broad-brimmed straw hat and stay in the cool shade.

"I don't remember leaving the island or even what happened

immediately after I found Theo in the gazebo. Mother had a school friend who'd married an Englishman and was living in Bermuda, where he had been posted as an adjunct of some sort to the governor. After I was out of danger, she and I went to stay with them in Hamilton for the rest of the fall and on into the winter.

"When I returned, my entire world had changed."

Faith was very close to her sister, Hope, one year younger. The thought of losing her was unbearable. Theo had been older, but the siblings appeared to have had a similar bond, especially on Ursula's part.

"It must have been terrible to return to the house, knowing he was gone from it forever," Faith said.

"The thing was that it wasn't my house."

Faith nodded. "It must have seemed like a totally different place without him."

"No, it really wasn't my house. While we were gone, Father sold the Beacon Hill house and moved us to Aleford."

Seeing Faith's astonishment, she added hastily, "Mother knew all about it, and on the steamship back, she told me we'd moved, but I hadn't fully taken it in until Father picked us up at the pier and we drove past the Boston Common without slowing down.

"He'd managed to hold on to the firm without declaring bankruptcy on Black Tuesday, but barely. Uncharacteristically he'd been investing heavily in the market and lost everything. And then there were Theo's debts. I learned all this later. At the time, I was protected as much as possible from the grim financial reality my parents were facing in the midst of their intense grief. And guilt. Mother blamed herself for leaving, although I don't see how she could not have gone. How could she have known? And her sister did have a close call. I believe, though, that to the end of her life, she wished she had insisted that the guests leave. Mother thought Mrs. Miles, the housekeeper they'd hired for the summer, would watch over things—she was quite a martinet—but she'd slipped out. Probably to meet someone to go to Illumination Night. Mother rued hiring her. And Father blamed himself for just about everything from renting the Vineyard house to not being strict enough with his son, although he may also have privately reproached himself for being too strict.

"During those times creditors did not expect to be paid—no one had money—but Father felt honor bound to settle Theo's accounts and his own even if it meant selling everything. The building with his offices and the house both went. The Pines in Sanpere didn't, but that was just because no one wanted to buy a big place like that on an unfashionable island. I believe for a while he thought that Mother and I might live there and he'd rent a room near where he'd rented office space. He let the servants go. When I think back, it must have been a terrifying time for him. Many of his wealthy friends were weathering the crisis, but an equal number were going under."

Then as now, Faith almost blurted out.

"He was too proud to ask anyone for a loan. Fortunately he had many loyal clients who stuck with him, although their reduced incomes meant a reduced income for him. Years later, after his death, Mother told me that he had worried all that summer about a fiscal crisis, but he was in the market too deep to pull out. He thought he'd suffer losses, and then he lost it all.

"Mother had inherited a house in Aleford from a maiden aunt and it had always been rented. Now it was to be our new home. I'll never forget arriving from Bermuda in the late afternoon—it was quite dark—driving down Main Street, which looked very pokey to me after Commonwealth Avenue. The house was on Adams Street, up the hill from the green. It's changed hands many times since we lived there and I barely recognize it. The current owners gutted it and added another story and all sorts of enormous windows."

And, Faith thought, probably a home gym, media room, spa,

great room, and heaven knows what else—retromedieval banquet hall?

"It was a fair-sized early-nineteenth-century Colonial, but the ceilings were low and Father looked even taller coming through the doorways, which the top of his head just grazed. A local woman, Mrs. Hansen, helped Mother with the housework and the cooking—you've heard me talk about my Norwegian friend, Marit. That's how we met. Mrs. Hansen was her mother and Marit was my age. Mr. Hansen was a builder, and there was no work during the Depression, so they went back to Norway a few years after we moved to Aleford."

"I thought you'd been born here and grew up in this house," Faith said.

"After so much time, it seems like it, but my parents were both still alive and living in the Adams Street house when I got married and moved into this one . . ." Ursula paused. "You must be wondering about that."

"Arnold Rowe, the tutor. Your husband? Yes?"

Faith had hoped that Ursula would start with an explanation after her dramatic revelation the previous time, and it had been all she could do to keep from asking her about the Professor. Ursula, however, was telling her tale in her own way.

"It's the rest of the story and it's quite complicated," Ursula said.

"That's all right. Complicated is fine. The kids are with friends; Tom is with . . . well, himself and his maker, and I have as much time as you want."

"Good—but Dora will be cross if I don't eat. I've started going down to the kitchen for some meals. She left something in the fridge. If you'll take my arm, we can go see."

Dora had left what amounted to a ploughwoman's lunch—a more delicate version of the ploughman's wedges of cheddar cheese, relish, butter, and crusty bread. There was cheese, but

thinly sliced, some chutney, the bread and butter plus salad, and
with a nod to the Hanoverians, a modicum of Ursula's favorite—
liverwurst.

After settling Ursula with a full plate and putting the kettle on
for tea, Faith excused herself to make several phone calls with her
cell.

"It's terribly rude, I'm sorry, but I wasn't able to reach two of
the people I'm hoping can come for Sunday dinner after the service tomorrow."

"Don't be silly. I just may make Samantha happy and get one
of those things myself. They're awfully convenient," Ursula said.

Seeing James Holden, the newest Tillie, had caused Faith a
restless night until suddenly in the wee hours of the morning she'd
had an idea, a plan to "catch the conscience of a king." She wasn't
going to stage a play, but she was going to set a trap, and if it did
not snare a mouse, it would at least have been baited.

She was going to give a dinner party, or rather a Sunday dinner party. She often invited people for postchurch luncheon, so it
would not seem out of the ordinary, and she was going to seed the
guest list with her friends the Averys. Will and Patsy Avery were
not members of First Parish, so had no idea of the current situation—otherwise Patsy would have been on the phone to Faith
immediately. They had adopted siblings Kianna, age five, and her
brother, Devon, age three, last fall after a prescient doctor asked
them whether they wanted to reproduce themselves or raise a family together. For Patsy and Will, the answer was family, and they
had found one in these harder-to-place older children, who were
now also an extension of the Fairchild family. Ben didn't mind it
one bit that Devon worshiped him—and Faith suspected he liked
the opportunity to play with LEGOs again. Amy and Kianna
were equally inseparable and the four children would consider it a
treat to have their lunch in the kitchen, away from the grown-ups,
before going out to play on the swing set. Tom and his brothers

had constructed it shortly after Ben was born, much to Faith's amusement. It would be some years before the infant could climb the tower or go down the slide, but the Fairchild boys had worked in a frenzy to get it ready—and it did seem in retrospect that Ben was on it in a very short time.

The other grown-ups she was inviting were the Reverend James Holden—Faith intended to steer the conversation to boat purchases—and Eloise Gardner, the education director, who was also on the list Tom and Faith had drawn up. Eloise was a clotheshorse. A few pairs of Manolos, a Prada bag, plus trips to Sonia Rykiel, Ralph Lauren, and Burberry would eat up the missing money in a flash.

She hadn't left messages on their machines when she'd called earlier, wanting a definite reply, and she was in luck. She reached them both and they would be happy to come. James had been previously, but Eloise hadn't and expressed particular delight at the opportunity to sample some "real food," confessing that her own "cuisine" was limited to the boxes in the freezer with "Lean" in front of the word. If Eloise turned out not to be the guilty party, Faith resolved to invite her for meals often. No one should be subjected to that kind of life.

Albert Trumbull, the parish administrative assistant, and Lily Sinclair, the former divinity school intern, as well as the vestry members on the list, would have to wait their turns for scrutiny.

She noticed she had a text and, after opening it, was pleased to find a response to the e-mail she'd sent to Zach Cummings Wednesday night. He apologized for not getting back to her sooner—and told her to call. He'd be around all weekend. He'd written, "Another mystery?" and added a winking smiley emoticon.

Things were looking up.

"Pour the tea and let's sit here awhile. I love to look at the river, no matter what the weather," Ursula said.

It was still pouring steadily and a pool had appeared at the bottom of Ursula's yard that hadn't been there earlier in the day. Faith hoped Tom had remembered to turn on the sump pump, so the parsonage basement wouldn't flood. For a brief moment she thought longingly to the time in her life when she'd had no idea what a "sump pump" was.

"Here's where I say, 'Reader, I married him,' although not for many years. It was, in fact, quite a while before I thought of Arnold Rowe at all. It never occurred to me that he hadn't gone on to law school, completed his studies, and joined the ranks of desperate job seekers. I didn't know about the trial and had blocked the image of him in the gazebo from my conscious mind. My unconscious was not so cooperative. That first year I was plagued by nightmares, waking with feelings of terror; but not wanting to disturb my parents, I would turn on the light and read until sleep, uninterrupted, returned.

"The same aunt who'd owned our house was an alumna of the Cabot School here in town and had left a substantial endowment for scholarships. Mother approached the headmistress, and upon returning from Bermuda, I was enrolled there as a day student. Life took on a semblance of normalcy with new routines. Father took the train into town; I walked to school; and Mother managed the house, although her heart was in the garden. In the spring, that's where I'd find her, sometimes with tears in her eyes and I knew she'd been thinking of Theo. I missed him dreadfully and I didn't have anyone to talk to about him. Mother and Father never mentioned him, or what had happened. There were no visible pictures of him in the house, nothing to indicate he had ever existed."

"Why do you think this was?" Faith asked. It seemed so extreme. Theo hadn't committed a crime. He was the victim of one.

"Mostly because it was too painful—and people didn't 'let it all hang out' in those days, remember—but also because Aleford represented a new beginning for the family. The trial started in late October. Any reports would have been eclipsed by the day's more dramatic accounts of bank and business failures. In addition, although Aleford was the same number of miles from town then as it is now, much more distance separated the two when it came to communication at that time. It was truly a backwater.

"Earlier, in August, there had been a quiet funeral at King's Chapel and afterward he was buried in the Lyman family plot at Mount Auburn cemetery. I was too ill to be present."

Ursula sounded as bereft now as she was then. Faith's heart ached for her. Barely out of childhood, she had had the initial loss repeated over and over again with no one to talk to about her brother, no one with whom she could remember the happy days, years that had preceded his untimely death.

"He always kept Butterfinger candy bars in his pocket for me. They were my favorite. I haven't been able to eat one since . . ."

Ursula hated Aleford. She kicked a stone on the sidewalk. It felt so good, she kicked another. Cabot wasn't anything like Winsor, her old school. The day students, especially the ones on scholarships, were second-class citizens so far as the boarders were concerned. And how did they know—these girls who brought their own horses and talked of summers in the Adirondacks? Horses. Cabot was a very horsey school. Ursula had never ridden. The only horses she ever saw had been the ones the mounted police rode on the Boston Common.

She missed her friends. In the first months after the move, her mother had said not to worry, that they'd keep in touch and that Ursula could visit them often. And there had been a few letters back and forth, no one saying what they must all have been thinking, but these had petered out. The visits never materialized, and the only time she went to town was to go to church and see her cousins afterward. Even that wasn't every Sunday. Her parents had started at-

tending First Parish out here. It was nothing like King's Chapel. A boring white church with a steeple just like every other one you saw on the greens of New England. King's Chapel was made of stone, soaring pillars in front and inside vaulting that took your eye to the beautiful sky-blue ceiling above. It was the oldest church in Boston and didn't have a steeple. So there. She kicked another stone.

It was wicked to feel this way. She knew that, and in a flash she thought that Theo would have understood. He would have said, "Don't worry about it, squirt. Everything's going to be hunky-dory." But it wasn't and hadn't been.

She'd shot up the first spring here. Not surprising given how tall her parents were, but she felt like Alice after she'd nibbled the cake labeled "Eat Me." The Cabot girls her age were petite and dainty. She hated them. If it wasn't for Marit she didn't know what she'd do. And even with Marit, she wasn't able to talk about Theo.

Theo. She missed him all the time, and it seemed each day brought a fresh reminder, fresh pain. Last week she had been looking in the living room bookshelves for something about King Arthur and came across one of Theo's books from his course on medieval history with his name and address printed in his sprawling handwriting on the title page. The Professor ran the study sessions for the course, which helped Theo pass, and that's why Father had hired him to tutor Theo over the summer. Ursula had dropped the book, but picked it up immediately and rearranged the others to fill the space it had occupied. She took it to her room, searching in vain for any notes or underlinings Theo might have made, and slipped it behind her Little Colonel books in her own bookcase. Theo had given her a copy of his formal freshman portrait. The photo and now the book were all she had of him. His gift, her treasured wristwatch, had disappeared, lost that night or during the days that followed. She didn't want another one, and in any case, they were too expensive for the Lymans now.

She turned on Adams Street. It was the beginning of their third

*fall in Aleford. Nineteen thirty-one. Soon it would be 1932. Father
had been able to let Sanpere for the last two summers at what Mother
said was a "giveaway price," but it was something. Ursula hated the
thought of strangers at The Pines. Maybe next summer . . .*

*Would things ever get better? She'd heard Father tell Mother
that so many shoe and textile factories, the mainstays of Massachusetts manufacturing, had closed that former workers' children were
barefoot and in tatters. People were going hungry, too. Several Sundays ago they had passed a long line of people on Tremont Street,
and when she asked what it was her mother told her they were waiting to get served at a soup kitchen. One man facing the street had
a placard around his neck saying he would work for food. That his
children were starving.*

*She was wicked. She had food and a very pleasant roof over her
head. A school to go to when so many others had none of these
things. She pinched her arm and vowed to stop being so self-centered.*

*She was almost home. Adams Street was lined with tall maples
and oaks. The leaves were brilliant reds and golds and would start
falling soon. Falling, too, on Theo's grave. A grave she'd never seen.
She blinked back her tears, wiped her eyes, and stood up straighter.
She didn't want to upset her mother.*

*Aleford. What a stupid name. She hated this place and was
counting the days until she'd be old enough to leave and never come
back.*

"Well, your two lovebirds are certainly discreet," Patsy Avery said
to Faith as she came in through the kitchen door. Will and the
children went straight through to the living room.

"Lovebirds?" Faith was startled, but not so startled that she
failed to take the sweet potato pie from Patsy's outstretched hands.

"Didn't you say you'd asked the Reverend Holden to come? I
recognized him, but not the woman. They were holding hands as

they walked down the church driveway toward the cemetery, but dropped them as soon as they got to where you might see them from your back window. There they are now coming around to the front door."

"The woman is Eloise Gardner, our education director. Are you sure their hands didn't just touch in a sort of friendly accidental way?"

"Nope. This was fingers entwined. Nothing accidental about it, unless you call love an accident, which it certainly can be."

The front doorbell rang.

"Tom," Faith called. "Could you get that? It's our other guests."

Eloise and James. This was definitely a new twist, Faith thought. Tom hadn't mentioned anything about a budding romance between the two, but then, it wasn't the sort of thing he'd notice, not until he was invited to the wedding. And Faith rarely saw the two together. Eloise was around after Sunday school, but she generally didn't attend coffee hour—too many parents wanting to grab her attention, Faith assumed.

Did Patsy's observation make Faith suspect either individual or both more, or less?

She turned her attention to the roast. Faith was a firm believer in traditional Sunday dinners. Today it was a leg of lamb with new potatoes and asparagus. The first asparagus was coming in from California and Faith was roasting it at the last minute in the oven with olive oil and garlic, a drizzle of lemon when she took it out. The tips would be slightly crunchy, the stems tender. The potatoes had been steamed and were in the pan with the fragrant lamb to brown. She'd seasoned the roast with more garlic and rosemary. If James and Eloise were an item perhaps she should leave some breath mints on the table at the end of the meal.

"What's this?" Patsy asked, pointing toward a small dish filled with some sort of red jelly.

"I refuse to spoil lamb with mint jelly, no matter what my husband got used to as a child. But he still wants something like it, so that's red pepper jelly."

"Will has to have Heinz catsup with his scrambled eggs and the eggs have to be almost burned because that's how his mother made them. What will our children be laying on their poor spouses, I wonder?"

"Given what you put on your table, they're going to have a hard act to follow," Faith said.

"Ditto, but I plan on teaching both of mine to cook—a gift to whomever. And you've already taught Ben and Amy to do more than push a button on the microwave."

This was true, although there was plenty of button pushing, but both kids had always enjoyed messing around in the kitchen with mom, something Faith had never experienced.

Things were going well. There was nothing like good food and a glass or two of wine—a nice, full-bodied 2008 Porcupine Ridge Syrah from South Africa—to make people feel relaxed. Will was talking about how growing up in New Orleans, he and his friends would sneak into Preservation Hall and other jazz joints when they were young teens.

"The music never left and the rest of the city is definitely coming back," he said. "That Super Bowl win didn't hurt."

"Didn't hurt," Patsy cried. "Folks are still hanging their Saints banners all over the place and don't even think of wearing a cap or T-shirt anywhere in Louisiana with another team's name."

Faith decided it was time to try to steer the conversation in the direction she'd intended.

"Are you a sports fan, James? I know you must follow things like the America's Cup." She addressed the whole table. "I learned last night that James is an accomplished sailor when he was inducted into the Tiller Club. Have Faith catered the dinner."

"Congratulations," Will said. "My time on the water has been strictly limited to trying to get crawfish in the bayous, but I've always wanted to sail."

The Reverend had flushed at Faith's words. Yes, she'd been pretty obvious and now she was going to push it even more.

"James just bought a new boat, the club chairman told me. I don't remember exactly how big it is, though."

"Not that big," he said quickly. "I was able to get it for a very low price. The owner was forced to declare bankruptcy."

"So I heard. A great bargain. What was it? Ten—"

Before Faith could finish the sentence, everyone's attention turned to Eloise Gardner, who'd spilled what was left in her wineglass down the front of the light beige blazer she was wearing with a black pleated skirt.

"Club soda," Patsy said, getting up.

"I'm so sorry, but I don't think any went on your tablecloth or the rug," Eloise said.

"Don't worry. Patsy's right about the club soda and I have plenty in the kitchen," Faith said. The three women left the table, and as Faith went through the door, she heard James say, "So what kind of law do you specialize in, Will?"

Captain Holden had seized the tiller and was steering in another direction.

Club soda worked its magic and the wine had not spilled on Eloise's ivory-colored silk blouse or the scarf she was wearing draped across her shoulders.

"Your jacket should be dry enough to wear by the time you leave," Faith said.

"Even if it isn't, I won't need it. It's so warm today. Winter may truly be behind us."

Patsy straightened Eloise's scarf. "There, you look fine. And I love the nautical pattern."

Faith loved it, too. The scarf was from Hermès—the Christopher Columbus model to commemorate his supposed discovery of America. Hermès scarves like this one cost about $400.

"It was a gift from—a gift from a friend." Eloise stumbled over the words.

Patsy gave Faith a knowing look.

"Well, that must be a very thoughtful friend—and a good thing the wine missed it. As long as we're out here, why don't we give these starving children some dessert and put the pie in to warm?"

There were cheers from the round table by the window where the kids had been watching the cleanup. Nobody had spilled anything at their table, they seemed to be saying.

Eloise, Patsy, and Faith returned to the dining room. Clearing plates, Faith thought to herself, as Sigmund had said, There are no accidents. . . .

The party broke up after dessert. Will took the children home—Devon needed his nap—but Patsy insisted on staying to help Faith and headed for the kitchen. Eloise expressed her appreciation for the "gourmet meal," retrieved her damp jacket, and left. As Tom was seeing her out, Faith was left alone in the dining room with James.

"A delicious meal, as always. Thank you," he said.

His stern expression was at odds with the appreciative words.

"I'm glad you were able to make it," Faith said.

"I come from a family of sailors," he said abruptly. "Holdens have always owned boats. Airing First Parish's dirty laundry in public is not my style and I wasn't about to respond to your innuendos, but I can assure you that I am not involved in any way with Tom's problem."

Faith felt as if he had slapped her. He might as well have. And

"Tom's problem"? The good Reverend was firmly distancing himself.

"I'm not sure I know what you're getting at, James."

"Oh, I think you do and I'm telling you to stay out of my business. Boat buying or anything else I do on my own time has nothing to do with my commitment at First Parish."

Faith knew he was speaking of "commitment" as in "calling," but it certainly suggested "confinement." She realized that she didn't know much about James. Although he'd been at the church almost two years, she still thought of him as newly arrived. He wasn't particularly outgoing, but both Tom and the vestry seemed happy with him, and she hadn't heard any complaints from the congregation. She hadn't heard much praise, either.

Tom came in. "Care to sit in the living room for a while, James? Another cup of coffee?"

"Thank you, no. I have to be in Cambridge soon."

I'll bet you do, Faith thought. Eloise lived near Inman Square.

He left and Tom went out to join the kids in the backyard. When Faith went into the kitchen, where Patsy had already filled the dishwasher, she could see her husband, rake in hand, heading for the thick winter leaf cover on the perennial beds.

There wasn't much food left, but Faith put it away and was starting on the roasting pan when Patsy said, "Leave it to soak and pour me another cup of coffee. One for you, too. I want to know what's going on."

Faith had been waiting for this. Like her husband, Patsy was a lawyer, a juvenile public defender. Faith and she had been involved in two investigations over the years and Faith had learned that nothing much got past Ms. Avery. She couldn't tell Patsy what was going on at First Parish, but if Patsy guessed . . . Faith laughed to herself as she admitted this was one of the things she'd hoped would happen today.

"Tom barely said two words all through lunch and he's attack-

ing those poor flower beds as if the leaves were hiding Satan him-
self," Patsy said. "You start telling us about some boat and Reverend
Holden looks like he's been caught with his hand in the Poor Box."
Faith tried to suppress her gasp at Patsy's apt description.

"So that's it," Patsy said slowly. "Money. Of course. A financial
irregularity at First Parish. You don't have to say anything. I know
you can't. You suspect James Holden and maybe the Sunday school
director, too."

Faith lowered her head toward her coffee to take a sip. It could
also have been seen as a nod.

"But somehow Tom is being blamed, judging from the way
he's behaving—and the look on his face. One of those 'My dog is
lost; can you help me find him?' kinds."

Faith took another sip.

"Does he need a lawyer?"

"He has one," Faith blurted out. "Sam. He's away for the rest
of the week, though."

"Okay, I didn't hear anything. Sam Miller is a good choice,
especially as he knows the cast of characters. But before I leave,
answer me one question: Why did Ms. Eloise pour her wine down
her jacket so carefully? I saw it and she did a fine job of dribbling it
so it missed her very expensive scarf and white blouse. Hmmm?"

"Hmmm," was all Faith could think of in reply.

Dora had come in Ursula's kitchen door the day before, closing
her wet Mary Poppins umbrella behind her. She'd smiled broadly
at the scene. Ursula's plate was almost clean. She was popping a last
bit of liverwurst in her mouth. Faith had been afraid Dora would
chase her away, but instead she had suggested she make a fire in
the living room fireplace. "You can stretch out on the couch, Mrs.
Rowe, and Mrs. Fairchild can keep you company a bit longer. Her
visit today looks like it's done you a world of good."

Faith was conscious of a gold star about to be pasted next to her name in the Book of Dora.

Once Ursula was ensconced in front of the fire with an afghan that Faith recognized as Pix's handiwork, she began to talk.

"As I said, I hadn't given any thought to Arnold Rowe. I tried not to think about that night at all, although it was always with me, not far from the surface. I was very restless in Aleford and had never settled into the Cabot School. I thought of myself as a city girl.

"Time went by, I turned sixteen and shortly afterward two things happened that changed my life forever. The first was finding a box of clippings about the murder and the trial. The Adams Street house had a large attic and things from our Boston house that Mother wanted to save, but didn't have room for downstairs, were stored there. She never liked to go up in the attic—mice and spiders—but I loved it. There were two small round windows at either end, so it wasn't dark. I'd often take a book and curl up on a chair that I'd dragged closer to the light at the end overlooking the garden. The trunks and boxes didn't interest me, but one day Mother asked me to go through them for some curtains when I went up to read. She thought she could have Mrs. Hansen cut them down for the kitchen. The Hansens were going back to Norway, much to my dismay—I was already missing Marit—and Mother wanted to get as much sewing as possible done before they left.

"I found the curtains after much searching and was about to close that trunk when I saw there was a letter file in the bottom. These were large hinged boxes covered with marbleized paper where people used to file correspondence. My father had rows of them on the shelves in his office and I wondered what this one was doing here. I opened it and saw that the folders were filled with newspaper clippings and letters from a Boston law firm.

"I knew what it contained even before reading a single word— and why it had been tucked so far away. Perhaps that wasn't a bad idea, and I considered leaving it where it was, unread. I was torn between not wanting to be reminded of that summer and wanting to know what had been happening during the time I had been ill. And then one of the headlines caught my eye: 'Sentenced to Life: Tutor Convicted of Murdering Pupil.'

"I felt sick. All the time that I'd been going about my little life, Arnold Rowe had been in prison for his life—the Charles Street Jail, to be precise."

Faith wondered whether Ursula knew that the jail, closed in 1973 because overcrowding violated the constitutional rights of the inmates, had reopened in 2007, after extensive remodeling, as a high-end luxury hotel ironically named the Liberty Hotel. Faith wasn't sure whether such features as the Alibi Bar in the old drunk tank, the Clink restaurant with its vestiges of the original jail cells, and even the phone number (JAIL) represented a witty or totally inappropriate sense of humor. In its day, just before the Civil War, it had been hailed as a step forward in prison architecture with four wings to segregate prisoners by gender and offense extending from a ninety-foot-tall atrium. The multitude of arched windows set into the granite structure let in light and air, but didn't let anyone out, of course.

"I started to read straight through. The first clippings described the murder itself and I immediately knew something was wrong with the reports. First of all, the party was described as a 'small gathering of friends,' and then there was a reference to an eyewitness who saw Theo go toward the gazebo at midnight followed by Arnold Rowe. I felt terribly confused. Certain parts of the night were as clear in my memory as they had been when they happened and I knew that Theo had been in the gazebo arguing with someone, a man, well before midnight. I'd been asleep and they'd awakened me. My watch had a luminous dial, quite a new thing, and it was eleven-thirty. I wasn't able to identify the man's voice, just Theo's, but I did know it wasn't Arnold's. So who was there earlier with Theo? I read through the rest of the articles on the murder, including the news of Arnold's arrest. There were far fewer about the trial, which was held in Edgartown at the Dukes County Courthouse. By that time, the country was caught up in the aftermath of the stock market crash. People were more concerned about their next meal and a roof over their heads than what was characterized as a fight turned deadly between two Harvard students. The trial was short and the guilty verdict swift. A court-appointed lawyer represented Arnold. I couldn't find any indications of his line of defense. Without the proper facility on the island, Arnold had been immediately transferred to the prison in Boston."

Ursula had been only sixteen! Faith pictured herself at that age. Her sister, a year younger, had mapped out her entire future— Pelham College undergrad, Harvard for an MBA, summer internships at the appropriate firms, and finally partner with a corner office on a top floor with multiple-figure bonuses. And it had all come true. Faith meanwhile had been busy thinking up ever new excuses to get out of gym and ways to get Emilio, the very cool Italian exchange student, to notice her. Ursula at that age was dealing with issues an adult would have had difficulty with— complicated by grief over an irreplaceable loss.

"Finding the box was both liberating—I now knew more about what happened—and depressing—there were still so many unanswered questions. Had there been a thorough investigation? And what about the reporters' mistakes? It was not a small party, but a very large one. There was a single sentence mentioning a 'fierce' argument earlier in the evening between my brother and Arnold Rowe. Yet, at the time when it supposedly occurred we were at Illumination Night. The word 'fierce' surprised me, too. Theo could get annoyed, but even when he'd overly imbibed—in fact especially then—he was always very easygoing, and I'd never heard the Professor raise his voice.

"I returned often in the following weeks to reread the contents of the box until I had it virtually memorized, and then there was the second stroke of luck. Or divine intervention, if you will. I firmly believe in both.

"Mother and I had taken the train into town to see Aunt Myrtle. My cousins, whom I had thought would be there, weren't at home. Seeing that I was at loose ends, my aunt sent me to Stearn's to buy gloves on her account. I'm sure she noticed the ones I was wearing were outgrown. In those days you didn't go into town without a hat and gloves. The department store was on Tremont Street across from the Common. I wish you could have seen it—it closed in the late 1970s. Such elegance."

"My mother and I still miss B. Altman in New York—it sounds like the same kind of place."

"I had selected a lovely pair of gray kid gloves when I heard a couple talking behind me. The man was urging the woman to buy a coat she had just tried on. He was tired of shopping and didn't want to go to another store. She was resisting. I recognized both their voices immediately and told the saleswoman I wanted to try the gloves on in brown so I could remain at the counter. The woman was Violet Hammond and the man was Charles Winthrop. They hadn't changed much, especially Violet. She was still turning heads.

"When the saleswoman brought the gloves for me to try on, my hands were shaking. Violet and Charles were continuing their discussion directly behind me. He was growing increasingly angry and I didn't simply recognize the voice of the man who had been a guest at the Vineyard, but I recognized it as the man who had been arguing with Theo in the gazebo. Charles Winthrop was there well before Arnold. Charles Winthrop was the one who was desperate for money. Charles Winthrop had killed Theo."

"Are you all right, miss?"

"Yes, just a bit faint. I'll be fine in a minute."

Ursula desperately needed to sit down. She was leaning against the counter, the neat rows of gloves arrayed on the shelves beneath the glass. So many kinds of gloves. Long, short, even the arm-length kind debutantes and brides wore. They began to swirl together in front of her eyes. She closed them to keep from passing out.

Charles Winthrop. The voice. The other noises. He'd hit Theo. In her mind she heard her brother again, "Whadya have to smack me for? Thought we were friends." The thumping noise. Charles must have hit Theo again, hit him too hard. The sound she'd assumed was both of them running back to the party had been Charles alone. Charles running away to do what? Involve Arnold Rowe. Find someone else to blame. Maybe it was an accident. It had to have been. People didn't go around killing people like that. He'd hit Theo too hard. It had to be that.

No! It wasn't supposed to be at all. Theo was dead and Charles was guilty. Not the young man in a cell a short walk away.

"I'll be a good little wife, Charlie. Calm down. People are starting to look at us. It's a perfectly adorable coat."

The couple moved off. Ursula told the saleswoman she'd take the gray gloves. By the time they were signed for and wrapped, she had regained her composure.

"The couple behind me just now. Do you know who they are?"

The girl answered readily, "Oh yes, miss. That's Mr. and Mrs. Charles Winthrop. Very good customers."

Ursula had had to be sure. And she was also sure of her next stop. Her mother and her aunt would talk for hours more. She tucked her parcel in her purse and turned her steps toward the Charles Street Jail.

✳   ✳   ✳

The fire was burning low, but Faith didn't want to interrupt Ursula by putting another log on. Outside the rain had tapered off, but the sky was still dark.

"I've never told anyone about all this, except Arnold of course. A few days ago you and I were talking about coincidence. Cosmic coincidences, a dear friend used to call them. If Aunt Myrtle hadn't sent me to Stearn's it's unlikely that I would ever have seen the Winthrops. I was seldom in town, and in any case, we didn't travel in the same circles.

"Unlike today, that day was beautiful. Early spring, like now. As I walked down Tremont Street past King's Chapel and, yes, continuing on through Scollay Square into the West End, where the jail was located, I felt a warm presence. It was as though Theo were near. It gave me courage and strengthened my resolve. I thought I knew now who had killed him, but even so I realized I had known all along that Arnold hadn't."

Ursula paused, staring into the embers in the fireplace.

"That being so, I was just going to have to unmask the real murderer myself."

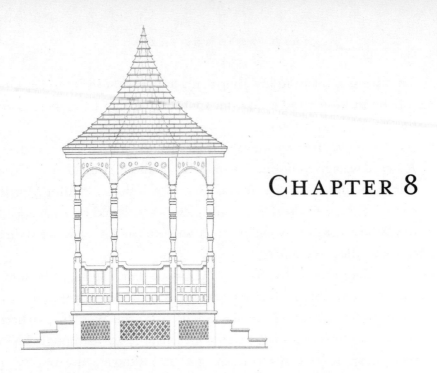

CHAPTER 8

It took Faith about twelve seconds to decide Lily Sinclair was a total bitch.

Hoping that face-to-face contact would give her an advantage in discovering any involvement on Lily's part, Faith didn't call the young divinity school student, but took a chance at finding her home early on a Monday morning. Lily lived in Somerville off Davis Square. Faith was meeting Zach Cummings at a nearby Starbucks at ten. Zach lived in Somerville, too. Somerville was a very happening place, much more affordable than Cambridge. New restaurants, bars, cafés, and shops had sprung up like mushrooms, fortunately not displacing old favorites like Redbones barbecue.

The face-to-face was not going well. Yes, Lily was home, but for a while it seemed Faith's interaction with her would begin and end quickly on the front porch of the double-decker's first-floor apartment. Lily's name, plus two others, was listed by the buzzer. Lily had answered the door, but didn't take the chain off. The opening was wide enough to reveal that her visitor was someone known to her and not an assailant, but she still didn't make a move. Her face was impassive.

"Hi, Lily. It's Faith, Faith Fairchild."

"Yes, I know. What do you want?"

That's when Faith rapidly jumped to her conclusion. At the same time, she realized that she really didn't know the people with whom Tom worked anymore. When they were first married— and continuing on to when the kids were younger before she had started the business again—she had had much more contact with everyone working in the church offices. Walter, James Holden's predecessor, had been a dear family friend.

Lily had been one in a string of interns that were little more than names to Faith, but she thought she had parted on good, if not close, terms with the young woman. She'd brought Lily a going-away gift her last Sunday in church back in January and had received a smiling thank-you. What had happened since then?

"May I come in?" Faith was beginning to feel like someone selling encyclopedias.

The door closed, and then opened wide. Lily, who was wearing Hello Kitty pajamas, led the way down a short hall into the kitchen at the rear of the apartment. It was obviously shared. Dishes were piled in the sink and a pot of what might have been chili was on the stove, its burners encrusted with many other offerings. Lily sat down and picked up the spoon sticking out from a bowl of cereal. She didn't offer Faith anything—neither a seat nor food. Faith was happy at this particular rudeness as it meant she wouldn't have to say no. It wasn't that the place was a health hazard, well maybe, but it certainly was unappetizing.

"I know why you're here," Lily said, crunching her granola.

"You do?" For a moment Faith herself had lost the thread. She was distracted by a makeshift clothesline strung from a knob on a cabinet to a catch on one of the windows. It was adorned with rather gray BVDs and decidedly not gray thongs.

"Look, I didn't take the money. I never even knew about the fund. And if you must know, my time in Aleford, or should I say

Stepford, convinced me a parish ministry is the last thing I want. I've taken a leave from the Div School." She put her spoon down and drank the milk from the bowl.

Faith concentrated on the first words.

"How do you know about the missing money?"

Lily shrugged. "I guess it's no big secret. Al told me."

Albert Trumbull, the parish secretary, or rather administrative assistant. Faith didn't really know him all that well, either. Certainly she wasn't on an "Al" basis with him. She longed for the good old days with Madame Rhoda and her psychic powers, a mystery at first when the woman appeared to be living a double life, but oh so much more explainable than all this young weltschmerz. Albert was on leave from the Div School and finding himself, too. *O tempora, O mores.*

Faith thought she should express concern over the second half of Lily's remarks. The missing money could wait a bit.

"It sounds as if you weren't happy at First Parish and I hope your time with us didn't contribute to your decision. You know Tom is always available to talk with you."

Lily flushed and pushed her bowl away. "Oh, he's a talker, all right, and let's just say my time with you didn't 'contribute,' it *caused* my decision."

Before Faith could say anything more, Lily got up and moved toward the door to the hall. The interview was clearly over. Faith had no choice but to follow.

As Lily virtually pushed her out, Faith managed to ask, "Do you have any idea who might have taken the money?"

Lily smiled wickedly. "I'd suggest you ask your husband. The talker."

Walking back toward Elm Street and Starbucks, Faith's mind was filled with questions for her husband, but they didn't have to do with the missing funds. They concerned Ms. Lily Sinclair.

* * *

Faith was on her second latte—she'd indulged in whole milk for the first one to soothe her troubled soul and was now nursing a skinny one—when Zach Cummings walked in. She'd scored two comfy armchairs, placing her jacket on the unoccupied one and ignoring an occasional angry look. Let them displace some of the other customers who seemed to have moved in with their laptops permanently—and nary a cup of joe in sight.

She waved Zach over and handed him her Rewards Card.

"Go nuts. Get whatever you want," she said. Zach was taller than he'd been when she'd met him at Mansfield Academy years ago, but still as thin, and still dressed in black. His legs looked like pipe stems and he was wearing a T-shirt with a screwdriver pictured in white that read I VOID WARRANTIES.

He reached into a pocket and waved his own card.

"I've got it. You good?"

She nodded. It was hard to remember he was an adult now. Or almost.

He returned with what appeared to be a Venti of black coffee.

"So, what's up?" he said.

"I need to know how someone could get access to someone else's bank account through an ATM, withdrawing a significant amount of cash over the course of a year."

"Same machine?"

"Yes—and twenty transactions."

"For the limit each time?"

Faith nodded.

"And this is all theoretical, right? You're helping someone write a book or something so everything you say is off the record and vice versa?"

"Completely theoretical, hypothetical, even rhetorical. I'm a little muddled—it's been a bad morning."

Zach shook his head. "I'm sorry, Faith." His expression indicated he was talking about more than her morning. He set his coffee down.

"Well, to start, have you heard of shoulder surfing?"

"Yes, but I don't know that much about it except it's a way to get a PIN by peeking over a shoulder somehow."

"It's the simplest way, especially for a nonhacker. All you have to do is act casual and watch someone enter their PIN at an ATM or a place like this—a cybercafé that has WiFi, even a library. At crowded airports, they sometimes use miniature binoculars to look at people using bank terminals. Shoulder surfing would be the first thing I'd consider, especially as it's the same location for each transaction. Try to recall who was close by before the first withdrawal. Was it a stranger or someone our theoretical person knew?"

"Okay, what next?"

"It gets a little more complicated, but not by much for anyone with a modicum of computer smarts. These are all phishing scams, spelled with a 'ph,' and are what they sound like—throwing out some 'bait' to see what gets caught in the net, on the Net. They try to trick you into revealing things like your Social Security number, passwords, credit card numbers—you get the picture. You'll get an e-mail or IM that seems to be an authentic one from your bank or the IRS. It purports to be alerting you to a serious problem. In order to correct it before it gets even worse, you must respond immediately with your information. It may even take you to a Web site that looks exactly like your bank's. A recent scam claimed to be from UPS and had you enter your credit card number to track a recent attempted delivery. Most people are getting stuff all the time, or if not, might assume someone had sent a gift, so this was very effective until it was flagged."

Faith was stunned. "I had no idea that there were all these risks. It's a wonder anything online is safe."

"This is just the tip of the iceberg. I'm assuming your, sorry, your friend's account was a random attack—caught in that big net. But it may have been targeted—'spear phishing.' Again, there would have been an e-mail message or IM, but addressed specifically to the account's user. There's also 'spoofing,' which is forging data, particularly an address, so that it seems as if it's secure. Misspelling one word, for example, which most people miss."

"Spoofing, phishing—who thinks these things up?"

"Oh, hackers are fun guys. Look at me," Zach said.

Faith did—hard.

"Whoa, I'm a White Hat. One of the good guys. I get paid to try to hack into systems and find out where they're vulnerable. It's a nice gig."

"What else?"

"Ask the person if they've received a message to call the bank, or a phone call purporting to be from the bank or your credit card company giving you a number to call. Again there's an urgent problem. The phone number you punch in takes you to the phisher's, or in this case visher's—voice phising—VOIP account, where you are asked to enter your bank account number and so forth."

"VOIP?"

"Voice over Internet Protocol—basically what it comes down to is making 'phone calls' over the Internet. You have no idea that it isn't originating from a regular phone number."

"I don't think there have been any calls like this, but I'll check."

"If you could arrange it, the best thing would be for me to take a look at the person's computer. What is it, by the way?"

"There are two—an old MacBook and a newer Dell." The Dell was in Tom's office and had replaced his previous PC a year or so ago. She gave a start.

"What's wrong?" Zach asked.

"The PC. I'm pretty sure the withdrawals started at the same time it arrived."

"Interesting." Zach got up and stretched. "I need more coffee. Want anything?"

Faith shook her head, but asked him what he was drinking. Black coffee seemed pretty boring and Zach was not a boring guy.

"They have something I like called the 'Gazebo Blend.' That with two shots."

Skimming over the thought of all that caffeine, Faith focused on the name, and the coincidence. "Gazebo." There are no accidents, she said to herself. It was getting to be a mantra.

When Zach returned he said, "Of course, the easiest way to get into someone's ATM account if you have stolen the card is to guess their password. That provides access into anything password-protected on their computer, too."

"With all the possibilities, I'd have thought this would be the most difficult."

"People are innately trusting—or lazy. They go for the simplest to remember and they use one password for all their accounts. 'One, two, three, four, five, six'—occasionally with more numbers in sequence—is the number one password, followed by 'QWERTY,' an individual's birthday, phone number, pet name. You get the idea. Your password should have at least six letters—longer makes it more difficult for a hacker, as does mixing letters and numbers. And you should change your passwords with some frequency, but people don't. They're afraid they'll forget a new one—and they're . . ."

"Lazy," Faith finished for him. A whole world of possibilities had opened up. Tom wasn't lazy, but he was trusting. Very trusting. It went with the territory.

"If this is someone you know, I'll bet you can guess his or her password." He drained his cup. "Gotta run, but I can come out next weekend and have a look at all your computers. Check them out. Make sure you have the proper spam filters."

Ben would be in heaven. Zach was a god so far as her son was concerned, and the highlight of his year to date had been a trip to MIT's new Media Lab with Zach.

"You've been an enormous help. I wish there was something I could do in return."

"You kept me out of jail, remember? I'd say that should do it for anything you want for the rest of your life," Zach said, smiling.

Faith's phone was vibrating. It was Tom.

"I need to take this," she said.

"Go ahead. I have to get to class, so I'll say good-bye."

Faith answered the call, giving Zach a swift hug as he left.

"Hi, honey. I was about to call you. I'm still in Somerville."

She had told Tom about meeting with Zach, but not about trying to see Lily. After both encounters, she was now itching to get home and talk to her spouse.

"What did he have to say?"

"Too much to go over on the phone. I'll be home in half an hour. Can you get away?"

"Shouldn't be a problem. I'll make lunch."

Faith hung up. She had certainly married the right man. He had his priorities straight.

Tom had made toasted cheese sandwiches, or toasted "cheesers," as he called them. It was his comfort food, together with Campbell's cream of tomato soup. While Faith maintained that "food snob" was a compliment, especially in her case, she had relaxed somewhat as the years passed, realizing that one person's caviar with the appropriate accompaniments (her ultimate comfort food) might be another's processed soup. The Fairchild pantry always had some cans of tomato and cream of mushroom soup, Tom's other mainstay, for times like this.

Before she told him about Lily, she gave him a summary of what Zach had said—she'd taken notes on her phone— and recommended they accept his offer to go over all their computers.

"According to Zach, because I know you so well, I should be able to guess your password. First we eliminate your birthday, or the birthday of anyone close to you."

Tom nodded.

"And it's not our phone number or a series of numbers in order starting with one."

"Nope." Tom seemed proud of himself. He'd avoided the usual traps.

"Then it's 'FAITH,' and you use it for everything."

His face fell. "How did you guess?"

"I know you, honey."

And so did a whole lot of other people. She pictured what now seemed the most probable scenario. Take the keys from his desk, unlock the file, remove the bank card, stroll over to the ATM, enter the PIN, and voilà, a wad of cash in your pocket. Reverse steps. It wouldn't have taken more than fifteen minutes total, a bit more if you had to walk around the block until the ATM was empty. Wouldn't want any witnesses. Of course, it could be someone local who had an account at the bank, too, in which case it would seem completely normal to be waiting to use the cash machine.

She went over it with Tom. "Next time you talk to Sam, sketch this out for him."

"I feel like an idiot," Tom said.

"Why should you feel anything except ripped off and furious? You haven't done anything that millions of Americans don't do every day. Pick a PIN they can recall easily. You are not a crook."

Bypassing the Nixonian echo in her head, Faith went on to reassure Tom that she was positive they were on the right track.

"I'm certain we know how and where it happened. We just have to find out who. And now, please tell me why Lily Sinclair hates us, and Aleford, so much."

"You went to see her, too." It was a statement.

"Before Zach. She referred to Aleford as Stepford, said her time at First Parish caused her to abandon the idea of a parish ministry, ,and has currently dropped out of the Div School. She knew about the missing money. Albert told her. Oh, and she thinks you took it. Plus, I'd say she is not your greatest fan. Many references to you as a 'talker.'"

Tom rubbed his hand across his forehead. Faith thought she saw a new line. At this rate, the furrows were beginning to resemble a south forty.

"She had some difficulty around this time last year running the youth group and I had to speak with her. Several times. I guess she thought of them as talking-tos. I would have called them pastoral counseling, something she might emulate even. That sounds a little stuffy, I know, but my other interns never seemed to mind. In retrospect her silence during them might have been hostility rather than what I took as embarrassment over her behavior. Even though she'd been through four years of college and a year at Harvard, she seemed very young to me. When problems surfaced, I put them down to her immaturity."

"What kinds of problems? I don't remember that you mentioned having any issues with her."

"I didn't think they were major. She had trouble establishing boundaries with the kids, and the first talk I had with her, aside from our regular meetings about the internship, was after one of the mothers called me to tell me that Lily had been telling what the mother thought were inappropriate jokes and using inappropriate language."

"Sexual?"

"No, just thoughtless remarks about how stupid adults could be, parents in particular. How they didn't understand their own children. When I mentioned it, Lily told me that she wanted the kids to open up about problems at home, but someone was getting it all twisted around. I made some suggestions about other ways to create trust and she seemed to be listening, but she did demand to know who the mother was pretty emphatically. I'd used 'she,' so it was clearly a female parent. I didn't tell her, of course."

Hence the Stepford reference, Faith thought. And although she knew Tom wouldn't tell her, either, she had some candidates—as Lily must have also.

"When another mother called a few weeks later with virtually the same complaint, I may have been a little more forceful in my criticism. That was the time she said almost nothing.

"And then there was that business at the end-of-the-year Sunday school picnic," Tom said.

This Faith did remember. As people were leaving, two boys in the seventh grade class began to pelt their friends with water balloons from a stockpile they'd stashed in the cemetery. They bombarded Lily, too, who thought it was great fun. Her sopping wet T-shirt made it clear that she wasn't wearing a bra. It wasn't a case of *Girls Gone Wild*—flat-chested Lily was not a candidate— but one of the mothers had hastily run up to her and thrown a tablecloth around her shoulders. Lily started to shrug it off and then, seeing Tom's approach, apparently had second thoughts, wrapping it tight before heading into the church. Faith could still see the defiant "F-You" look Lily had flung over her shoulder at the crowd as she stomped off. "Immature" didn't even begin to describe it. She'd made her youth group seem like a gathering of elders.

And there were the Hello Kitty pajamas the other day, although that didn't necessarily mean anything. Faith knew any number of adult women with this unaccountable taste in clothing and accessories. Hope had given Amy a darling Hello Kitty pocketbook last summer. A note of whimsy, wit for Faith's own spring wardrobe? She gave herself a mental slap.

"Plus," Tom said, "I heard later that she really lost it running the Christmas pageant. I was still laid up, but Eloise filled me in when I was writing Lily's evaluation in January and asked everyone for input."

This was a hard one. The Christmas pageant. Taken by itself, she would have been solidly on Lily's side. Faith had considered adding "but not running the Christmas pageant" after "in sickness and in health" to their wedding vows. She'd seen what it had done to her mother the very few times she'd caved and become involved. Parents got crazy—"What do you mean, my child is going to be an ox!"—and as the big day drew near, the kids got crazy—"What if I have to pee when I'm watching my flocks!"

"What happened?"

"Not a mother this time, but a father. Apparently he'd set his sights on Mary for his darling daughter, and when he arrived at a rehearsal and saw she was Angel Number Three, he told Lily to make the cast change. She told him to stuff it and banned parents from coming to rehearsals. He organized a protest, pulling his child from the pageant and getting several other parents to do the same. Eloise had to smooth a lot of ruffled feathers."

"Thank goodness we were away!" The Fairchilds had been on Sanpere for the holidays while Tom recuperated and it had been heavenly.

"Eloise knew Lily would be leaving soon and she only told me so I could make some subtle suggestions in the evaluation about controlling one's temper when interacting with parishioners."

Tom reached for another toasted-cheese sandwich. He'd made a stack of them. "I'm not surprised Albert told her what's happened," he said. "They became close friends, brought together, now that I think of it, over doubts about their calling. Maybe she came to First Parish with them; maybe her time with us created them—or Albert did. He certainly stoked the fire. I guess I haven't talked about her much with you because I feel as though I failed her. When she finished the internship, I knew she wasn't happy. Maybe I should go see her."

"No! Bad idea. Very bad idea. Nothing you could say will make Ms. Sinclair change her opinion of you, or the town. Or even about the ministry. Stay away from her. I'm sure Sam would tell you the same thing."

"I wasn't going to mention anything about the Discretionary Fund," Tom said. "Just see if she wanted to talk about leaving school."

"Fine, but that decision isn't going anywhere for a while. See if you think it's still a good idea when this is all over."

When we find out whether Lily's to blame for more than bad taste and stupid remarks, Faith added to herself.

"Tom, how do you suppose Albert found out about this? I'm assuming you told James."

"Actually I didn't. I planned to, but he already knew and the conversation ended before it started."

"Again, how did these people find out? I thought vestry meetings were executive sessions—confidential?"

"They are," Tom said slowly. "We know Albert told Lily and I think we can assume James told Eloise."

Faith had filled him in on yesterday's display of affection. Handholding might seem tame to the layperson, but it was the equivalent of second base for the clergy.

"Eloise and Albert are pretty tight. A lot of what she's in charge of for the Sunday school and youth group involves the calendar and Albert oversees scheduling. They live near each other in Cambridge. I heard him tell her about a new restaurant in their neighborhood and she said they should try it out."

So her husband wasn't as oblivious as Faith thought. She might not be the only eavesdropper in the family. She was sure, though, that he hadn't reached her skill level.

"That leaves James," she said. "Is there anyone on the vestry who might have leaked this to him?"

"Dear God. There is. Sherman Munroe. They have some sort of connection."

"A connection?"

"Yes. Sherman was the one who brought James to the attention of the search committee."

"Hello, Mother."

"Pix dear, how lovely to hear your voice."

"And yours sounds much stronger than it did on Saturday morning when we talked. How do you feel?"

"Much more like my old self, which is a very old self, of course."

"Mother!" Pix hated to hear Ursula talk this way.

"Tell me about the shower. I wish I could have been there."

"I wish you could have, too. It was wonderful. Our hostess lives in a beautiful home across from the Battery, the promenade overlooking the river. From the house's portico we could see Fort Sumter. Oh, and Mother—her garden! She kept apologizing because it wasn't at its peak yet and looked 'scrawny,' but it was gorgeous. Carpets of daffodils and tiny anemones, and then huge camellias, azaleas, and of course magnolias. Everywhere in Charleston you can smell jasmine, and redbud trees thrive here— all the ones I've tried to grow have died. The shower was in the garden with the food set out under a pergola covered with wisteria. Each guest received one of Charleston's famous sweet grass baskets, small ones filled with sugared almonds. I took a lot of pictures."

"I'm sure Rebecca was thrilled. She's a lovely girl. Mark is a lucky man."

"We're all lucky. I know it's a cliché, but I do feel as if I've gained another daughter. It was a nice old-fashioned shower. Samantha made the bridal 'bouquet' from all the ribbons, and the gifts showed that they had been chosen with care by everyone."

Care—not poor taste. Pix had attended a shower for the daughter of a friend a few months ago, and it turned out to be a lingerie shower with the offerings so raunchy that Pix, who did not consider herself a prude, was mortified. Flavored panties that dissolved at the crotch! She hadn't read the invitation carefully, just noted the time and date. When the bride opened Pix's set of pots and pans, the room grew quiet and then burst into laughter. Apparently the young woman, who was in law school, used her oven as an annex to her overflowing closet and the flat cooktop as a place to pile textbooks. No one said "dinosaur," but Pix had felt her skin beginning to look scaly.

"It sounds like you and Samantha are having a fine time," Ursula said.

"We are. The Cohens have been the perfect hosts, both at Hilton Head and here. And Cissy has included me in everything. Saturday we went to Becca's final fitting. She looks like a princess in her gown. It's ivory satin, strapless—very simple—but they've had a little jacket made from some antique lace Cissy found, which makes it unique. But I don't want to tire you out talking. I'll call again tomorrow."

"Give my love to everyone—and I want to hear all about your dress, too, darling."

Ursula's interest in fashion hovered between zilch and nada, so Pix took the comment for what it was—a nice thing for a mother to say to her daughter. She closed her phone and resumed her walk. She was strolling down King Street, basking in the sun—and the anonymity. She loved Aleford, but it was rather nice to be in a place where everybody didn't know your name—or the names of your children, husband, pets, and so forth. Plus any number of other details about your life. She snapped another picture of a palm tree. She wasn't in a rush. Life had slowed down almost to a crawl. The Cohens had arranged for Pix and Samantha to stay in Cissy's brother's guesthouse, a short walk away from their home. The kitchenette had been stocked for breakfast and it meant that Pix didn't feel they were outwearing their welcome by staying with the Cohens.

Tomorrow Cissy and she were meeting with someone at the Planter's Inn to finalize the menu and other arrangements for the rehearsal dinner. The following day Cissy had declared to be a day off from wedding plans and the ladies were going to head out to Sullivan's Island to a beach house that belonged to someone in Cissy's family. Pix was beginning to think that between the two of them, Cissy and Stephen were related to almost the entire population of South Carolina. Every time a name came up, one or the other would explain to Pix that it was a cousin twice removed or the sister-in-law of a brother-in-law. Mark had said the wedding would be a big one. That could be a major understatement.

She paused to look in the window of an art gallery featuring the work of a number of Gullah artists and caught sight of her reflection. Maybe Faith was wrong. Maybe she bore so little resemblance to the college girl she'd been so many years ago that there was no way Stephen could have recognized her. Okay, it was still bothering her. Every time she'd found herself alone with him for a few minutes—like last night on the brick patio behind their house drinking a glass of wine while Samantha helped Cissy and Rebecca's sisters in the kitchen—Pix had been tempted to say something. But what? "That Yankee in your bed Green Key Weekend was me"?

She turned away and continued her walk. No, that would be tacky in the extreme. She had to let it go and be content with who she was in the present—the mother of the groom. The past was past.

Wasn't it?

✳   ✳   ✳

One of the things Tom and Faith had discussed in between every-thing else they seemed to be discussing was why Ursula seemed so driven to tell her story now. Tom thought it was because she'd been ill. He'd often had individuals confide long-held secrets to him as they approached death, and although Ursula was on the mend, the intimations of mortality had been strong during the winter months.

"But she keeps alluding to something she wants me to do when she's finished talking," Faith had pointed out. "That sounds like something specific has happened that's caused her to tell me all this now."

"Possibly, although what she wants you to do could be as sim-ple as helping her tell her children about their father. With Pix out of town she has the time to be alone with you to work it out."

The next day back with Ursula, Faith thought Tom might be right about Ursula's wanting her help, not in telling Pix and Arnie, but in deciding whether to tell them at all. Yet the thought that this wasn't the whole impetus for revealing her secret nagged at Faith nevertheless.

"Pix is having a wonderful time in Charleston. She called yes-terday."

"I talked to her, too," Faith said. "The Cohens are going to be wonderful in-laws."

"I'm looking forward to meeting them at the wedding."

"Me, too." Nothing was going to keep Ursula away from the wedding of her first grandchild, and Faith hoped she would be at all of them.

Ursula abruptly changed the subject, plunging back into the past.

"I never thought the guards wouldn't let me see Arnold. That's how naïve I was. Or that he wouldn't want to see me. I walked into the jail, told them that I wanted to visit Arnold Rowe, that I

was a relative—a fib, but I thought, given the circumstances, jus-
tifiable—and one of the men at the desk told me to wait. I'm sure
they thought I was a great deal older than sixteen. I was wearing
a suit, hat, and gloves plus I was quite tall for my age. He brought
a chair for me to sit on. I assumed it would be a while and I began
to worry about what I would tell my mother. Fortunately he returned soon and escorted me to a nice little room. I later learned
it was the warden's sitting room. A guard came in with Arnold
and then left us alone. I scarcely recognized him. He was so pale
and thin."

"Miss Lyman, what on earth are you doing here?"

*Arnold Rowe had been curious to find out who his "cousin"
might be since both his late parents had been only children. Possibly
last on the list he'd considered as he made his way through the series
of barred doors was Theo's sister.*

*Ursula had planned various openings, but as soon as she saw
Arnold the words that were uppermost in her mind came spilling out.*

*"I know you didn't have anything to do with my brother's death
and I think I know who did."*

"I think we should sit down," Arnold said. "I know I need to."

*He indicated the horsehair settee next to the fireplace. It was
slippery and slightly scratchy; Ursula sat on its edge as Arnold started
to speak.*

*"First of all—and the most important thing—is to say how
sorry I am about Theo's death. There are no words that can convey
the depth of my sorrow. He was not just my student, but also my
friend, and the guilt that I feel will be with me every day for the rest
of my life. I should never have left the house that night."*

Ursula started to speak, but Arnold held up a hand.

*"No, there isn't any excuse. I should have demanded he end
the party when we returned from Illumination Night. It was get-*

ting quite wild. At the very least I should have stayed with Theo. I've never been able to say these things to your parents. I asked the lawyer the court appointed for me to deliver a letter with these sentiments, but he, for reasons of his own, would not. At some time you might deem appropriate I hope you will convey what I've said."

Ursula shook her head. "They never speak of him—or that night. I only learned recently that you had been convicted of . . . convicted of his murder."

"I am guilty of it in my negligence, but please believe me, I had nothing to do with the act itself."

"I do believe you." Ursula looked straight into his eyes. "As soon as I read the newspaper accounts of the trial, I knew the wrong person had been arrested. That the wrong person was in prison. To-day by mere coincidence I got final proof of it."

Arnold looked astounded. "Proof?"

She quickly told him first about the time discrepancy and then about the conversation she'd overheard just before the murder took place.

"I've often wondered how you came to be there. The sight of you, so young, beside Theo's body, is one I can never—and should never—erase from my mind." He had tears in his eyes and Ursula felt her own fill.

"It was definitely Charles Winthrop speaking. I'm positive."

She described being at Stearn's and hearing the voice again, the voice that had been reverberating consciously and unconsciously over the years.

"I don't think he planned to harm Theo, but he was not in control of himself." She shuddered slightly as she recalled the vehemence of his words: "You're not going anywhere."

She told Arnold what she believed had happened. A night that had begun in innocent, albeit self-indulgent pleasure, gone terribly wrong as an argument over money turned deadly.

"*But what doesn't make sense to me is how there was enough evidence to try you. Let alone convict you.*"

"*The first year I was here I thought of nothing else. I was innocent. How could it have happened? My lawyer was young and very impressed by the names of those involved in the prosecution—wealthy Bostonians, prominent old families. The owner of the house you rented pushed for a speedy trial. He made it clear to my lawyer that he was out for blood, my blood, on behalf of your family. I had a hard time even getting my lawyer to listen to my account of that night. And I had two eyewitnesses who saw me, me alone, going down the path toward the gazebo after midnight. He finally interviewed them, but said afterward he wouldn't call them to testify.*"

"*Who were they?*"

"*Mary Smith, who worked in the kitchen, and the gardener, Elias Norton.*"

"*I know, or rather knew, Mary. She was deaf and I learned to sign from her.*"

"*Elias is deaf, too. I thought that was why the lawyer wouldn't put them on the stand, but that wasn't it—there were plenty of interpreters available on the island. He said they weren't friendly witnesses. I wanted to talk to them myself. I'd learned to sign, too—the whole phenomenon of the Vineyard deafness and subsequent sign language had interested me—but there was no way I could contact them except through him. And the most damning testimony of all came from Violet Hammond.*"

"*She's Violet Winthrop now, remember.*"

Arnold nodded. "*I'm not surprised. She was after him all that summer and poor Theo was like a lovesick calf. I tried to talk to him—Violet was costing him a lot of money, and had been during the school year what with champagne suppers at Locke-Ober and the like. He wouldn't listen. I thought she'd find someone else and leave him alone, but she enjoyed stringing him along, even though Charles was the one she wanted. I wish I had been more persistent.*"

Ursula interrupted. "He wouldn't have listened. I saw the way he looked at her, too, and she is very beautiful. What was her testimony?"

She had a feeling she knew. . . .

"She testified that she overheard a violent quarrel between the two of us and that I threatened Theo to the point where he ran out of the house, apparently in fear of his life. She said she saw me follow him and immediately got Charles Winthrop to go after us both. She said we'd been drinking heavily. Winthrop corroborated her story. He described going after us as soon as she alerted him, coming upon us in the gazebo when it was too late.

"But they lied!" Ursula flushed angrily. "Didn't your lawyer challenge them? And what about your testimony?"

"He didn't question them at all and he'd told me early on that he wouldn't put me on the stand. That the prosecutor would, as he said, 'eat me for breakfast.' "

It was getting late. Ursula knew she should leave, but not yet. She needed to hear more.

"What made you go out to the gazebo? How did you know Theo was there?"

"As I said earlier, the party had become wild. Word of it had spread all over the island and cars filled with crashers kept arriving. Most of the servants, including the housekeeper, had disappeared, no doubt to the Illumination, but also to avoid any involvement. I saw a young lady tuck a small silver cigarette box into her bag, which I promptly retrieved, much to her fury. The house was filled with valuables. I knew we might need to call the police, but I didn't want to do it without telling Theo first. I thought I could get him to announce the party was over and tell people to leave himself—a face-saving gesture. No one had seen him. I went out to the pool. It was filled with partygoers, some had shed their clothes. I was at my wit's end and then someone, a man, told me he'd seen Theo heading in *the direction of the gazebo quite a while ago. I thought he must have arranged to meet Violet there as I hadn't seen her, either."*

"So this man saw you, too? Who was it?"

"I didn't know him, had never seen him before, and even though I begged the lawyer to put an announcement in all the papers seeking his help, nothing ever came of it.

"And then several people began shouting at me that Theo was in the gazebo and wanted me there. They seemed to think it was some kind of joke."

"And they were never questioned, either?"

"No."

"So you went after Theo—and found him." Ursula's voice trembled.

"Yes." Arnold put his hand briefly over hers. "Would that I had gone sooner."

"What can I do?"

"Nothing. You've been kind enough to listen." Arnold's expression was resigned. "It's not as horrid here for me as most. I've been teaching classes in all sorts of things from basic reading and arithmetic—many of the inmates never learned—to history. Civic groups donate books. We never know what we will get. As time has passed I've been granted certain privileges like seeing visitors without a guard, although you are my first."

"What about your classmates at Harvard? The professors? Surely they would take up your cause!"

"That's not how things work, Ursula. Again, it was wonderful of you to come, but I think you'd best not visit another time. This is no place for a young lady."

Ursula stood up. She'd tell her mother she'd taken a long walk, which was partially true, but even a lengthy promenade about the parts of town where she was permitted wouldn't have taken up this much time.

"I intend to return, Mr. Rowe—and I intend to get you out of here. The best way is for me to find out as much as possible about what really happened and present the facts to my father. He is a fair man and he would never want an innocent person to be unjustly confined. If need be, a judge will have to order a new trial."

Arnold Rowe shook his head slowly. "You make it all sound so easy. I'm afraid you are going to be terribly disappointed—and hurt."

"Perhaps—but I have to try. We know that Charles Winthrop was desperate for money and that Violet Hammond was, if not his fiancée at the time, about to be. They had every reason to lie. I'll say good-bye for now."

Arnold opened the door and the guard showed her out.

"Good afternoon, miss," he said.

Ursula walked down West Cedar Street toward her aunt's house on Louisburg Square. She felt as if she had passed from one world to another and was struck by how normal things looked in this one. The people she passed nodded and smiled slightly. The old, wavy amethyst glass in the windows of the Beacon Hill houses were unchanged, the brass door knockers and handles as bright as the day they were installed. The brick sidewalks uneven from years of use. Cars passed slowly. It was all as it had been before she'd rung the bell at the Charles Street Jail, but it would never be the same for her again.

Arnold Rowe had been framed. She was certain of it.

Her mother barely noted her tardiness and rushed her off to catch the train back to Aleford. On the way Ursula showed her the gloves and the purchase was met with approval. The motion of the train, the sound of the tracks, was soothing and for a moment Ursula allowed herself to feel happy. Arnold had looked a shadow of his former self—emaciated and deathly pale, but there was no pallor in his warm brown eyes or the smile that crossed his lips several times. She had found him; she was going to help him.

And she would start now.

Charles Winthrop had needed money right away. Theo hadn't had any to give him, nor was there any money in the house. As she'd walked back to her aunt's, Ursula had thought of something. She needed to ask her mother a question and the sooner the better.

"I know it's very hard to talk about Theo, Mother, but I've been thinking of him so much today. Perhaps, in part, it was being near the old house. I would like to have something of his as a keepsake. Would you and Father let me have the pocket watch Father gave him when he turned eighteen?"

It had been gold, and was a reward for not smoking or drinking.

Her mother looked very tired.

"In all the confusion of that night, some of his things were lost. We don't have the watch."

"Or his signet ring?"

All the Lyman men were given these rings with the family seal when they were confirmed.

"That was lost, too."

Ursula had her answer. It was as she thought.

The train was slowing down for the Arlington station. She watched the landscape come to a halt, but she wasn't seeing the town center, she was back in the gazebo caressing her brother's hands. His fingers were bare.

The ring was already missing.

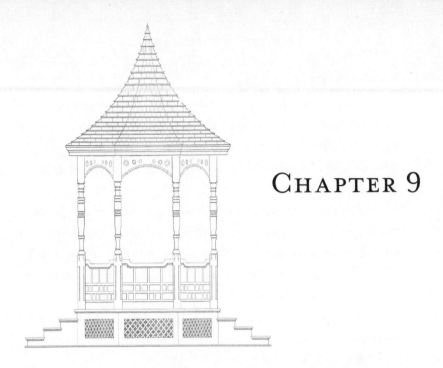

CHAPTER 9

"My greatest problem was figuring out how to go off to Martha's Vineyard for an entire day. I couldn't tell my parents. Finally the simplest solution was the most obvious one. I cut school."

Faith had been reeling from Ursula's account of her sixteen-year-old self marching up to the Charles Street Jail, gaining admittance, and embarking on an investigation to free a convicted murderer. And now this? Cutting school? This was the kind of thing people like Ursula, and her daughter, never, never did without at the least a gun to their heads.

"I told Mother that I was involved in a project that required my presence both before and after school. I would have to leave early and might be quite late. Mother was not particularly interested in academics, although she was a reader—she was quite fond of Mazo de la Roche's novels, and all she ever wanted as gifts were the newest Jalna and a box of Fannie Farmer chocolates. I knew she wouldn't ask me any particulars, so I told myself I wasn't really lying. I did have a project. A large one.

"We'd been in Aleford for some time, but I didn't know many people in town. Since I attended Cabot, not the public school, I knew I wouldn't run into any fathers on the train who might recognize me. In any case, I took a very early one before rush hour. I changed to the train for Woods Hole and the ferry in town. Before I boarded I called school. Mother and I had very similar voices and people often mistook us for each other on the phone. I simply told the secretary, Miss Mountjoy—you can imagine what fun the girls had about that name, especially since she always looked as though she'd received dire news and perhaps she had."

Ursula got back on track. "I said that Ursula would not be at school today, but would return tomorrow. She said, 'Thank you for calling, Mrs. Lyman,' and I hopped on the train."

At this point Faith was no longer reeling—nothing further would surprise her, she was sure—but had a strong sense that the nation had lost a valuable resource. FBI agent? Spy? G-woman?

"I had time to think on the ferry over. It was a beautiful spring day, so warm it could have been July. . . ."

Ursula stood on the deck watching the gulls circle overhead and wished she could be a little girl again on Sanpere sailing with Theo in his beloved catboat. It had been built on the island and he'd helped, a little boy himself at the time. Friends had much larger boats and Theo never turned down a chance to go "yachting," but she knew he was never happier than when he was in his own boat sailing down Eggemoggin Reach up into Jericho Bay.

The trip was taking longer than she'd remembered and her time on the Vineyard would be shorter than she hoped. She knew that neither Mary Smith nor Elias Norton had been live-in employees. Mary lived in Oak Bluffs with her family, happily not far from the ferry landing. She'd pointed the house out to her once when Ursula had received permission to walk into town with Mary, who was doing various errands for Mrs. Lyman. Ursula didn't know where Elias lived.

The salt air had dried her throat out and she walked quickly to the Smiths' house. Mary would give her a glass of water and they'd talk. Everything was going to be all right. Ursula closed her eyes for a moment. All morning she had steadfastly pushed any thoughts about the enormity of what she was doing from her mind, as well as any thoughts of failure.

Outside the tidy Cape, a young woman was weeding the front garden. Ursula started to speak, then, seeing her resemblance to Mary, signed instead. Her effort was returned with an appreciative smile. She was relieved to know that her signing skills were still intact. Mary and Elias had married and were living only a short walk away. There wasn't a cloud in the sky as she set off.

Even if it had been possible—if they had been able to hear and speak—Ursula would not have wanted to talk with them on the phone. Nor had she wanted to write to them. She had wanted to appear unannounced, wanted to present Arnold's case, her case, and gauge their reactions without their prior knowledge.

Mary opened the door, and the first thing Ursula noticed was that the woman's obvious surprise seemed more like fear. Elias stood behind his wife in the doorway. Neither of them moved or responded to Ursula's signed greeting. Ursula hadn't thought beyond finding them and getting them to tell her what they'd seen that night. That the couple might not want to cooperate, not agree to see her, simply hadn't occurred to her. She congratulated them on their nuptials. The well-wishes triggered a polite response. Mary invited her in and Elias stepped back, both still visibly ill at ease.

"Would you like tea, miss? Or something cold?" Mary signed.

"I'd love a glass of water, thank you," Ursula replied.

They both disappeared to what Ursula assumed was the kitchen in the back of the house. The parlor was small, spotless with a few cherished possessions on the mantel—a framed wedding portrait, a pair of brass candlesticks, and an iridescent glass vase filled with blue hyacinths.

When they returned, Ursula's heart sank at the look on Mary's face. The woman was blinking back tears and her hand shook slightly as she handed Ursula the glass of water. In contrast, Elias's face was blank, his mouth set in one firm line.

The only thing to do was start from the beginning and tell them everything—finding the newspaper articles, encountering the Winthrops in the department store, and finally her visit to Arnold in jail. Mary gave a gasp at this last piece of information and started to lift her hand, but dropped it back in her lap. Elias had sat impassively throughout Ursula's account. When she stopped signing and drank some water he stood up, firmly taking charge.

"We're very sorry about young Mr. Rowe, but we don't know what we can do to help him." He tapped Mary on the arm and she jumped up. No other kind of sign was necessary. The visit was over.

"Please," Ursula implored. "Please sit down again and just tell me what you saw that night in the woods. Arnold saw you both. You must have seen him, too."

"It was a long time ago. We talked to the lawyer fellows when it happened and it's all over now."

Mary's hands were clasped behind her back. Ursula stood up and signed her thanks. Despair slipped over her, threatening to engulf her completely, but she had to leave the house, get back to the ferry, and make her way home. At the door, she signed one last question.

"Is Mrs. Miles, the housekeeper, still on the island?"

A look of disgust crossed Mary's face, the expressive face Ursula remembered so well from their times together. Mary's emotions were always close to the surface.

"That one! A she-devil to work for and she took off that night for good. I haven't laid eyes on her since she went out the back door in her Sunday best before it was even dark, neither has anybody else."

Elias took Mary's hand and held it.

What did he want her to keep from saying, or was it a gesture of affection? Ursula wondered. She thought the former, and after wishing them well—she could tell Mary was expecting and, from the lack of any children's toys or things in the room, assumed it was their first—she went out the front door.

As soon as she heard the door close, Ursula darted around the side of the house. She was sure they would be discussing her visit and thought she might be able to see into the room from a side window, but Elias's green thumb had produced forsythia bushes and spirea in such abundance that it was impossible. She was about to give up and head for the landing when she heard steps on the back porch of the cottage. She had a clear view of the yard from where she stood and stepped farther into the cascading blooms, blessing them now for their protective cover.

Mary was carrying a basket of wash to hang on the line and Elias was following her, signing away like mad even though her back was turned. He reached out to stop her; she dropped the basket and began to sob. It was all Ursula could do to keep from running out to comfort Mary herself.

"Run after her, Elias. The ferry won't be leaving for a while. What we did was wrong!" she signed frantically.

"We didn't tell any lies."

"We didn't tell the truth, either." Mary wiped her eyes with her apron. "We saw that boy lying in the summerhouse as plain as day. You thought he'd passed out from drink. And we never checked! Somebody else was nearby in the woods, but we couldn't see. It wasn't Mr. Rowe, because we did see him close to where the path started at the house. He was running toward us and it was after we'd gone by Mr. Theo."

She stopped signing when she saw Ursula emerge. Elias seemed to be battling two warring instincts; his expression was tormented.

"I guess I know when the Almighty is trying to tell me something," he signed to Ursula. "All you told us, and your coming here today, was meant to be. We did see Mr. Rowe, but we don't know how your poor brother came to die and that's the truth. Let's go inside and sit down again. We'll tell you everything. If you miss the ferry, I'll run you over to the mainland in my skiff."

Tea appeared rapidly—and a plate of oatmeal cookies. As they sat in the parlor, Ursula remembered that Arnold's lawyer had said Mary and Elias would not be friendly witnesses. A better description would have been "terrified" ones.

Elias signed that the prosecutor had warned them that he would bring up what he imagined they had been doing off in the woods if they took the stand.

"It was a lie. I respected my Mary, but people want to believe the worst! He told us he'd make sure it got out and no one would hire servants with such low morals. It didn't matter how good we were at our jobs."

Ursula was shocked. She felt as if she had left the few remaining remnants of her childhood behind over the course of the afternoon, a childhood where, before Theo's death, she'd believed that all adults told the truth and nothing bad could happen to anyone she knew.

Mary looked tired, and Ursula told them she would be in touch. In fact, she didn't know what her next step would be, other than toward the ferry, which hadn't left. She hugged her old friend, now restored to her, and Elias went with her. As the ferry pulled away, he waved once.

She waved back and went to the prow of the Naushon. As she faced Woods Hole, crossing Vineyard Sound, the world seemed newly made and she imagined herself as a kind of figurehead—a sort of Winged Victory.

It was after dinnertime when Ursula walked into the house. She had planned to phone, but had just made both trains. Her mother rushed over to her.

"Ursula! Where have you been? We were just about to start calling around!"

"I've been to Oak Bluffs and I need to tell you why."

Her earlier exhilaration had left her and now she was exhausted.

Her father got up from his chair.

"Sit down. Have you eaten today? And I think a drop of brandy might be a good idea."

Mr. Lyman had thought the whole notion of the Thirty-second Amendment was misguided, making criminals out of otherwise law-abiding citizens. He wasn't much of a drinker himself, but saw no harm in keeping decanters of port and sherry as well as a bottle of brandy.

Ursula was not used to spirits and choked at the first swallow, but soon the alcohol's warmth suffused her body and she realized she was hungry. She made short work of the sandwich her mother brought.

It took a long time to tell her parents what had transpired and her mother had not wanted to hear any of it at first.

"It won't bring Theo back. Why stir things up again?"

"I'm sorry to disagree, Dorothea," Mr. Lyman said. "If what Ursula has been telling us proves to be true, we must do everything in our power to clear Arnold Rowe."

At midnight, Ursula knew she couldn't talk any more. Her mother had gone to bed with her usual Ovaltine and her father told her to go, too. He wanted to make some notes. While he believed her, he wasn't totally encouraging.

"I'm not sure how to proceed," he said. "The only evidence against Charles Winthrop is a young girl's recall of an extremely traumatic night. Lawyers for Winthrop would be able to easily discredit your testimony, questioning why you hadn't mentioned it at the time to anyone—the fact that you were ill and didn't know any of the particulars of the charges, or even the outcome of the case *against Arnold, will not make a difference, I'm afraid. They'd also bring up the notion of false memory after so many years. They will also"—Theodore Lyman hesitated—"put your motivation down to a schoolgirl's crush."*

Ursula started to protest.

"No, daughter. I believe you, but the Winthrops are a very powerful—and proper—family. They are not about to have it come out that their son was in debt to the worst sort of bootleggers and involved if not actually in committing the crime of murder, then in covering it up. Young Charles knew his actions, had they come out, would have resulted in his estrangement from the family— emotionally and financially."

On this note, he kissed her good night and told her not to set her alarm. He'd call the school to tell them she'd be late.

She thought she would have trouble falling asleep, but Ursula sank almost immediately into oblivion—sleep, the sweet escape.

"Ursula," Faith said, "this has been an amazing story. I know it has a happy ending"—she assumed they had reached it—"otherwise there wouldn't be a Pix or an Arnold junior. I wouldn't be sitting here, either."

"This part *did* have a happy ending, but it's not over. I'll explain shortly. To finish up about Arnold's imprisonment—Father consulted his own lawyer, William Lloyd, taking me with him. The next day both men went to the jail and spent a long time talking to Arnold. After that everything happened quickly. A judge in Dukes County ordered a new trial, but before they got to jury selection, Mr. Lloyd asked that the charge be dismissed in light of new evidence that exonerated his client beyond the shadow of a doubt. Of course it had all been worked out beforehand. Mary and Elias had been deposed, as was I. Arnold's full account was presented to the judge also. The charge was dropped and the case was left open: 'Murder by person or persons unknown.' It was hard on Mother. Not that she wanted Arnold in jail, but she had hoped that justice would be done. That Charles Winthrop would be punished—she'd come to believe he'd been responsible. But there wasn't enough evidence to arrest him. Both he and his wife stuck to their accounts of that night."

"And Arnold was freed right away?" Faith said.

"That very day. Father eventually found him a position as private secretary to a business acquaintance who was very open-minded—difficult to find any sort of job in those times and there was Arnold's incarceration, however mistaken."

"And what about you? It must have been hard to go back to Cabot after all these dramatic events."

"It was. I'd never felt very comfortable there. I missed my old school. By the time I graduated it was understood that Arnold and I would marry. It was merely a question of when. He came out to Aleford often at my parents' invitation. No one could ever take Theo's place, but they began to rely on Arnold for advice and I think he brought them a measure of comfort—he'd been so close to Theo. I know it did me.

"Things had improved somewhat for Father, but I knew that going to college would stretch their finances considerably. I went to Katie Gibbs instead and got a job as a secretary in a large law firm—lawyers seem to figure prominently in this tale. Arnold wanted me to go to college—Wellesley, in fact, where dear Samantha went. I told him he could be my college and he took the job seriously. He would have made a wonderful professor, but his life went in another direction. We were married quietly at The Pines on Sanpere on my nineteenth birthday. Arnold had risen in the firm and eventually became a partner, but that was much later. We wanted to be near my parents and bought this house. You know the rest—or most of it.

"The day Arnold was freed, he came to the house for dinner. At the beginning of the meal, Father gave thanks. We all said 'amen' and Father added that from then on, we would never talk about what had happened again. And we didn't."

"Not even with your husband?" Faith found this almost beyond belief. She knew New Englanders were tight-lipped, but this was taking things to a whole new level.

"I imagine it's hard for you to understand. You were raised in such a different time. It wasn't a guilty secret, but it wasn't something we wanted to trumpet from the rooftops. We needed to have a normal life again. When the children were born, we did discuss whether to tell them or not. We certainly wouldn't tell them when they were young, and by the time they were older, there didn't seem to be much point."

Yet they had arrived at a point now. The point where the story ended and its purpose began.

"What do you want me to do, Ursula?" Faith asked. "Be with you when you tell Pix? Or tell her myself? Perhaps with Tom, as well?"

Ursula shook her head. "Not yet. I can't think of that now. Go over to the window seat. There are two envelopes tucked underneath the cushion. The first arrived some weeks ago, just before I went to the hospital. The second more recently. Bring them here, if you would."

Faith removed the envelopes and gave them to Ursula, who handed one back.

"Please open it and look at what's inside."

Faith read the contents, glancing quickly at the newspaper clippings, focusing longer on the words on the single sheet of paper:

Are you sure you were right?

"And now this one." Ursula handed her the other envelope. It contained only the sheet of paper, apparently the same kind as the other. Again a single sentence:

You saw the knife in his hand.

"Do you know who's sending these? Why would—"
"Wait, dear." Ursula slipped a third envelope from her pocket, removed the letter, and handed it to Faith. Two lines this time:

Time will tell.
I'm waiting, but not for long.

"It came yesterday," Ursula said. "I've been expecting it."

Normally the Uppity Women's Luncheon Club was Niki's favorite gig. Years ago Sandra Katz, who lived in Aleford, decided that she had women friends she enjoyed being with who should get to know each other. What started out as a December holiday luncheon, which Have Faith catered, became an informal club meeting at various members' houses several times a year. The only rule was no cooking—no pressure to match or surpass a fellow Uppity's prior menu. For such a small gathering, only Faith or Niki needed to be there. After a while, it became clear that the women were getting a kick not just from Niki's great food, but her sense of humor, and it became her assignment.

The women were married, divorced, or never married. They ranged from stay-at-home moms to a college dean, and were all now somewhere in their forties. Sandra, who worked raising funds for nonprofits, was the unofficial president and the person who got in touch with the catering company. Thinking spring, Niki thought of eggs—hard-boiled on the seder plate, hard-boiled and colored in an Easter basket. That took her to the idea of breakfast for lunch. Before she was married, exhausted after working all day, she'd often had breakfast for dinner—crispy bacon, maybe a sausage, scrambled or poached eggs with toast. Faith and she had been experimenting with an eggy breakfast puff. The batter was poured over a peach or pear half placed in a ramekin, and when it looked like a golden-brown popover it was ready [see recipe, p. 250].

Sandra loved the idea of the puff, and Niki thought she'd add mini BLTs using turkey bacon with tiny grape tomatoes. She'd also put out a large bowl of fresh strawberries—they were coming in from Watsonville, California, now and delicious. She'd toss them with a little bit of sugar to release their juice and set separate small bowls of several flavors of yogurt—the Greek kind, of course—alongside. The Uppities wanted a salad, so she'd do a simple one of fresh spring greens with a lemon–poppy seed dressing—also on the side. Some of the Uppities were always doing Atkins, Pritikin, or the grapefuit or cabbage soup diet. Before they sat down to eat, she'd serve Kir Royales—crème de cassis and champagne—both alcoholic and non, with cheese straws. A mild cheese so as not to interfere with the taste of the drink.

There would be more cheese for dessert. Sandra had said they were celebrating their tenth anniversary together and she wanted a cake—a chocolate cheesecake. What she'd actually said was, "Screw carbs. This is a celebration and we all look pretty damn good. Besides, isn't chocolate supposed to be healthy now?"

Niki was with her on that one, and there *was* evidence that dark chocolate lowers both blood pressure and cholesterol, and it has eight times the number of antioxidants of some fruits, to protect the body from aging. The Uppities would appreciate this last tidbit of knowledge.

The food was packed and she was ready to leave. Should have left. Faith was at Pix's mother's house and Tricia was over at the Ganley café making sure everything was going smoothly there.

Niki slumped into one of the beanbag chairs Faith had placed in the play area for her kids. It felt great. Maybe she could just sit here, letting the chair cushion her, for the rest of her pregnancy. It was appropriate. She'd resemble a beanbag herself by the end of it.

She got up, locked the door, and set out for the job. She hoped the women wouldn't expect her usual "wit and charm"—a compliment passed on through Faith. She felt funny today, but not funny ha-ha.

Today's hostess lived in a beautifully restored Arts and Crafts house with a decidedly nonperiod kitchen. It didn't take Niki long to set up and another Uppity luncheon was launched. Going in and out of the dining room, she heard snippets of their conversation, which ranged from spouses to kids and a lot about politics in between—"My skipped period was early onset menopause! I was so relieved! The only diapers I want to change in the upcoming years are my grandchildren's!" and, "It's so nice when he's away. The bed's a snap to make and I can have a glass of wine and soup for dinner. But then if it's too long, I don't like it." And, "Honestly, if I talked to my mother the way she talks to me, I wouldn't have seen twenty." The dean had addressed the whole table at one point. "'Underachiever'! The boy's drag-ass lazy, but if I told his parents that, I'd lose my job in a heartbeat—plus we could kiss those all-important future donations good-bye. These days my job is ninety-nine percent fund-raising and one percent education."

The rhythm of their conversation, their lives, was ordinarily very comforting, but today Niki found herself feeling more and more depressed. What were she and Phil going to do? With a blatant view to the future offspring, both sets of parents had given the newlyweds the money for a down payment on a small house in Belmont. "Good schools," her mother had assured her. She'd memorized *Boston* magazine's annual ranking list. "And good property values." She'd bought that issue, too. But now they couldn't keep up the mortgage payments with what Niki alone made. In the past, various restaurant owners and chefs had offered her jobs that paid more money. She'd turned them down, cherishing not just the relationship she had with her boss, but the freedom she had to experiment with new things in the kitchen and her flexible work schedule. Three years ago, she'd taken several months off to travel, ending up in Australia and almost settling there. She knew that with the current economy the jobs she'd been offered before—and many of the restaurants—no longer existed. Even if she could tear herself away, it wasn't an option.

True, the cheesecakes were selling well, but woman cannot live by cake alone. At that thought, she lighted the numeral ten candle she'd stuck on the top of the cake and opened the door, singing "Happy Anniversary to You."

Sandra blew out the candle and Niki started to cut slices.

"I'll do that. Why don't you get the coffee, and Lisa, please get a chair so Niki can join us?"

Niki had been dreading this moment. Not joining them—she always did at the end—but the coffee.

"How about I serve and maybe someone else can bring in the pot?"

She'd plugged in the coffeemaker earlier and so far so good in the olfactory department. Pouring it out would be another matter.

Sandra raised an eyebrow. She'd never heard Niki say anything but "Sure" to a request.

"No problem, I'll get it. Why don't you sit here?"

Niki flushed and sat down at the head of the table, right in the limelight where she absolutely did not want to be.

"Great lunch as usual, Niki. I love that puff thing. Is it hard to make?" Pamela was tall and slender with the kind of short haircut that only the best stylist could deliver. She was a Wharton graduate. She and her husband had moved into town now that their children were out of the house. They lived in a condo at the Four Seasons and Niki was pretty sure Pamela's cooking nowadays was room service.

"It's very easy. I'll e-mail the recipe to anyone who would like it." Sandra returned with the coffee and started pouring.

"I know you want some, Niki. And you take just milk, right?"

"I'll pass today, thanks."

"On the milk?"

"No, the coffee."

"Okay." Sandra pulled the chair Lisa had brought in up to the table. "You've been looking like you lost your best friend since you got here. What's going on?"

"Nothing," Niki said, and started to add a further denial, but one of the other Uppities interrupted.

"Come on, sweetie. You know all our secrets and then some."

It was true. Over the years Niki had heard them unburden themselves to one another in sorrow and in joy.

She burst into tears.

"You're pregnant!" Sandra happily clapped her hands together. "The smell of coffee and hair-trigger hormones, oh Niki!"

"We'll make the next luncheon a shower," Pamela said. "I love to buy baby things, and given my daughter's track record with men, I'll be a grandmother at eighty."

"Is that biologically possible?" the woman next to her teased. "Isn't your daughter twenty-eight?"

"So, she'll adopt. I should only be so lucky."

It was inevitable. Niki found herself spilling her guts to the roomful of sympathetic women. "Spilling her guts" was an apt phrase, she thought, as a torrent of words spewed forth. She told them about Phil's losing his job and not wanting to burden him further with her news. And described how depressed she was feeling most of the time. During the rest, she was feeling nauseous.

She'd hardly finished when the Uppities whipped out their BlackBerries and iPhones, looking up contacts; making notes for themselves about Phil's qualifications; and entering how to reach him.

"You may have heard about the old boys' and old girls' networks," one said. "But they're nothing compared to the Uppity Women's."

This was the woman, Niki recalled, who had a bumper sticker on her Lexus that read, WOMEN WHO SEEK TO BE EQUAL TO MEN LACK AMBITION.

"Now you go home and tell Phil everything," she said. "It's time for you to start enjoying being pregnant. Not the morning-sickness part, but the rest—and believe me, there will be plenty of joy."

"Tell me about it," Pamela said. "I never got so much action. I was horny; he was horny. That's why pregnant women have such a glow."

"It was the big boobs that did it for my husband," Sandra said. "He went nuts."

This led to a few more comments on sex and a discussion about getting picked up at Trader Joe's, especially on Saturdays at the Sample Station.

"Forget Costco, it's all families, although there is stuff to try that you'd normally never eat—deep-fried pizza last time I was there. The Roche Brothers cheese counter is good, too. I love the come-ons, 'Do you think this Brie is ready—subtext, I am.' Even you married gals should give it a whirl; it's great for the ego."

Niki began to laugh so hard she had to make a mad dash for the bathroom to pee. This was beginning to happen a lot lately and she'd seriously considered getting those nonsenior Depends-type things that Whoopi Goldberg was advertising to keep from "spritzing."

They helped her clean up and sent her on her way. She decided to go directly home and bring the van back to work later. The Uppities should be cloned, she thought, and then changed her mind. She wanted to keep them all to herself.

"Who do you think is sending these?" Faith repeated her earlier question. She'd moved back to the window seat and had spread the letters out on the cushion.

It was still raining heavily, as it had been on and off for days. Every night the news showed footage of people near the swollen rivers being evacuated from their homes by Zodiacs and even canoes. Faith had received two reverse 911 calls from the Aleford police announcing road closures, and this morning she'd seen ducks swimming on her front lawn.

But it could have been brilliant sunshine and eighty degrees. Her mind was on the papers beside her.

"Who?" she repeated. "It has to be someone who saw your husband in the gazebo—and knows that you were there, too."

"Which most likely means it's one of the people who was staying in the house, although I suppose it could be any of the partygoers—the few still alive." Ursula shook her head. "Very unlikely. It just had to be said. No, it's one of the four, and easy to eliminate two of them. Charles Winthrop was older than the rest and I'm sure he's been gone awhile. I know that Schuyler—Scooter—Jessup died just after Arnold. His wife, Babs, is alive, however. We used to run into each other in town at the Chilton Club from time to time over the years, but of course we never mentioned that night."

Of course, Faith thought. Not the thing to do.

"Which leaves Violet Hammond, Violet Winthrop. The envelope has a New York City postmark and the Winthrops left Boston before the war so Charles could run the family's Manhattan office."

"How did you know? They wouldn't have kept in touch, would they?"

Ursula shook her head. "No—thank goodness. I didn't want anything to do with either of them, but I did want to know where they were, especially early on. I suppose I was nurturing notions of, well, revenge. I used to think I'd uncover some kind of evidence that would bring Charles to trial. As time passed, there were other things to think about, especially during the war years and after the children were born."

During the last few minutes, everything had become clear to Faith. The cause of Ursula's illness, the need to tell someone what she believed to be the truth, and now the kind of help Ursula wanted from Faith.

She was asking Faith to prove her husband's innocence—a task she thought she had accomplished almost seventy years ago. A closed book—until the letters arrived sowing their insidious seeds of doubt.

Yes, Ursula wanted Faith to solve Theo's murder, irrefutably.

"Tell me what you want me to do first."

"We don't have much time. I'd like to get this settled before Pix gets back, or near enough. And then, there's the implied threat in the third letter. I think I know what it means."

Faith did, too. "That the writer intends to use information about the crime to hurt you in some way? Knows, perhaps, that it was kept secret and plans a tell-all story, but where? I can't imagine the media would be interested in such old news."

"Nor can I, although it might make a splash for a while in the Aleford and Boston papers. And I wouldn't want to see my family's private affairs in the headlines." Ursula pursed her lips.

Faith knew that Ursula belonged to the school that believed a lady was only mentioned in the press three times: when she was born, got married, and at her death. No, she wouldn't like the notoriety at all.

"The writer means to go public in some way and I have to find out how. And find out what it is she believes happened that night.

Yes, she. It has to be Violet because of the postmarks—and I think she was a rather unscrupulous woman. She's a very old lady now and I suppose this is her idea of fun. She used to enjoy stirring things up—she was quite sarcastic, but that voice of hers tended to make even the meanest remark sound melodic. I don't know why she's waited so long to go after me—and my family. Perhaps something reminded her of that summer recently."

"All will be clear." Faith wished she felt as confident as she sounded. Ursula was asking the impossible—that Faith trace this old crime and unmask the culprit. Yet truth dealt with the possible, not the reverse, and Faith intended to do everything she could to reveal it.

"So," she said, "I'll find out where the old witch lives and go talk to her. Tell her to stop bothering you or we'll get some kind of restraining order. She *is* making threats."

Ursula nodded in agreement.

"She lives on East Seventy-second Street. I have the phone number."

"How did you get this? I thought four-one-one wouldn't give out an address."

"I didn't call information. I called that nice reference librarian Jeanne Bracken, and she got it for me. She said something about 'Googling' the name, but I think we had a bad connection because of all this rain. The wires must be soaked."

Faith decided there were more important things to discuss, but she made a mental note to explain to Ursula sometime that "Google" was not a form of baby talk.

"I could go Thursday, or maybe even tomorrow," Faith said. She could take the shuttle and if there was time swing by Zabar's on the West Side for deli.

"Thursday would be fine. And tomorrow, do you have time to pay a call on Babs Jessup? I have her address and phone number, too. If you agree, we could call now."

Faith was a little mystified.

"I thought you were sure that it was Violet Winthrop who is responsible for the letters."

"I am, but forewarned is forearmed. I have a feeling that Babs might tell you what Violet has been up to all these years. I don't think she liked Violet. In fact, I'm sure of it, but the Jessups and Winthrops were related."

"So she'd know?"

"Yes. Should we make the call now? Probably sometime in the morning would be best for her. She's an old lady, too. We all are—and that's generally when we feel the best."

Faith hated to hear Ursula refer to herself as an old lady.

"Anytime in the morning would be fine." She'd been mentally rearranging the next two days, who might pick Amy up for ballet, what to take out of the freezer for dinners.

The call was made and a woman who identified herself as Mrs. Jessup's companion told Ursula eleven o'clock would be a good time. After she hung up, Ursula reported the companion had said that Mrs. Jessup enjoyed visits and would be delighted to meet Mrs. Rowe's friend. Faith was all set.

Phillip Theodopoulos was sitting in the little room off their bedroom, which they'd made into an office. He was hunched over his computer at the desk and didn't hear Niki come in. She put her arms around his neck from behind his chair and he started in surprise.

"Hi, honey. How'd it go? Fun with the Uppities?"

He always enjoyed hearing her accounts of these luncheons, even though at times he felt like a target, along with the rest of the male sex.

"Not just fun. I have three things to tell you. First, I saved you a big slice of cheesecake—chocolate hazelnut. Second, the Uppity

Women's network is on the job, or rather going to find you a job. I'm a little surprised your phone hasn't rung yet."

She hugged him tighter.

"And the third?"

"You're going to be a dad."

CHAPTER 10

Standing at the front window, Faith pulled the drape farther to one side so she could watch Amy get on the bus. Mothers with younger children were gathered at the stop. Faith wished she could join them, but that would only make Amy more of a target—"Kindergarten Baby Amy has to have her mommy walk her to the bus" or some other taunt. The bra had offered an enormous amount of support—psychological, not physical. Amy marched out each morning, chest—what little there was—forward, a smile on her face. If she'd known the song, Faith imagined her daughter would have been belting out "I Am Woman." Time to teach it to her.

The bus stopped, the children got on, and Faith turned away. Amy had moved and was now sitting in the front seat. She said the teasing had stopped. Faith wasn't complacent. Mean girls were devious and sometimes smart. They'd find something new, or someone. The school was implementing a more current antibullying curriculum. That would help. And meanwhile, she would continue to ask her daughter how her day had been much more thoroughly.

Amy looked like a child—long, straight fine hair the color of good butter; eyes the color and sheen of wild blueberries. She was growing fast and it was a pleasure to watch her move on the sports field and off. She loved to dance. Yet Amy wasn't going to stay a child for long, especially not in twenty-first-century America where the media was constantly bombarding kids with messages to grow up fast, inventing a whole new market: "tweens."

Her appointment with Babs Jessup—Mrs. Schuyler Jessup, she corrected herself, picturing a Beacon Hill grande dame—was not until eleven. She'd drive to the Alewife T, where she could park the car and take the Red Line to the Charles Street stop near Beacon Hill—an impossible place to park.

It was too early to leave, so she put in a wash and changed sheets. At nine the phone rang. It was Tom.

"Albert just called. He's picked up some sort of bug and won't be in today. He said it's not bad. He just needs a day or two. The thing is, I know he meant to take a folder home with him yesterday that has articles he's collected on how to make the church greener. He's preparing a report for the congregation's consideration."

"I assume by 'greener,' you mean a paperless newsletter and toilet paper recycled from grocery bags or what-have-you."

Tom laughed. It was good to hear.

"Yes. No plans to repaint our pristine white clapboard. Anyway, could you drop it off at his place on your way? I'm sure he'd be very grateful and you know how conscientious he is. He'd hate to waste time even while recuperating. This would give him something to read in bed."

Faith quickly rearranged her plans. She'd have to leave a little sooner and park in the garage under Boston Common after she dropped off the folder in Cambridge.

"I'll come and get the folder in a few minutes."

"Meet you halfway in the cemetery?"

"Oh Reverend Fairchild, you do say the most romantic things!"

It all seemed to be coming to a close. Tomorrow Faith would fly to New York and confront Violet Winthrop. Given the woman's age, it would have to be done gently, but given the woman's actions, firmly. Faith had called her sister, Hope, and made a tentative arrangement to meet for coffee in the late afternoon before returning north. This was still Ursula's story, not hers, so she'd alluded vaguely to having to meet with someone on the Upper East Side. Hope was born with a client-confidentiality gene and never pried—not overtly anyway.

Sam Miller would be back tonight and was coming straight to the parsonage from the airport. Pix was leaving Charleston—reluctantly from the sound of recent conversations—on Friday morning.

The rain had finally stopped.

She was driving down Route 2 toward Cambridge. Magic 106.7 FM was playing Dan Fogelberg's "To the Morning." What kind of a day was it going to be? Faith wondered, listening to the words of the lyrics. She felt more optimistic than she had since Tom had come home from the emergency meeting of the vestry called by Sherman Munroe. The man himself, or his name, had been popping up ever since. Was he the "shoulder surfer" or other kind of hacker? Was it all a setup to get rid of a minister he didn't like? Church politics were never pretty. Yet, why not confront Tom directly if he was dissatisfied? Of course, Faith imagined Sherman was always dissatisfied and probably always devious. She realized that he was a man who enjoyed manipulating others, and reveled in his own power. This may all have been a game to him; one he thought he couldn't lose. Everything remained unresolved. And Tom would always have the implicit accusation hanging over his head. The vestry had wanted to avoid police involvement from the first—dirty linen and all that. Thank goodness Sam would arrive soon. He might insist the authorities be informed and a proper investigation conducted.

The song was ending. *There is really nothing left to say but / Come on morning.* A beautiful voice. A beautiful song. Faith hummed the tune and thought, Okay, come on, morning.

Albert had lived off Kirkland Street near Harvard Square since moving to the Boston area. Miraculously Faith found a place to park. She'd never been to his apartment, and when she went up the front steps, she realized that there was no way to leave the folder in an entryway or tucked behind a storm door. Both substantial outer and inner doors were locked. She pushed the buzzer next to his name and waited by the intercom. It was a nice brick building, and obviously secure. She'd never given much thought to where he lived, but was a little surprised at how nice the building was. The rent would have been high for a student, although he was making a decent salary now. Maybe he had roommates, although his was the only name listed. She rang again. He must be asleep. She hated to get him out of bed when he wasn't feeling well, but Tom had seemed to think Albert wanted the material. She gave it one more try and called Tom.

"Albert's not answering the bell. Did you call him?"

"I did, but he wasn't answering the phone, either, so I left a message on his machine. I figured he was asleep, or maybe in the bathroom."

Faith didn't want to dwell on the possibility of stomach flu.

"Give me his number and I'll try."

"Okay, and if he still doesn't answer, look and see if his car is there, although I can't imagine he'd go out. He has a parking place next to his apartment and you know the car."

Faith did, as did her kids. They wanted a Mini Cooper just like Albert's, complete with the Union Jack roof.

"All right."

The phone rang four times before the machine kicked in. Faith told him she was leaving the packet for him propped up against the door. It wouldn't be seen from the street, and didn't contain anything of value. Rain wasn't predicted, and if it did shower, the porch had a roof. She hung up and went around to the side of the building. The only car there was a Honda Civic of a certain age. From the look of the tire pressure, it had been there awhile.

There was a small yard enclosed by wire fencing and the other side of the building was separated from the next by an alleyway. No room for cars. She walked up the street to Broadway. No sign of the Mini Cooper. She walked the other way to Kirkland. Nothing there, either. She called Tom again.

"Are you sure he said he was home?"

"Absolutely. This is very odd. Do you think he had to go to the doctor's, or even the hospital?"

"I wouldn't start to worry yet," Faith said. "He told you it wasn't serious. Do you have his cell?"

"No," Tom said slowly. "I've asked him several times—in case I need to get him in an emergency—but he's been kind of funny about it. I've had the feeling he didn't want me to know."

It was a little past ten o'clock. She had an hour to get to Beacon Hill.

"I'll talk to you later, sweetheart. Stay by the phone, okay?"

"Faith, what's going on? Where—"

She switched her phone off and got in her car. Albert was definitely not home and Faith had an idea where he might be instead.

Albert Trumbull's Mini Cooper was parked on Cameron Street in front of Lily Sinclair's apartment. Faith didn't know whether to feel glad that she'd been right or sad that she'd been right. She pulled up next to it and called Tom.

"Honey, I think you should come and have a chat with Albert. I'm at Lily's apartment in Somerville and his car is parked in front."

She could hear Tom's sigh over the phone.

"Maybe he loaned it to her while he was sick?"

A person could drown clutching at straws, Faith thought. She also thought it was time for her too-nice husband to get tough.

"I doubt it and I doubt he's making some kind of pastoral call. If you want me to check it out, I'll go see. But Tom, get going now. You need to talk to him. To them. Call it a hunch."

"But Albert?"

"Tom!"

"Okay. I'm leaving."

Faith double-parked, deciding to take her chances on getting a ticket. She might get lucky even if the Somerville police did cruise by. The Mini was so small that her Subaru wagon looked like someone had inexpertly parked too far from the curb. She sat for a moment. Faith trusted her hunches, but she realized she might be able to get some confirmation if Zach was available. She dialed his number.

"Hey, what's up? We're still on for Saturday, right?"

Zach was coming out to go over the security programs on their computers.

"Saturday is still fine. I was wondering if you could take a quick look at a Facebook page for me? Her name is Lily Sinclair."

"Sounds like someone working in a gentlemen's club. It's real?"

"Oh yes."

Lily had been enrolled at the Div School. Despite what Zach thought, "Lily Sinclair" couldn't be an alias.

"Here she is. Not bad. And her face isn't, either."

"Zach!"

"Just kidding. Actually she looks very nice. Cool taste in music."

"Just tell me if there are any photos or comments about a boy-friend."

"Would his name be Al? And would he be an Anglophile—his Mini Cooper has a British flag painted on the roof?"

"Yes, and yes. You're a doll. Thank you so much! See you Saturday."

"I take it you don't want me to friend her?"

"Absolutely not."

A hunch had just become a fact. She got out of the car.

Before she rang the bell, she took a look around. The double-decker backed onto another the next street over. It was attached to its neighbor on one side and separated from a single-family dwelling by a narrow driveway on the other. She'd blocked Albert's car in, but he could still leave from the back door and get to the street down the drive. She pictured herself chasing him into Davis Square and hoped it wouldn't come to that. Not only would she feel ridiculous, but she didn't have the time.

She rang the bell and heard steps in the hall.

"I'm coming, hon. Silly girl, you left your keys on the table."

The door opened wide, and while Mr. Trumbull, sometime divinity school student and administrator at the First Parish church in Aleford, was registering extreme surprise at seeing his boss's wife on the doorstep, said wife stepped across the lintel and closed the door behind her.

"Tom's on his way. We need to talk. Lily out for coffee? Or something else to cure what ails you? By the way, glad you're feeling better."

Albert was wearing pajamas—pale blue cotton ones like the kind Brooks Brothers sold. Faith didn't think young men wore these, opting instead for more casual nightwear or nothing specific. Albert had frozen in place. The only thing moving was his mouth and this was opening and closing like a fish out of water desperately gasping for air.

"Why don't we sit down over here while we wait for Tom—and Lily?" Faith wasn't worried anymore that Albert might try to take off. She was, in fact, wondering if she could get him to move into the living room and sit on what she recognized as an Ikea couch and one of their Poang chairs. She gave him a little nudge and he shuffled into the room, collapsing on the couch.

"I . . ." He stopped and didn't start again, just rubbed his hand over his eyes and bowed his head. Faith hoped he was praying. He needed to.

She got up, went into the hall, and opened the front door, leaving it ajar. She wasn't counting on Lily to be as docile as her boyfriend. This way, having forgotten her keys, Lily would think Albert had left the door open for her while he was getting dressed. If Faith answered when Lily rang, she would most likely make a run for it.

Faith returned to the living room and looked at Albert closely. Definitely bed hair. They sat in silence for what seemed like a very long time. Faith didn't want to start without Tom—or Albert's significant other.

"Where is Lily?"

"Starbucks," he whispered.

"What is she getting?"

"Iced mochas and apple fritters."

Faith nodded. The mocha might be a little sweet, but she'd suffer. No way was Albert getting it. He could have the fritter, though. Unless Tom was peckish. Faith had pretty high standards for fritters.

"Where are you? Why is the door open?"

Lily was home.

"In here," Albert said hoarsely. Maybe he did have a sore throat. Faith resolved not to get any closer. "Mrs.—" Once more Albert clammed up, but this time it was because Lily interrupted him.

For a moment Faith thought the young woman was going to toss the cardboard tray holding the drinks and pastry at her.

"I knew you'd figure it out. Your sanctimonious prig of a husband couldn't in a month of Sundays! And, you." She whirled around and took several steps toward Albert. Faith was hoping she'd get close enough for Faith to snatch a coffee. She needed it. "You probably told her everything."

Albert cowered. Faith had never actually seen anyone do this, but that's what it was. He put his arms above his head and folded himself into a sitting fetal position.

His behavior had an immediate effect on Lily. She put the tray down on the floor, sat next to Albert, and threw her arms around him.

"My poor baby! Has she been horrible?"

The bell rang and Faith sprinted to the door. She didn't trust Lily not to disappear with her "baby" into the kitchen or elsewhere, barricading them both in. The woman was in tigress mode. The look she'd shot at Faith bore the promise of much harm, bodily harm.

Tom had his hand raised to ring again. She didn't want to think how fast he must have been driving, although Aleford wasn't that far from Somerville, a straight shot out Route 2.

"It's been Lily and Albert all the time," Faith said, "and I've only got five minutes before I have to leave for my appointment with Mrs. Jessup. Come on." She pulled him into the living room, skirting the Starbucks tray. The ice in the coffee was no doubt melting, but Faith had changed her mind. She didn't like mochas that much anyway.

"Why don't you tell me what's going on, or rather what's been going on." Tom addressed the two of them. He looked very tired and very stern.

Lily released Albert and he sat up straighter.

"It was all my idea. Albert has nothing to do with it." She looked a lot like Sydney Carton approaching the guillotine.

"I'm assuming you're talking about taking the money from the church's account."

Albert's face was ashen. He croaked out, "It wasn't just Lily. I'm equally to blame. More so." He cleared his throat; his next words came out louder and stronger.

"You shouldn't have treated Lily the way you did, Tom. Talked to her the way you did. It wasn't fair. She was just trying to do her job, and in my opinion, she was doing a damn fine one!"

"Wait a minute." Faith hated to leave, but she had to get going. Before she did, she needed to inject a little reality into the situation.

"The two of you stole ten thousand dollars from the church, cast the blame on an innocent person, and somehow it's my husband's fault?"

It was Lily's turn.

"You bet it is! We wanted to turn the tables on him. See how he felt being treated like a criminal. And aside from what he did to me—I was committed to my calling before he sowed all those seeds of doubt—the parish needed to see that their emperor had no clothes. He's fooled parents into thinking he's so in touch with their kids, but he has no idea what's going on with them and the issues they have. I heard that his own kid was in trouble at school, too. The way Tom is alienating the younger generation, his sainted First Parish is going to find itself without a congregation when all his suck-ups die off. And he had no right to rake *me* over the coals. I have a father who does that!"

Seeing the look that passed between Tom and Faith, Lily added, "And don't start with any psychobabble. This has nothing to do with what's happened between my father and me. It's all Tom's fault. Period."

During Lily's diatribe, the Reverend Thomas Preston Fairchild had turned beet red. Faith had seen him lose his temper a few times. It was scary. When Lily had mentioned Ben's trouble at school, Faith thought Tom was going to explode, but he'd waited. Steam rising from the center of Vesuvius, but not the main event. That was coming now. He was going to lose it. And he did. For the next few minutes the "sanctimonious prig" let Albert, still cowering, and Lily, suddenly sobbing, have it. About the laws of man, and yes, God, that they had broken. About their self-centeredness. About the betrayal of their calling, and on and on.

"We didn't spend the money," Lily interrupted at one point.

Faith had been wondering about this. Starbucks was pricey, but Albert had had the car before the thefts and Lily wasn't shopping on Newbury Street, except maybe at the Second Time Around. What had they done with the loot?

Albert brightened. "Yes, it's all here. In an envelope with the withdrawal slips under Lily's mattress. We'd always intended to give it back."

Tom blew up again. The lava flow wasn't quite as monumental as before, but still very impressive, fed by the force of the anguish he and Faith had suffered over the last twelve days. The idea that they had been toying with his life—with the life of his church—was intolerable. Under the mattress, indeed!

Reluctantly Faith took her leave as Tom was calling Sam. It was like skipping out before the last act of a play, a play like *The Mousetrap*. Tom would tell her about it later. She couldn't keep Mrs. Jessup waiting. She couldn't let Ursula down. Not at this point.

Mrs. Schuyler Jessup was wearing a daffodil-yellow nubby wool suit over a delphinium-blue and white striped silk blouse. Faith was immediately reminded of the flowers she'd seen as she walked from the Common to the Mt. Vernon Street address. Everything bloomed earlier in Boston and it had been a nice reminder of what was to come in Aleford.

Introductions were made and Mrs. Jessup instructed Faith to call her "Babs."

"My family called me 'Babby' for many years, but I put a stop to that when I married Scooter. It was bad enough being Babs and Scooter. Will you have coffee or tea?"

Faith hesitated. From the look of the room—the export porcelain, Chippendale and Sheraton furniture, damask upholstery, walls crammed with artwork collected by many generations—she was sure the tray would be loaded down with the appropriate sterling vessels. If she chose coffee and Babs normally had tea, the companion, a pleasant-looking, slight middle-aged woman hovering at the door, would never be able to carry it all.

"If you're wondering what I take, it's coffee. I know 'elevenses' is a British custom, but I've never been a tea drinker. Besides, there's all that fuss with strainers, lemon slices, and extra hot water pots."

"Coffee is fine—it's what I prefer, too."

Entering the room, Faith had been struck by the thought that ninety really is the new seventy when it came to Ursula and now the woman before her. She recalled that Babs had been described as athletic in her youth and she looked as if she were still scoring below par. Her spine was ramrod straight and the only softness evident were her skin and snowy white curls, kept away from her face by a headband that picked up the blue in her blouse. She was wearing pearls the size of pigeon eggs.

Coffee and a plate of tasty-looking macaroons arrived. The companion poured out and then discreetly disappeared.

"I'm sorry to hear that Ursula has been ill. Our families knew each other, but I'm afraid we lost touch when the Lymans moved out west."

If Faith hadn't known Babs was referring to Aleford, a twenty-minute drive, she would have assumed the woman meant the Territories.

"She's on the mend and I'm sure will make a full recovery."

"There. We've taken care of all the niceties, so why don't you tell me what she's sent you to see me about?"

Faith had been afraid she'd have trouble changing gears from larceny to murder. The present to the past. Driving over, she'd been euphoric—and furious. She'd called Tom as she was walking down Charles Street. Sam was sending one of the firm's associates over. No crime had been reported, so Tom couldn't call the police in at this point, nor did he want to—however, a crime had been committed. He didn't know how to proceed. Sam was trying to get on an earlier flight and meanwhile had told Tom to stay put. Lily and Albert were definite flight risks. The associate would be reinforcement, and a witness. Tom told her that Albert had stopped cowering and started crying. He was continuing to break into tears at regular intervals. Lily, however, had regained her composure and had refused to say anything further except to call Tom several names that were not going to help with Saint Peter, should she get that far. The scene was pretty much what Faith had thought it would be.

At the Jessup house, the turmoil of the morning receded the moment she'd stepped into the downstairs hall and walked up the curved stairs, the mahogany banister soft and gleaming after centuries of use. By the time she was ushered into the sun-dappled living room, Faith was imagining herself stepping into a Henry James novel or Marquand's *The Late George Apley*.

"It has to do with the death of Ursula's brother, Theo."

Babs put her cup down. "We loved Theo. He was my husband's best friend. Scooter never got over his death. We were so young and this sort of thing had never happened to us—I mean, a tragic accident, a death, illnesses. Those were supposed to come later in life, and at that point we didn't think past the next week."

"You do know what happened afterward? About the way Arnold Rowe was cleared?"

"Oh yes. I must confess that I didn't really notice Ursula much at the Vineyard. She was just Theo's little sister, although now the age difference scarcely matters. At the time, there was a great deal of talk about the way she marched into the jail and some people were rather scandalized. It all died down quickly. There was other, bigger news during those Depression years and then the war."

Faith went on to tell her about the letters and handed over the copies she'd made for Babs to read herself. She handed them back, holding the papers in her fingertips as if they were contaminated with something.

"I'm afraid I still don't understand why you're here. Pleasant as it is. What does Ursula want?"

"Any information you might have about Violet Winthrop. That's who she thinks is sending these. She doesn't know anything about her, or her husband, except that he was transferred to New York some time in the thirties. I'm going to New York tomorrow to speak with her."

Babs gave a wry smile. "And since, unfortunately, we are related by marriage, I'm the one to fill you in."

"Yes. We're trying to figure out why she might be doing this. Ursula thinks it could be boredom. I'm not so sure."

"And you would be right, knowing Violet. I doubt it's that simple. Let's get some hot coffee. I need another cup and it's time for some sandwiches." She pressed a spot in the design on the Oriental rug and the companion appeared so quickly she must have been sitting near the door. She said she'd brew some fresh coffee and bring another tray, whisking away the one on the table in front of Babs.

The old lady settled back in her chair. Faith noticed a malacca cane next to it, the only indication that Mrs. Jessup needed help getting around.

"Tell me about yourself while we're waiting. I know your husband is a minister. I'm afraid I would have been quite inadequate as a clerical spouse. For one thing, I have a tendency to laugh in church."

Babs was a kindred spirit and Faith soon had her laughing with stories of Faith's life.

The sandwiches were egg salad, freshly made, with a little chive, on sourdough—not the usual WASP equivalent of Wonder bread with the crusts removed. More coffee was poured and Babs started talking about Violet Winthrop, née Hammond.

"She was quite a piece of work. I disliked her intensely and we were thrown together quite a bit because Theo was madly in love with her, as was Charlie Winthrop. Neither of them would have married her. She was a fling, and common sense, plus family pressure, would have prevailed. I still don't know how she managed to get Charlie to propose, but he did, very shortly after Theo was killed. Perhaps he was feeling his own mortality. And Violet was extremely beautiful. It was something to walk down the street with her. People, men and women both, would stop to stare at her. And oh, how she loved the attention.

"She had been considered fast at school. I think it was Miss Porter's, maybe Rosemary Hall. My mother wasn't happy about my going around with her, but I told her I couldn't very well not, since Scooter was such good friends with the men she dated. Mother needn't have worried and I told her so. Violet liked men. Period. She didn't have, or want, girlfriends. She certainly wouldn't have had any influence over me. We were both females, yes, but chalk and cheese—you can decide which was which. This doesn't help you, though. Ancient history.

"They moved to New York soon after they were married. It was a small wedding at her people's out in Chicago. Charlie wasn't terribly bright and he was in the way in the office here, according to one of our Winthrop cousins. The New York office had a

spot for him where he couldn't cause much damage. Essentially
it was a place to go every day—the family taking care of one of
its own. The Winthrops did make rather a lot of money during
the war years and he came in for a great deal of it just by being
one. There's a daughter, Marguerite. Charlie wanted Scooter to
be her godfather, but I told him absolutely not. I think he said
he was an agnostic or something and wouldn't do a good job. It
wouldn't have fooled anybody else, but probably fooled Charlie,
who wouldn't have paused to consider that at the time Scooter
was a junior warden at church. There were no other children and
Marguerite never married to my knowledge. Charlie died many
years ago and the last I heard mother and daughter were still living
in the same town house they'd been living in at his death. On the
East Side somewhere. You have to understand, I didn't just dislike
Violet because she was always quite awful to me—made me feel
like a kind of freak because I enjoyed sports, terrible catty remarks
about my muscular calves. Those things hurt when you're young
and insecure. No, I also disliked her because I thought she was
completely amoral. No heart. However you want to put it. She
used people. The only person she cared about was herself. Poor
Charlie."

And poor Theo, Faith thought, and said, "This helps a great
deal." They hadn't known about Marguerite Winthrop. Could she
be responsible for the letters?

"Although," she said, "I still don't know why she, or perhaps
her daughter, would decide to torment Ursula at this point. Malicious mischief? She wants some kind of last thrill?"

"Dear Faith, don't kid yourself. Violet did a lot of things for
thrills, but I doubt this is her object now."

"Then what?"

"Money, of course."

"Ursula and I talked about the possibility that it was blackmail
of some sort, that the letters were veiled threats to bring the whole

thing up again. But she's a wealthy woman. Why would she need money?"

"Not 'need,' 'want.' When you go to see her, how about a little wager that she has one of those needlepoint pillows with YOU CAN NEVER BE TOO RICH OR TOO THIN on it."

It was a sucker bet. Faith politely declined and, after a heartfelt promise to visit again, took her leave. She had a great deal to think about.

There was a time when flying had been fun. That time was long past. First there had been a long wait in the security line, then a further wait when someone's laptop case strap got caught in the conveyer belt, bringing everything to a halt, and finally a wait by the gate while the plane—late arriving—was serviced. The wad of gum below the window and crumpled napkins at her feet were evidence to the contrary, but Faith didn't care. She just wanted to get to the city.

With only her handbag, she was out of the terminal quickly and grabbed a cab. Despite her errand, her spirits lifted as soon as she saw the familiar skyline. She was home.

It was odd to drive past her family's apartment ten blocks north of her destination. Her parents were in Spain, a rare vacation that presaged more, longer ones. For some time now, her father had been urging the congregation to form a search committee and engage an interim. "I may have to actually quit in order to make them realize I can't keep being their minister forever." Jane Sibley, a real estate lawyer, had gone part-time some years ago. She was urging her husband to retire, as were his daughters. Faith was happy they were away. The last time she'd seen them her mother looked wonderful, as always, but her father looked extremely tired. He'd never bounced back after a serious heart attack several years ago. While she understood how hard it would be for the church to let go of their longtime leader, she was entertaining thoughts of standing outside a Sunday service leafleting the congregation with a letter begging them to let him leave.

She'd called Hope when the plane had landed and they were meeting at the Viand coffee shop on Madison, not far from the Winthrops' town house. Faith was in need of an egg cream, that quintessential New York delicacy consisting of U-Bet (and only this brand will do) chocolate syrup, very cold milk, and very fizzy seltzer. No eggs involved. It went very well with Viand's pastrami sandwich—not to be compared with Katz's, but that was too far downtown.

As soon as she was finished with Mrs. Winthrop, and perhaps Miss W. would also be there, Faith was to call Hope. She put her number on the screen and activated her iPhone's GPS tracker, In-staMapper, which Hope had insisted she install and was now in-sisting she use. It would allow the mistress of time management to schedule her arrival at the coffee shop to coincide with her sister's arrival there, thus not wasting a minute of Hope's billable hours.

Faith had called the Winthrop house from Ursula's on Wednes-day and left word on an answering machine that Mrs. Rowe was not able to come herself, but someone else representing her would arrive on Friday morning and to please call back if it was not con-venient. There had been no call.

Faith paid the cabdriver and approached the house with some trepidation. Compared to the others on the block, the place looked shabby. The evergreens in the large urns on either side of the front door were dry and most of the needles brown. The brass knocker and door handle needed polishing. The door itself could use a fresh coat of paint.

Noting that she seemed to be arriving unannounced often lately, Faith pushed the bell. She hadn't given her name when she'd called; she wasn't sure why, but the whole enterprise seemed to call for anonymity—and even stealth.

She could hear a chime sound faintly within. She waited and pushed again. Nothing. She stepped back and looked at the façade. All the drapes were drawn. Perhaps they were away. Perhaps she should have called from the airport. The house certainly looked unoccupied. As she was considering whether or not to stay, she saw one of the drapes twitch. Someone was peering out a second-floor window. She stepped back and rang again.

The intercom crackled.

"Yes? Who is it?" The voice was firm and clear.

"My name is Faith Fairchild. I'm here on behalf of Ursula Rowe."

"Her daughter?"

"No, but like one."

Faith wanted to establish her bona fides.

The door buzzed and she opened it, stepping into a large foyer tiled in black and white marble. It was hard to see the pattern, however, because of all the mail, junk and otherwise, strewn about.

"Well, don't just stand there. We've been expecting you."

The voice came from the back of the house. Faith walked toward it through a dining room, the furniture covered with dust so thick it would have provided hours of scribbling pleasure for a child. Several botanical prints hung on the wall, which also showed the outlines of other artwork that had been removed. The room smelled musty.

"We're in here. Come on." The voice was impatient.

"Here" turned out to be the kitchen and the disorder continued. Empty cans of cat food were piled in one corner and the sink was filled with dirty dishes. There was a small patio beyond a pair of French doors and the only light in the room was coming through the grimy glass. Faith, endowed with the native New Yorker real estate instinct, immediately began to see the place scrubbed clean, staged, and up for sale, calculating the price as she looked about for the house's owner. It took a moment to distinguish the human occupants from the cats, as both looked gray with tangled coats. In the case of the nonfelines, the coats were layers of sweaters and hair that badly needed cutting—and washing. One of them stood.

"I'm Marguerite Winthrop and this is my mother, Mrs. Charles Winthrop," she said regally. Faith wasn't sure whether to extend her hand or curtsy. In the end she did neither, but took the chair Marguerite had indicated.

Apparently, however, it was Violet's show.

"I knew Ursula would have to respond." It was the same voice Faith had heard over the intercom. Faith tried to hold her temper. She thought of what the letters had done to Ursula. The crone in front of her suddenly reminded her of Sherman Munroe. Both their voices were filled with smug entitlement. That whatever they did would always have been justified merely by who they were.

"Mrs. Rowe was literally made ill by your letters. If you don't stop sending them, we intend to seek legal action."

Violet laughed. It was a deep, throaty laugh and Faith thought if she closed her eyes, she might see the beautiful young woman Violet had been. The woman whose voice sounded like money, like Fitzgerald's Daisy Buchanan. There were also traces of a younger Violet beneath her rather grotesque makeup—a slash of red lipstick, purple eye shadow, powdery white foundation, and dark brows that had been penciled on in thin, surprised half-moons.

"Did you hear that, Marguerite? Little Ursula is threatening me with legal action. I suppose I should be quite terrified."

Faith stood up. "This is obviously a waste of time. Mine, that is. I don't know why you sent those hateful letters, but this is not a threat. If you send more, or attempt to contact Mrs. Rowe in any way, we will get a restraining order."

"I believe the only one being restrained will be you. Now, Marguerite!"

Marguerite grabbed Faith and shoved some kind of cloth over her face. The woman was surprisingly agile and all those sweaters were concealing a strong body. Warm sweaters. Faith was feeling very warm herself. Very, very warm. Her body was on fire. She tried to pull off whatever it was Marguerite was holding over her nose and mouth. It had a sickeningly sweet smell. I have to breathe! I have to get away from these women! From this house! were Faith's last thoughts for some time.

When she slowly became conscious again, she was indeed restrained—tied securely to the chair with ropes and bungee cords. Her vision cleared. The two women were drinking something from mugs advertising a local blood bank. She hoped the liquid was tea or coffee.

"Ah, you're back," Violet said.

After trying to move, Faith discovered her ankles were tied to the front chair legs and her arms, extended straight down, were pinned to the back ones. Her hands were free and she could move her fingers. Not that this did her any good. She had no idea how long she'd been out and she had a foul taste in her mouth. Her head ached.

"As soon as you feel you've recovered—it shouldn't be long, we practiced with the chloroform on each other—you're going to call Ursula and suggest a trade. What was the amount, Marguerite?"

"We thought a hundred thousand dollars was a nice round number."

"Of course," Violet said. "We want it transferred directly into our bank account here. Ursula was so thoughtful sending you on a weekday when all this business can be taken care of quickly. We were afraid it would be a weekend, which would drag things out."

"Wait a minute. You must be insane! You're holding me hostage until Ursula pays you?"

"That's been our plan from the start, although we thought she'd send her actual daughter, or her son."

They *were* insane. Faith felt as if she'd been transported to a remake of the film *Grey Gardens*.

"I'm not calling her," she said. "And in any case, she doesn't have that kind of money."

"Oh, but she does, or she can get it easily. And I think you'll find it increasingly unpleasant here if you don't call."

Faith willed herself not to let the terror she was starting to feel show. This couldn't be happening. She was in the middle of New York City—on the Upper East Side, for goodness' sake!

"It's nothing personal. We've been driven to this by that crook Bernie Madoff. We should be tying him up—or that wife of his— but that would have been more complicated, and Bernie, at least, is not reachable. He ruined us! At this point we can't even pay the electric bill."

"Wait a minute. You may have lost your money through Madoff, along with a huge number of others"—Faith was tempted to add, Who are not tying people up, yet thought it wise not to dwell on the situation—"but your house is worth many millions."

Violet looked aghast. "Sell our home! I'd starve to death first. I'll have you know my husband, Charles Wendell Winthrop, bought this house for me when we first moved to New York City and he intended that I should live here for my entire life, as did he. When I do die, it will of course go to my daughter."

Faith had the feeling Violet was now regarding her as some sort of malevolent real estate broker who had happened by to try to swindle her further.

"I won't call Ursula. That's final."

Violet's smile was nasty.

"Marguerite, dear, it's time for you to practice your piano." She added, "My daughter is an accomplished pianist who could have had a brilliant career were it not for the petty jealousies and dirty politics of the concert world. 'Marguerite' is French for daisy, a name that would have been too common. From birth I had intended her for great things. My husband used to call us his two flowers."

The younger flower left, disappearing into the gloom of the dining room and thereafter to parts unknown.

"She's a sensitive girl and I didn't want her to overhear us."

Faith could feel sweat start to trickle down various parts of her body.

"I've killed once and I will kill again, Mrs. Fairchild," Violet said matter-of-factly. "If Ursula doesn't wire the funds within twenty-four hours, you'll be dead."

It was the first part of what she said that struck Faith.

"It was *you,* not your husband—and certainly not Arnold Rowe. *You* killed Theo."

Violet nodded. "Such a long time ago that it doesn't really matter anymore. Not then, either. Theo Lyman was getting to be quite a bore. Every time I'd turn around, there he would be, acting like an idiot, trying to impress me. Oh, they had money, the Lymans, I'll grant you that, but it was gone soon enough. Thank goodness I had the sense to stick with Charlie. And he with me. But then, he rather had to." Violet smiled in reminiscence. "He was grateful. Oh yes, very grateful—starting that night—and I made sure he stayed that way. Yes, starting all those years ago on a warm summer night on Martha's Vineyard . . ."

"What's happened? You look terrible. Have you been in some kind of fight?"

"Violet, my God! You've got to help me. I don't know what to do. It wasn't my fault. He wouldn't give me the money!"

"What are you talking about? Calm down! Here, come into the library. Nobody's there."

She stood with her back against the door so they wouldn't be disturbed. Charles sat down on one of the couches and put his head in his hands. After a moment he looked up; his face was streaked with tears.

"I killed him. Theo's dead. I swear it was an accident. He was laughing and wouldn't listen. I pushed him. Maybe I hit him. I don't remember. He fell against a bench." Charles jumped to his feet and came toward her speaking rapidly.

"I never meant to hurt him. Just wanted to scare him a little. Oh God! What am I going to do? I'll go to prison. No one will believe me!"

"I believe you, Charles. Start at the beginning. Where were you?"

"I need a drink. There must be something to drink in this place. What does he need with all these things?" Charles gestured wildly at the weapons displayed throughout the room.

"I'll get you a drink in a minute. Tell me what happened from the start." Violet kept her voice steady and calm. "Sit down again."

Charles sat on an ottoman closer to Violet and looked up at her.

"I owe some men some money. A lot of money. If I don't pay them first thing tomorrow morning they'll go to my father—and they'll hurt me. Said I wouldn't be playing tennis for a long time. I kept telling Theo. Out in the gazebo in the woods. I didn't want anyone to hear us. He was pretty loaded. Just laughed and wanted to go back to the party. Kept saying he didn't have any money. Everything's a blur. I got mad. You've got to believe me. I never meant to hurt him. He was so still. Didn't move. I ran back here to find you."

Violet nodded. "We don't have much time. First, you were never in the gazebo tonight. Nobody saw you leave, did they?"

Charles shook his head.

"Next, I want you to give me ten minutes and then find a couple of people, people you don't know—that won't be hard in this crowd; I have no idea who these crashers are. Tell them Theo wants

the Professor out in the gazebo right away. It won't make sense to them, but they'll think it's a game and start shouting for him. Then find Rowe yourself. Keep an eye on him, but don't let him see you. As soon as you see him leave the house, follow a little ways behind. Get Scooter and some others to go with you. Tell them something's happened; you don't know what. Now repeat it all back to me— and don't have anything more to drink until later. When you leave now, go wash up and pull yourself together."

Charles repeated what Violet had told him to do and left the room. She walked slowly about. It was her favorite place in the house and she'd often thought she'd like to meet the man who collected all these weapons, bagged the game. A real man. Not like Charles, or Theo. But Charles was going to do just fine. Charles with all that Winthrop money and position. Nobody was going to snigger at Violet Hammond behind her back again. She knew what people said about her. It was coming to a happy ending a bit sooner than she planned—so long as Charles did exactly as he was told. And he would. Tonight, tomorrow, and in the future. After all, a wife couldn't testify against her husband, could she?

She picked up the stiletto letter opener on the desk with her handkerchief and climbed out the window. It didn't take long to get to the gazebo.

Theo was unconscious. There was almost no pulse, such a slight flutter that she almost missed it. She shuddered in repulsion—his face already resembled a death mask—but quickly pulled herself together and took his gold watch and his signet ring. They would have to keep the bootleggers—she knew what Charles had been up to—happy for now. If Charles's father got even a whiff of scandal regarding his son, he'd cut him off for good. And that wouldn't do at all.

Someone was coming—walking rapidly down the path. She heard Rowe call Theo's name.

Theo wouldn't be answering.

She plunged the stiletto into Theo's chest and slipped out the door into the woods to wait.

It was perfect. She heard the Professor's anguished cry and Charles's arrival with the others. When she went back into the gazebo, slipping in with several others, she saw that Arnold had pulled the knife from Theo's chest and was standing over him. She screamed—and kept on screaming.

Everything was going to be fine.

"My family has always been devoted to music, particularly the piano," Faith said. "I'd love to hear your daughter play. What kind of piano do you have?"

Violet rose to the bait.

"We have two, of course. A Steinway grand in the living room and a Baldwin in her music room. When she began to show her talents, we converted one of the bedrooms into a studio for her. It's soundproof, otherwise you could hear the music from here."

"What a shame I can't. It would be such a treat."

Would overweening pride overwhelm Violet's judgment? It was the only way Faith could think of to get the woman to untie her.

"Oh no you don't, Miss Smarty-pants. When I get word that the money has been transferred, perhaps Marguerite will give us a brief concert. For now, you'll be staying right where you are."

Pride did not go before a fall. They sat in silence for a while and then Violet burst out, "Now are you going to make that call or aren't you? My patience is wearing thin."

Faith was about to say no again when she realized that each time Violet had voiced the demand, she'd insisted Faith make the call. Why couldn't Violet make it herself, or even darling daughter Marguerite? Surely they had the number and they could hold the phone up to Faith so she could speak to prove she was actually here—and in extremis. Maybe, no probably, the phones were landlines and not portable. Violet would have to untie her and she wouldn't want to risk it.

So, Faith had to make the call using her cell. Violet was isolated from the world, but not completely. She'd assumed whoever came would have one.

It was a glimmer.

"All right. Bring me your phone," Faith said, feigning defeat.

"Don't you have your own? It's a long distance call. I don't see why I should have to pay for it."

The illogic was breathtaking—and breath giving.

"My phone is in my purse, which must be somewhere on the floor." They must have taken it from Faith's shoulder when she was knocked out. She hated to think of what it rested on. "The phone is in the outside pocket." She'd placed it there so she could call Hope easily.

Violet got up. She may not have been as athletic in her youth as Babs Jessup, but she still had excellent posture and didn't seem to require a cane or walker to get about.

"Is this it?" Violet asked dubiously. She held up the iPhone. Clearly cells in all their incarnations were a novelty.

"Yes. I have Ursula on something called 'speed dial' so I could get in touch with her once I made contact with you. Just run your finger across the screen and the number will ring. Hold it to my face and I'll tell her what's going on."

Please, Hope, catch on. Please . . .

"Are you there yet?" As always, her sister got right to the point.

Faith interrupted quickly. She couldn't have asked for a better opening.

"Yes, I'm here with Violet, Mrs. Winthrop, that is. And Ursula, I'm afraid things haven't gone well. For us, I mean. Mrs. Winthrop and her daughter, Marguerite, had the misfortune to lose a great deal of money with Bernard Madoff. They are demanding a trade.

In return for my safety, they want you to immediately transfer a hundred thousand dollars into their bank account."

Faith could almost see the stunned look on Hope's face as she rapidly processed the bizarre call.

"I see. Have they harmed you in any way?"

"No, Ursula, but they will if the money isn't in their account within twenty-four hours. At the moment I'm tied up in their kitchen. Actually, a lovely room with French doors leading to a back patio. The house itself is quite grand, although being on the ground floor, I can't say what the upstairs is like."

"Give me that thing." Violet was almost snarling. "You'd think you were going to move in! Now listen to me, Ursula Rowe, I have nothing to lose and everything to gain, so you'd better start getting the money together if you want to see your precious friend alive."

There was a pause. "She wants to talk to you again." Violet held the phone up.

"Keep the phone on. I'm setting all the wheels in motion. Good-bye."

Hope must have assumed she was on speakerphone. Bless her. She could be counted on to think of everything.

"She's getting everything started. Just leave the phone on the table and she'll call back for your account information."

"All written down in this." She waved a large ledger—the kind Faith associated with Melville's Bartleby. "That wasn't so hard, was it? We'll have you out of here in no time."

Faith was sure that's exactly what Hope was planning, too.

Her sister had friends in high places, so when New York's finest shortly arrived, some at the front door, which Violet refused to open, but more over the wall and into the back patio, Faith was not surprised. She was, however, understandably enormously relieved. When the police shattered one of the glass doors to get in, Violet threw herself at Faith, knocking the chair to the floor, all the while screaming something about an unholy alliance on the part of Ursula, the Madoffs, and poor Faith herself. Marguerite was discovered deep in Beethoven's "Moonlight" sonata and the two women were bundled off to the precinct charged with an entire laundry list of felonies, and thence, Faith assumed, soon to Bellevue, where their tattered apparel would be exchanged for more appropriate—and restrained—white jackets. Hope arrived on the heels of the police and accompanied her to the precinct.

"It isn't that I think you need a lawyer; it's that you need a sister," she said. "Aside from wanting to see you safe and sound with my own eyes, I'm aware that the police don't know you the way I do. I haven't heard *this* story yet, but based on the past, I do know it will be a hard one to swallow."

Faith never did get her egg cream and pastrami on rye, but took a rain check. She spent the night at Hope's and left early in the morning. She wanted to go home. That home.

Aleford.

CHAPTER 11

No matter what form the wedding ceremony takes—in a church, a temple, or a field of daisies—the receptions all follow the same patterns. The toasts to the new couple, the first dance, breaking bread, more toasts, more dancing, neckties loosened, high heels slipped off, and late in the day or night, a feeling of great ease. Two families have become one—for the moment or forever. Degrees of separation disappear. Discoveries are made—"My sister Sally must have been in your class!" and "I was born in Orange Memorial Hospital, too!" The dancing becomes freer—and closer during the slow numbers. Time is suspended. Lights are lowered.

The reception had arrived at this point and Faith was sitting with Tom at the Millers' table. She was breathless from the hora that one of Rebecca's aunts had initiated, sweeping the women in the room into the circle, including Ursula, who knew all the words to "Hava Nagila," most others chiming in only at the chorus, but with gusto. Earlier the bride and groom had been hoisted on chairs for that hora, the dancers snaking about in a joyous procession as the song continued on and on. Joy. So much joy.

Tom, sans collar, had acquitted himself so well in Hebrew during his part of the ceremony at Kahal Kadosh Beth Elohim that the Cohens' relatives and friends were asking who the new rabbi was. The chuppah—the canopy under which the couple stood, which symbolized the home they would make together, a home open on all sides for anyone to enter—was composed of a blanket of flowers. Faith had never seen one quite like it, nor the flowers that were everywhere at the reception—roses, orchids, and other varieties in ivory, the palest of greens, and as many kinds of pink as Chanel's lipsticks. The bridesmaids wore midcalf pastel strapless sheaths and carried calla lilies. They looked like lilies themselves.

Their parents escorted the wedding couple to the chuppah. Cissy and Pix wore deceptively simple, flattering cocktail dresses, cut exquisitely in two slightly different shades of lavender; Sam and Stephen sported elegant pale gray vests under their tuxedos. Grandchildren escorted grandparents to their seats and Ursula in her garnet satin looked like royalty.

"Happy, darling?" Tom placed his hand over his wife's.

"Very," she said. "And we have two more days here all to ourselves. Well, there's the brunch tomorrow, which will be fun—but after that, it's just you and me, kid."

"Sounds perfect."

Faith moved her chair closer to Tom's and leaned back against his shoulder. She was content to sit and watch the dancers whirl by for now.

When Rebecca and Mark had stamped on the wineglass wrapped in the napkin at the close of the ceremony, Faith was reminded of the act's additional meaning, apart from being a historic reminder of the destruction of the temple in Jerusalem. That the breaking of the glass symbolized our imperfect world, and the act carried a message for all present—to work hard each day to mend it.

There had been much mending of various sorts since April's

dramatic beginning. After countless vestry meetings preceded by consultations with Sam, Tom—and First Parish—had decided not to prosecute Albert and Lily. In fact, Tom decided to keep Albert on for a number of reasons: he'd been doing an excellent job; was clearly not cut out for the ministry, yet very much wanted to be a church administrator; and perhaps most pressing—Tom wanted to keep an eye on him. At first Faith had been vehemently opposed to this "turning of the other cheek," but Tom had explained that although he didn't feel that he had brought the whole thing on himself as Lily had described, he cared deeply about the young man and setting him adrift just didn't make sense.

Lily was a different story, and while they were still struggling to sort out what to do, Lily herself came up with the solution, asking to meet with Tom and then the vestry accompanied by her mother. Her father was refusing to have anything to do with her at the moment.

She had confessed everything, describing the deep depression she'd fallen into at divinity school that had taken a manic turn during the internship. She was seeing a therapist and was feeling clear about what she really wanted to be doing—nursing. To start, she hoped to be able to work in Haiti with a view to returning to the Boston area in a year to enter an RN program, gaining the skills she needed to go back or go to another part of the world.

If Faith thought it was all a little too pat and the ends a little too neatly tied up, she kept her mouth shut. Sherman Munroe and others in the church were falling all over themselves trying to atone for their suspicions and she was unabashedly enjoying it. The Minister's Discretionary Fund, and everything else requiring passwords, PINs, and so forth, had been protected as only Zach could. He boasted that First Parish was now on a level with the Pentagon, although he had added that neither place should be complacent. Hackers weren't.

And there was further mending. Pix had arrived at Logan Airport late that Friday morning to find not only her own husband waiting for her, but Tom, in great agitation, waiting for his wife. "I seem to have missed something," Pix had said, never dreaming how much. Over the next few days she'd found out—mostly from her mother.

In the weeks that followed they learned that the Winthrop women were indeed destitute. When Charles Winthrop died, the family told Violet that she could expect nothing from them save a spot next to him in the family plot at Mount Auburn Cemetery and they did not wish to see her until she was ready to use it. Violet was thin, but she wasn't too rich since she refused to sell the town house. Faith strongly suspected the cat food tins had not been enjoyed solely by the Winthrop pets.

They also learned that Marguerite was adapting well to life in prison—three squares, clean clothes, and fresh bed linens. She had changed her name to Daisy and was entertaining the other women in the upstate prison with medleys of show tunes on an old upright whenever she got the chance. Her mother was in a secure psychiatric facility.

"They're playing your song. Shall we dance?" Tom said. The music had stopped, and was starting up again.

Faith stood up and began to sing along, "Start spreading the news . . ." as Tom led her onto the floor.

She'd been very careful about champagne, but Pix was still feeling very rosy. Aside from her own wedding, it was the happiest one she had ever attended. She only wished her father could have lived to see his beloved grandson as an adult, a fine young man with a lovely bride.

After Ursula had told Pix the whole story, Arnie flew in and Pix heard it again. When she and her brother talked later, they admitted that they had always suspected that there was something major their parents hadn't shared with them, but thought it might be that their father, older than their mother, had been married before.

Pix drained the glass she'd been nursing. It was hard to believe all that had happened while she had been enjoying the Cohens' hospitality, blissfully unaware, in South Carolina. Cissy and Steve were coming to Maine in August for a week of sailing, kayaking, and, in Cissy's case, painting. She was a talented artist and confessed she'd always wanted to do watercolors of rockier shores.

"Don't tell me it's Pix!" The man standing in front of her looked very familiar and it took only a few seconds for Pix to gasp, "Brian?"

Brian had been Stephen Cohen's Dartmouth roommate and Pix's Brown roommate's boyfriend. She knew Mindy hadn't married him, but obviously he had stayed in touch with Steve. He was laughing.

"Mind if I sit down?"

"Please do." Now what? Pix wondered. Would it all come out? Was he the type to grab the mic and make a joke about Green Key Weekend for the amusement of all?

"Just about missed the whole darn wedding. Car trouble and finally we just ditched it and rented one."

"You were from Savannah, as I recall." Pix tried to sound nonchalant. It wasn't working.

"Talk about coincidences! The mother of the groom and the father of the bride—"

"Please," Pix interrupted, and then was interrupted herself by Dr. Stephen Cohen, who had suddenly appeared at their side.

"Brian! You made it!"

"I wouldn't miss Becca's wedding for the world, old buddy. And the first person I run into is Pix . . . wait a minute, I've got it—Rowe. Mindy's roommate. She's still in Savannah, too. Hotshot lawyer and there's talk of a run for the statehouse. Married a cousin of my wife's and we're all family."

Pix was feeling dizzy and wondered whether it would be rude to excuse herself.

"Speaking of family. You two are family now!" His grin couldn't possibly get any broader, Pix thought dismally. Any minute now, he'd start spreading the news. No, wait, that was the song. Oh, she couldn't think straight at all.

"Yes, it's great," Steve said. "Pix and I have had fun talking over old times and the only fly in the ointment is that her husband can beat me at golf. I think Mark can, too, but he's smart enough to let me have a few strokes. Maybe now that they're married, it will change."

Pix knew they were talking about golf scores, but she'd stop paying attention after the part about catching up on old times.

"Well, I need to congratulate the bride and groom and dance with my wife. She had us taking lessons last winter, said we were getting stodgy. Y'all take care now."

"It was good to see you again," Pix managed.

Stephen gave his friend a hug and said, "Now, about that weekend. You understand it's Pix and my little secret."

"Not to worry." Brian zipped his lips and walked off.

"You knew it was me! All the time?" Pix didn't know whether to be indignant or jubilant. "I thought you'd forgotten."

"Wait a minute. I'd thought *you'd* forgotten. And yes, this is starting to sound like a bad sitcom," he said, laughing.

Pix was speechless. It was the one thing that hadn't occurred to her—or Faith. That Stephen would think Pix didn't remember *him*. It really was very funny and she started to laugh, too.

Sam and Cissy came dancing over, finishing with a flourish, both singing "New York, New York." It was that kind of song.

"Hey, you two, what's so funny?" Sam asked.

"Nothing," Stephen said, taking Pix's hand for the next number.

"Absolutely nothing," she said, stepping into his arms and matching her steps to his.

* * *

Ursula sat listening to a long story Rebecca's aunt was telling about someone. It wasn't clear whether this person was in the present or past, but it didn't seem to matter. Ursula had discovered that people in Charleston tended to regard the living and the dead much the same when it came to storytelling, even as to tense.

She watched the couples on the dance floor, her eyes picking out her own children and grandchildren with pride.

The living and the dead. Oh Arnold, I wish you were by my side—or whirling me about the way you used to when we would go dancing at the ballroom in Newton at Norumbega Park. So elegant—and you were, too, my darling.

The living and the dead. She saw Theo's face in Dan, her youngest grandchild, who was the same age Theo had been when he died. Arnold was buried on Sanpere, but Theo was nearby in Cambridge at Mount Auburn. Faith had taken her the week after her return from New York and the two of them had laid a spray of white lilacs on the grave. Ursula knew Faith was keeping the details of her trip from her and Ursula didn't mind. Being shielded was a blessing at this point in life. She suspected Violet may have told Faith that she alone was responsible for the murder. It didn't matter. Her brother was gone.

"It's a slow song, Granny. Would you like to dance?"

Dan had shed his jacket and tie. Like his mother, he had a habit of running his hand through his thick brown curly hair and it was no longer slicked down as it had been during the ceremony.

"I'd love to. Will you excuse me?" Ursula addressed the table and, taking her grandson's hand, walked onto the dance floor. They were playing Cole Porter. "Easy to Love." She hummed along as they danced and through half-closed eyes saw their faces.

Good night, Theo.

Good night, Arnold.

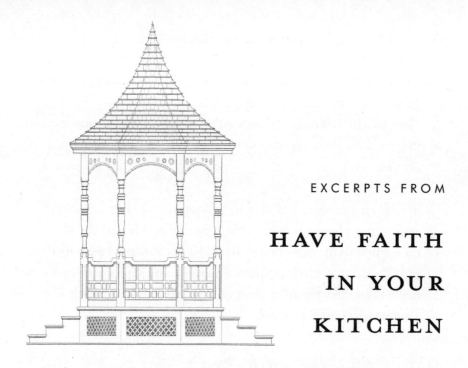

HAVE FAITH
IN YOUR
KITCHEN

By Faith Sibley Fairchild
with Katherine Hall Page

Borscht

1 small red bell pepper, diced	2 ½ quarts stock or water
3 tablespoons olive oil	2 bay leaves
1 large red onion, sliced	½ teaspoon thyme
3 cups peeled and cubed beets	Salt
(approx. 3 large beets)	Freshly ground pepper
Juice from ½ lemon	Sour cream

Heat the olive oil in a large soup pot. Add the onion slices and diced pepper. Sauté, stirring over medium heat, just until the onions start to give off some liquid. Add the rest of the ingredients except the sour cream. Bring to a boil and then turn to a simmer. Cook until the beets are tender.

Place in a blender or food processor, or use an immersion blender to process until the soup is smooth, but still has some heft to it.

Serves 4–6.

This is an easy summer or winter soup recipe. It is best made a day ahead. Serve it cold in the summer and hot in the winter topped with sour cream. To make the spiderweb garnish, pipe concentric circles of sour cream on the top of each portion. Drag the tip of a sharply pointed knife through the circles to create the effect.

Baked Chicken with Red Wine, Sage, and Root Vegetables

2 ½ pounds chicken

1 tablespoon olive oil

½ pound parsnips

½ pound carrots

1 large yellow onion

2 tablespoons fresh sage

½ teaspoon salt

½ teaspoon freshly ground pepper

1 cup dry red wine

Faith's family likes dark meat, so she uses four whole chicken legs.

Preheat the oven to 350°.

Rinse the chicken and pat it dry with a paper towel.

Drizzle the oil in a casserole large enough to hold the chicken and vegetables. Faith prefers the oval ones from France, but Pyrex is just fine, too.

Place the chicken pieces in the casserole.

Peel the parsnips, scrub (or peel) the carrots, and cut both into chunks, about an inch long.

Peel the onion and cut it into eighths.

Arrange the assorted vegetables around the chicken.

Strip the leaves off the sage stems. Roll them into a small cigar shape and slice into thin strips (a chiffonade). Sprinkle on top of the chicken and vegetables along with the salt and pepper.

Pour the wine evenly over the casserole.

Cover tightly with aluminum foil and bake for 1 hour.

Uncover, baste with a bulb baster or a spoon, and bake for another 45 minutes, basting occasionally. The chicken should be nicely browned. Let the dish rest for 5 minutes.

Serves 4 amply. Be sure to spoon some of the liquid on top of the chicken and vegetables when serving.

What is nice about this dish is that it omits browning the chicken, which you would do in a more traditional coq au vin. It takes less time to prepare and Faith created it as a heart-wise version for her husband. She uses a salt substitute and takes the skin off the chicken unless she's making it for company. You can vary the vegetables—turnips are good also. She serves it with the following:

Sautéed New Potatoes with Sage

Small red potatoes	2 tablespoons fresh sage
1 tablespoon unsalted butter	Salt
1 tablespoon olive oil	Freshly ground pepper

While the chicken is baking, start the potatoes.

Faith figures 3 potatoes per person.

Wash the potatoes, cut them in half, and steam them until you can pierce them with a sharp fork.

Set aside.

About 15 minutes before the chicken is ready, sauté the potatoes in the butter and oil. Unfortunately, a butter substitute does not work with this dish. Once the potatoes start to brown sprinkle them with the sage and add salt and pepper to taste.

The potatoes will be done at the same time as the chicken and should be slightly crispy.

Faith makes this basic recipe often to accompany meat, poultry, or fish, varying the seasoning. Rosemary is one of her favorites.

Fruit Breakfast Puffs

4–5 tablespoons unsalted butter, melted	¾ cup flour
4 peach halves, fresh or canned, or	¼ cup white sugar
pears, strawberries, or other fruit	¾ cup milk (whole, 2%, or 1%)
4 large eggs	3 tablespoons fresh orange juice

Preheat the oven to 400°.

Cover the bottom of 4 large (approximately 4 inches in diameter) ovenproof ramekins with 3–4 tablespoons of the melted butter.

Place the peach, or other fruit, on top and set aside.

Whisk the eggs in a mixing bowl and add the flour, sugar, milk, and orange juice, blending well.

Add the reserved tablespoon of melted butter and mix well again.

Divide the batter evenly among the ramekins and bake on a baking sheet for about 20 minutes or until puffed and golden. Serve immediately.

This is a very pretty presentation. The batter puffs up nicely, almost like a popover.

Faith adapted this recipe from a breakfast puff she had at the very charming Englishman's Bed and Breakfast in Cherryfield, Maine. Many thanks to the hosts, Kathy and Peter Winham.

Ursula's Rum Cake

2 ½ cups sifted all-purpose flour

2 teaspoons baking powder

1 teaspoon baking soda

½ teaspoon salt

2 sticks unsalted butter, room temperature

1 cup sugar

2 large eggs

1 cup buttermilk

Finely grated zest of 1 lemon

Finely grated zest of 2 oranges

1 cup chopped walnuts

Glaze ingredients:

3 tablespoons fresh lemon juice (from lemon grated for zest)

½ cup fresh orange juice (from oranges grated for zest)

1 cup sugar

5 tablespoons dark rum

Preheat the oven to 350°. Grease and flour an 8-cup kugelhopf or bundt pan.

Sift together the flour, baking powder, baking soda, and salt, and set aside.

Beat the butter in an electric mixer until soft. Add the sugar and beat to mix. Add the eggs one at a time, beating after each addition. On low speed, add the sifted dry ingredients in three additions, alternating with buttermilk, scraping bowl as necessary.

Remove from the mixer and stir in the zest and nuts.

Pour into the prepared pan, smooth top, and place in the hot oven. Bake for 55–60 minutes, until top springs back when pressed lightly.

Remove from the oven and set on a rack.

Immediately prepare the glaze.

Place the juices and sugar in a saucepan over moderate heat and stir with a wooden spoon until the sugar is dissolved and the mixture comes to a boil. Remove from heat, add the rum, and stir.

Pierce the top of the cake with a cake tester. Spoon the hot glaze over the hot cake (still in the pan), spooning a little at a time. When you notice glaze oozing around the edge of the cake pan, use a metal spatula or knife to ease the edge of the cake away from the pan, allowing the glaze to run down the sides. Continue this until all the glaze is absorbed. It will be absorbed, believe me.

Let the cake stand for 10 to 15 minutes, until the bottom of the pan is cool enough to touch. Then cover the cake with a plate, hold the plate tightly in place against the cake pan, and flip over the cake and pan. Remove the cake pan from the cake. Let stand for at least two hours until cool and cover with plastic wrap. Can stand overnight before serving.

Truth be told, this extraordinary recipe is not Ursula Lyman Rowe's, but Valerie Wolzien's—the author of many of Faith and my favorite books: the Susan Henshaw mystery series and the one featuring Josie Pigeon. Slice a large piece of cake and settle down with, say, *Murder at the PTA Luncheon* or *This Old Murder* or *Death in Duplicate*, or . . .

Author's Note

*"Life, within doors, has few pleasanter prospects than a
neatly arranged and well-provisioned breakfast table."*

I came across this quotation from Nathaniel Hawthorne's *The
House of the Seven Gables* during the dead of last winter, a very
cold, long one. Visions not of sugarplums but of eggs Benedict,
sour cream waffles, bagels and lox, streaky bacon, beignets, and
café au lait immediately danced in my head. Breakfast is my favorite meal.

The word "breakfast," from the Middle English, means just
that—breaking the fast engendered by a night's sleep. However,
our ancestors all over the globe ate a much heartier breakfast than
we normally do, as a necessity for the hard day's physical labor that
followed.

In the present day, those of us who eat at home do so lightly,
and well over sixty percent of us grab 'n' go—a doughnut and
coffee or some other combination from a drive-thru before physically, but not psychologically, less strenuous work.

Even before Kellogg's, grains have always played a prominent
role in breakfast composition and remnants have been found at
Neolithic sites. In the United States, the Pilgrims started the day
with maize—another one of those life-saving gifts from the Native Americans—grinding the kernels and mixing them with water to form "mush." It was not what the early colonists had been
used to—wheat breads, coffee or tea with milk—but when they
added maple syrup (tapping the trees was another skill they picked
up), the concoction was quite palatable. They drank hard cider
or ale to wash it down. This did not mean they went about their
labors pie-eyed—although I'm sure there were exceptions passed
out under the haystacks. These fermented beverages were safer to
drink than many water supplies throughout this period and earlier
world history.

The Victorians' mid- to late-nineteenth-century menus were
a breakfast lover's dream. Excessive in all things comestible, they
did not stint at the morning meal, and although Nellie Grant's
1874 wedding repast marked a special occasion, it was typical of
upper-class breakfast fare: Soft-Shelled Crabs on Toast, Chicken
Croquettes with Green Peas, Lamb Cutlets with Tartare Sauce,
Aspic of Beef Tongue, Woodcock and Snipe on Toast, Salad with
Mayonnaise, Strawberries with Cream, Orange Baskets Garnished with Strawberries, Charlotte Russe, Nesselrode Pudding,
Blancmange, Ice Cream Garnished with Preserved Fruits, Water
Ices, Wedding Cake, Small Fancy Cakes, Roman Punch (a rum
concoction), Chocolate, and Coffee.

In the South and some Mid-Atlantic states, Hunt Breakfasts,
which originated in Britain, were sumptuous affairs with staples
similar to what was still found some years later at the Edwardian
breakfast sideboard, resplendent with silver chafing dishes: Scrambled Eggs in Cream, Country Sausage with Fried Apple Rings,
Creamed Sweetbreads and Oysters, Capitolade of Chicken (a kind
of hash), Kidney Stew, Bacon and Fried Tomato Slices, Waffles,

Hominy Pudding, Broiled Salt Roe Herring, Baked Country Ham, Spoon Bread, Beaten Biscuits, Buttermilk Biscuits, Jellies, Apple Butter, Honey, Damson Plum Preserves, and Coffee plus Bourbon and Branch, no doubt in stirrup cups. Reading over this list transports me to breakfasts I've had in the South—nothing better in the morning than grits and eggs, a real biscuit, and a thick slice of country ham with redeye gravy.

These two menus are from the pages of *The American Heritage Cookbook and Illustrated History of American Eating & Drinking* (1964). If one turns up in a book sale, grab it. Not just fascinating reading, and some very interesting recipes, but a feast for the eyes, as well.

Hawthorne's quotation prompted me to think about my favorite breakfasts, starting in childhood. My father came from the generation of men who quite literally could not boil water. Somewhere along the way he learned to make pancakes, although I believe Aunt Jemima may have helped him out. He made them in shapes, some of which required a bit of imagination to define, but we loved them. My mother sent us off to school each weekday morning with a good breakfast under our belts—Cream of Wheat, Wheatina (not a general favorite), Quaker oatmeal, sometimes eggs and bacon, but always freshly squeezed orange juice. Frozen OJ had become available after World War II, but Mom didn't believe in it (or Tang or Pop-Tarts, introduced in the 1960s, which of course made them immediately desirable and exotic).

I grew up in the trading-stamp era and after a certain amount accumulated, we would each get a turn to select something from the S&H Green Stamps catalog, that Book of Wonders. My brother picked a waffle iron, and waffles with fruit and other toppings began to appear at weekend breakfasts. He later chose an ice-cream maker, the kind that used rock salt. It was wooden and you had to turn a crank, producing the best ice cream I've ever had, thereby showing not only an early appreciation for good food on his part, but also the recognition that if you wanted tasty things to eat, the best way was to learn how to do it yourself. I've always been grateful to him for this nugget of culinary wisdom. Meanwhile I was trying to amass a set of matching luggage. I got as far as a Black Watch plaid overnight bag and a cosmetics case.

My mother came from a Norwegian-American family. Breakfast in Norwegian is *frokost,* "early meal," and a meal it is. A number of years ago I was with my mother and my aunt in a hotel on the West Coast of Norway at breakfast time. A tour leader was looking for someone who spoke French to help explain the offerings to two sisters from Brittany. I was happy to oblige (they hadn't thought it necessary to know English, the language of the tour, as they would just be looking at scenery). I walked them past the vast array—herring in a number of sauces; *leverpostei,* a kind of liver pâté, I explained; smoked salmon; smoked eel; *gravlaks,* fresh cured salmon; shrimp in cream sauce; cold sliced venison; lingonberry sauce; sliced tomatoes; cucumber salad; a medley of cold and hot cereals; fresh fruit; *wienerbrød* (Danish pastries); a variety of breads; Ry-Krisp and other crackers; cheeses: Jarlsberg, *gjetost* (a sweet brown goat cheese, an acquired taste), my personal favorite, *nøkkelost;* and mounds of boiled eggs, to name some of the offerings. The women were aghast, searching in vain for a croissant or even a small toasted piece of a baguette. "*Le petit déjeuner norvégien, c'est bizarre,*" one said. Fortunately there was plenty of good strong coffee, the national drink after aquavit.

I long for these Norwegian breakfasts, but Kviknes Hotel in Balestrand is far away. We duplicate the spread on Christmas morning, but there's no fjord out the window.

I'm also extremely fond of a traditional British fry-up as served in Bloomsbury's Gower Street House Bed and Breakfasts in London. I also recently had the pleasure of a number of proper English breakfasts in Bristol at Crimefest, the annual international crime fiction convention "Where the Pen Is Bloodier than the Sword." The incomparable Colin Dexter was the guest of honor. Bristol is noted for its sausages, a delicious bonus to a wonderful four days. My French ladies would look just as askance at the British breakfasts—plates filled with fried tomatoes, fried mushrooms, fried eggs with fried bread swimming in baked beans, accompanied by streaky bacon, sausages, maybe a kipper, toast, lashings of butter, jam, and strong tea. Mueseli made an appearance at roughly the same time as crunchy granola in the U.S. and appears to be here to stay. I skip it, not only because I don't have room to eat it, but also because it puts a damper on all that joyful artery clogging.

This is not an activity I espouse on a regular basis, but sometimes the craving for a certain kind of breakfast is irresistible. In Maine, I head for the Harbor Café in Stonington and order two eggs over easy with hash browns, wheat toast (more a concession to taste than health), sausage links, and a bottomless mug of coffee. At the end of the meal, I always save a toast triangle, which I spread with one of those Kraft marmalade packets as a kind of dessert. My favorite marmalades have been produced by Keiller in Dundee, Scotland, since the 1790s. Legend has it that the spread was invented by Mary, Queen of Scots', French cook. I'm particularly partial to Keiller's Three Fruits variety.

Diner breakfasts are wonderful and cannot be replaced by Egg McMuffins. You are never going to hear "Adam and Eve on a raft with some joe" in a fast food chain.

So many of the breakfast foods we love were brought to this country by immigrants. Doughnuts came with the Dutch, "Oily Cakes," which are also ancestors of fried dough, that staple of amusement parks and fairs. Doughnuts became a national favorite with the invention of the doughnut machine in the 1930s, a fact that makes me think of the beloved classic children's book by

Robert McCloskey, *Homer Price* Homer's uncle has a diner and a doughnut machine that under Homer's hands becomes unstoppable, spewing out the toothsome confections much to the townspeople's delight and later consternation

German immigrants brought us sticky buns; the French, *pain perdu*—French toast—and croissants. Eastern European Jews gave us bagels and blintzes, congee and dim sum are from Asia, and huevos rancheros from Mexico. All now are breakfast staples.

My breakfast musings also took me back to A. A. Milne's poem "The King's Breakfast." Frederic G. Melcher, co-editor of *Publishers Weekly* and originator of the Newbery and Caldecott medals for children's literature, was a member of my church in Montclair, New Jersey. He used to come and read poetry to the Sunday school classes and this was one of his favorites. I can still hear his voice as the poor king, " 'Nobody,' / He whimpered, / 'Could call me / A fussy man; / I only want / A little bit / Of butter for / My bread!' " And isn't this just what we all want?

Breakfast in the twenty-first century is very much a social ritual. Retirees meet for breakfast, as do young mothers with strollers in tow; job seekers network at breakfast; the Scouts, fire and police departments, and all sorts of organizations, raise funds at pancake breakfasts. Brunch provides a special occasion to visit with friends and family. And brunch's basic eggs Benedict has been transformed into a multitude of versions, replacing the ham or bacon with smoked salmon, various kinds of sausage patties, duck, and even avocado slices. Eggs Sardou, created at the legendary New Orleans restaurant Antoine's, tops the English muffin with an artichoke bottom and anchovy fillets, and covers the poached egg with a hollandaise that includes bits of chopped ham and slices of truffle. Variations on this recipe omit the anchovies, ham, and truffles, substituting creamed or steamed spinach. There are several widely differing accounts of the origin of eggs Benedict, but my favorite credits a Mrs. LeGrand Benedict of New

York City, who, during the 1860s, asked Chef Charles Ranhofer at Delmonico's to devise something new for her to eat at lunch. Obviously a woman after my own heart.

Breakfast for lunch, breakfast for dinner, and above all breakfast in the morning.